FOLLY PARK

FOLLY PARK

A NOVEL

HEIDI HACKFORD

SHE WRITES PRESS

Published 2022
Printed in the United States of America
Print ISBN: 978-1-64742-271-4
E-ISBN: 978-1-64742-272-1
Library of Congress Control Number: 2022909334

For information, address:
She Writes Press
1569 Solano Ave #546
Berkeley, CA 94707

She Writes Press is a division of SparkPoint Studio, LLC.

To my dad, whose boundless curiosity
first inspired me to explore the past

Nations reel and stagger on their way;
they make hideous mistakes;
they commit frightful wrongs;
they do great and beautiful things.
And shall we not best guide humanity
by telling the truth about all this,
so far as the truth is ascertainable?

—W.E.B. Du Bois,
Black Reconstruction in America, 1860–1880

CHAPTER ONE

A plain, flat package had appeared on the dressing table in the dank basement room where the speakers waited before they were called to the stage. Inside, Temple Preston found an advance copy of a new book. It had a catchy title, and the back cover promised "a tell-all tale unearthing the scandalous past of a prominent Southern family." That family was hers, and she was the one who had released its ugly secrets. The time had come for her to make a choice—reject her heritage or be complicit in the enduring evils spawned from the deeds of her ancestors.

But there were consequences for challenging power and privilege. The price Temple paid was the loss of the place she loved most in the world.

IT BEGAN WITH AN EXPLOSION. Seconds later, the shriek of Folly Park's security alarm sent the dog darting into the closet as Temple scrambled out of bed. Jamming on tennis shoes, she sprinted up the gravel drive, praying the historic home that had been in her family for over two hundred years had not been damaged. Workers were blasting through rock to build a lake for a new golf course nearby, and for three days tremors had triggered the alarm.

The noise stopped abruptly as Temple opened the back door of the mansion, the sudden silence fizzing in her ears. She was just in time to see Al, Folly Park's groundskeeper, stretched to his full height, lowering the golf club he'd used to beat the alarm into submission. He could have climbed the ladder that leaned against the wall and flipped the manual switch, as Temple had pointed out yesterday. But although she was his supervisor, Al often ignored her suggestions. Temple told herself she didn't push it because Al had worked at Folly Park for so long and their friendship stretched back to her childhood. The real reason was because her people had once owned his people, and it troubled her deeply.

As they surveyed the ceiling where a jagged crack had appeared, a second blast rumbled in the distance. The crack split wide, and chunks of plaster came down in a flurry of dust. Something struck Temple above her left eye just as Al shouted, "Watch out!" and pushed her to the floor.

When the dust settled, Al helped Temple up. "You're bleeding," he said.

Pain throbbed in her forehead, and Temple's fingers came away spotted with blood. But she was only interested in what had hit her—a tin box about the size of a hardcover book. She pushed the debris aside as tiny stars sparked in her peripheral vision.

Al tugged a faded blue bandanna from the pocket of his khaki pants. "Let me check out that cut."

"I'm fine." Temple straightened up with her prize. "Look at this!" Al hovered over her shoulder as she pried open the box. Inside was a hinged case and a leather-bound book.

The case contained a framed ambrotype photograph. Temple immediately recognized two of the five people in it—General Thomas Temple Smith and his wife, Carolina, who were both tangled in her lineage. In the photo, likely taken just before he went off to fight, the general stood on the wide veranda of Folly Park in his Confederate uniform with Carolina seated in front of him. Beside her was another woman Temple could not identify. Nor could she name the dark-skinned man and a pretty girl at the edge of the frame, who were likely enslaved.

The unknown woman on the veranda looked about the same age as Carolina, who was nineteen when the Civil War began. Smooth dark hair framed an angular face, and her light eyes—probably blue—were intense in the black-and-white photo. Oddly, the general's hand rested on her shoulder rather than his wife's. And Carolina was leaning to touch the stranger's hands where they were bunched into fists on her lap. Easing the photograph from the frame, Temple turned it over to find only the date—June 17, 1861—scrawled on the back.

"Who's that sitting by Carolina?" Al asked.

"I don't know."

"Seriously?"

Since her grandfather died last year, Temple was the resident expert on Folly Park's long history, and the Civil War period was her specialty. She believed she knew all the important people in the general's life and most of the minor characters too. But this woman, clearly on intimate terms with the master and mistress of Folly Park on the very eve of the war, was unfamiliar to her.

Returning the photograph to the box, Temple opened the small book. It appeared to be a diary, but no name was written on the flyleaf. The first entry was headed, "Thursday, August 30, 1859," in an even, legible script.

Temple read, "I have resolved to record in this little book—an engagement gift from Mother—my daily skirmishes with self-improvement. There is, Mother assures me, much to be done to prepare me to be a wife."

Carolina had married the general in May 1859, Temple recalled, so this was not her diary. *Did it belong to the stranger in the photograph?*

"I wonder who hid this." Temple peered up at the hole. "The ceiling was damaged during the Civil War, so I suppose the box could have been sealed in when it was repaired."

"It's probably been weak ever since." Al poked a text into his cell phone with his forefinger. "I'll get a structural engineer to check things out. We can't afford to have it collapse on a bunch of tourists."

"We're supposed to call them guests, not tourists," Temple said. It was one of the many pointless changes Stuart Sprigg had made since coming on board. "We also can't afford to fix the hole."

"Sue the developers doing the blasting. Greedy crooks."

Al's habitual assumption of bad motives often had the perverse effect of making Temple defend people she didn't even know. "I suppose you can't really blame them for buying land people are willing to sell."

"Yes, I can. These new developments are making everything so expensive folks can hardly afford to live in their hometown."

Temple's own family had struggled to hang on to Folly Park. By any measure they were highly privileged, but her maternal grandfather, Chauncey Temple Smith, had inherited a quagmire of debt accumulated over generations. He had been forced to sell the estate to the nearby town of Preston's Mill, which allowed him to remain living on the second floor of the mansion while it operated the place as a tourist attraction. Unfortunately, the house's well-preserved appearance masked an advanced termite infestation, and the red brick sometimes crumbled when touched. Much of the foundation was shored up by I-beams, and the roof needed a complete overhaul. Temple's grandfather had wanted her to watch over the house, somehow regain ownership, and restore it fully. But it seemed like every chance was snatched away like a dollar bill in a wayward breeze.

"I'll try to get some compensation for repairs," Temple said.

"Should I tell Sprigg what happened?" Al had a mischievous glint in his eye. He liked to stir up their excitable new director.

"No, I will," Temple said hastily. "After I talk to the developers. And please don't say anything about the box until I can do some research." The strange woman in the photograph made her vaguely uneasy.

Al nodded, and a chunk of debris fell from his grizzled head. His brown face was caked with white plaster dust, and he snorted when he caught sight of himself in the beveled mirror on the wall. "Look at me. I could pass for White with the tourists."

"Guests," Temple said absently as she started down the hall.

OPENING THE FRONT DOOR, TEMPLE stepped out on to the wide, white-columned veranda—the same one from the photograph in the box she held. She had passed many quiet evenings here with her grandfather, who looked like he belonged to another century with his trim beard, string tie, and crisp white shirt. When he rolled up his sleeves and played old Southern ballads on his violin, she imagined the ghosts of long-gowned women and men in tall boots strolling in the shadows under the trees. But the spring foliage of the massive oaks on the front lawn seemed sparse this year, and Temple supposed they were nearing the end of their natural lives. They were already ancient by the time her great-grandfather inherited Folly Park in 1934.

Although the house tour covered the family history from colonial times to the present, Folly Park was a tourist attraction because of General Smith. He was one of the most effective cavalry commanders in the Confederate army, but in September 1863, his brigade had been defeated in the meadow below Folly Park. The night before, the general himself was accidentally killed by his own sentry while sneaking back into camp.

Whether or not the general had gone to see the Union commander and betrayed his men in a deal to save Folly Park was an enduring mystery for historians, but most people in the nearby town of Preston's Mill never questioned his loyalty to the South. They believed the general had been on a reconnaissance mission.

On long, drowsy Saturday afternoons when Temple was young, her grandfather had taken her and her brothers to the battlefield to search for bullets and other artifacts. Harry, the eldest, spent most of his time under a shady tree joking with the other treasure hunters when they took a break. Temple's younger brother, Beau, hunted field mice, which he killed with deliberate purpose when he could catch them. Occasionally, one of the treasure hunters, slowly uncoiling his back, would catch sight of Beau stalking his prey in the distance and remark benignly, "There's something wrong with that boy."

Temple shadowed her grandfather, absorbing his tales of the general's exploits and the old days at Folly Park, while the red dirt worked its way under her fingernails and into the sweaty creases behind her knees. She was seven years old the day she caught on that her favorite characters in her grandfather's stories—the "aunts" and "uncles" with the funny names and sassy attitudes—were Black people who lived with but weren't related to their White ancestors. She pressed her grandfather for more information, and he provided an explanation of slavery he probably felt was suitable for a child: people who came from Africa were given food, clothes, and houses for their whole lives in return for their work. But Temple sensed there was something wrong about it all, and she felt as if she'd somehow let down her beloved aunts and uncles just by being herself.

The front door squealed open, and Al emerged, swatting plaster dust from his arms. "What are you still doing here?"

Temple gestured at the lush lawn sloping down to a green river that curved through blue hills toward the distant Atlantic. "I love this view. It never changes."

Al seemed about to say something, but just then his wife appeared at the edge of the drive. "Look at you two! You're filthy!"

A sturdy, cheerful woman with a tawny complexion and a dash of freckles across her nose, Betty Jean ran the ticket office at Folly Park. Today, she had braided her hair in cornrows finished off with orange beads, and she was wearing a hot-pink blouse and black-and-yellow-polka-dot pants. Temple smiled. Betty Jean's colorful clothes were a sore spot with the new director. When Stuart told her she looked unprofessional, she remarked that in her experience only unhappy people were offended by bright colors.

"I'm happy," he'd said peevishly.

Betty Jean came closer, squinting, and Temple casually moved the box behind her back.

"What did you do to your face, honey?"

Al told Betty Jean about the ceiling while she fished a Kleenex from a capacious woven bag and wetted it on her tongue.

Temple knew it would be pointless to struggle, so she meekly submitted to Betty Jean's ministrations. In any case, she liked the way Betty Jean held her chin firmly while she dabbed at the cut, face puckered with concentrated concern. It reminded Temple of her mother.

A button pinned to Betty Jean's blouse read VOTE POE FOR MAYOR. Temple was interested to learn that Frank Poe was running in the special election. He was a public defender whose wife ran an organic farm on land that had been in Frank's family since Reconstruction.

"Put antibiotic cream on it," Betty Jean instructed as she let Temple loose.

"I will. Thanks." Temple turned to Al. "Can you please clean up the mess from the ceiling?"

Al drooped his shoulders and shuffled his feet. He whined in a falsetto voice, "Yes, Missus, I gets right on dat. Don' hit me, Missus! Don' whip yo' faithful darky."

As usual, Temple's cheeks flushed at this routine. "Very funny. Cut it out."

"Yes, Missus." Grinning, Al went back inside the mansion.

TEMPLE CROSSED THE GRAVEL DRIVE and peeled her soggy newspaper off the doormat. A thin local daily, the *Preston's Mill Progress* invariably ended up soaked by the morning dew. Chick, her fifty-pound mutt, was pushing a bulge into the screen door with his nose, and Temple let him out for a run. In the bathroom mirror, she examined the gash on her forehead and the beginnings of a bruise around her right eye. She had literally been beaten up by a house.

After a quick shower, Temple went into her bedroom and carefully eased out her dresser drawers so she wouldn't disturb the haphazard pile of paper stacked on top. The only mess in her tidy house, this was her dissertation, which she was supposed to be turning into a book. She had a contract with an academic publisher who wanted the complete manuscript at the end of the summer, but even though she was grateful to have such an opportunity, Temple just couldn't make herself work on it. At some point, a mouse had chewed through a good portion of the bottom margin, and she imagined its nest lined with her footnotes. It seemed as good a use for them as any.

When Temple entered the detached kitchen building where the offices were located, Martha silently handed over a handful of message slips. The star of her church choir, Martha abstained from speaking before ten o'clock because she believed morning air harmed the vocal cords. Stuart Spriggs's office door was closed, but Temple could hear him braying into the telephone. He seemed to think talking loudly made him sound confident.

The phone messages were all from Temple's brother Beau. He called her at work whenever she didn't answer her cell phone, refusing to leave a voicemail or text. Like their father, who believed information was power, he preferred to keep her guessing. Temple tossed the messages into the recycle bin and took the tin box from her work bag.

Carefully leafing through the diary, she found a letter slotted between the pages. The address was written in blotchy ink: Miss Jane Elliot to the care of Mr. John Elliot, Boston, Massachusetts. The wax seal was broken.

Folly Park, 6th Nov. 1859

Dear Jane,

How do I begin when I have not sent a Word in six long Years? That it was I who was too Idle to keep up a Correspondance does not surprize either of us I am sure dear Cousin—But I know <u>you</u> will not Condem me so true and Constant as you are and so I beg you to come to me. I need your Friendship & Councill despertly—I am married now and I have displeased my husband ~~and he~~ But the story will keep for when I see you. We are very ~~wellthy~~ Rich so ~~do not let~~ the Expence must not prevent you. I enclose Banknotes. You <u>must</u> come to me <u>at once</u> dearest Jane.

Your,
Carolina

Temple remembered the general had an aunt who married a man from Boston, likely the John Elliot on the envelope. His daughter Jane would have been a first cousin to both Carolina and the general because they were first cousins themselves. Temple wondered if the reference to displeasing her husband referred to long-standing rumors about an affair Carolina had with a neighbor resulting in a duel. All her sympathy lay with the general, as she had never felt much interest in Carolina. But the loneliness in the letter was palpable.

Temple took the photograph out of the box, wondering if the woman seated between Thomas and Carolina was Jane Elliot. She flipped through the diary until she found an entry with the same date that was written on the back of the photo.

June 17, 1861

A photograph was taken of us today by a callow youth traveling about the country with his contraption. Thomas and Carolina thought it just the thing to divert me on my first day out of bed in a week. I was so distressed by Thomas's insistence that I consider returning to Boston I had made myself ill. I am appalled by my weakness! When <u>he</u> is going off to fight and perhaps might be injured or—but I will not write it, or even think it.

The young man posed us on the veranda—Thomas tall and smart in his new uniform, Carolina beautiful as ever. I did not want to be in the photograph—I would mar any portrait with my plain face—but they insisted. Then the youth inquired if we should like to include any favored servants, and Carolina summoned King and Jewel.

All the while he set up his camera, the young man talked of his ambition to make a name for himself by taking scenes of the war. I asked if he would peddle pictures of men and boys dead and dying and seek to profit from horror and bloodshed. When he said indeed he hoped he <u>would</u> profit, I told him he was no better than a vulture. He retorted that even vultures are obliged to eat. Disgusted, I made to move *away, but Carolina took my hand and Thomas said we must all seize opportunity wherever we may find it. The youth grinned boldly and said this was indeed true, as he himself was not favored to have been born into wealth. Thomas replied that, just as a person may not be all he seems, the appearance of riches may be deceiving. The youth declared he would call the picture "Portrait of a Poor Planter on His Porch." He was shockingly insolent! But Thomas's hand upon my shoulder trembled with suppressed laughter.*

Thrilled to discover the stranger's identity, Temple looked at the photo again. Jane was at Folly Park in the spring of 1861, when the photograph was taken, and her diary had been hidden in the ceiling during the Civil War. She probably came south after she received Carolina's letter in 1859 and never left. King must be the name of the enslaved man in the photo and Jewel the pretty girl. There might be information about them in the archives.

Temple turned eagerly to the beginning of the diary to read as much as she could before the staff meeting . . . and was soon bored. Illness had kept Jane confined to her bed for months. She wrote brief summaries of the "improving reading" her mother had assigned and lamented that visits from her fiancé were prohibited. Finally permitted to go downstairs in September, ensuing entries described Jane's mind-numbing routine of studying, needlework, and practicing the harpsichord. Drama was rare, centered on disagreements with a brother named William and the youthful antics of another brother named Benjamin. A few passages described the family's divided reactions to the news of John Brown's failed raid on the federal arsenal at Harper's Ferry. William thought him a hero for attempting to free the slaves. Jane's father believed he was a lunatic for planning a race war. Jane did not record her own thoughts, and there followed more dull entries. Temple yawned.

Then she discovered a passage that changed everything.

October 25, 1859

I am a coward. That is the truth, though it is painful to see it in black ink on this staring white page. It is so bald a truth! Even the word itself looks weak and craven—the "c" curled over the defenseless "o," the "w" like a stammer, the long neck of the "d" peeping up as if to see if all is safe. Oh, I do despise myself! I have always suspected I might not be brave and steadfast in a crisis, and now it is proved with certainty!

Yesterday, I left Stringfellow's shop on foot and unescorted. Benjamin had not yet come with the carriage, and I was late returning home to help Mother with her tea for the Ladies' Committee. It began to rain when I had gone barely half the distance—sheets of water that made the cobbles steam so it looked as if fog had rolled in from the sea. I was nearly run down crossing the street, and the hostler shouted and shook his fist. I hurried into the alley not far from our house—the quickest way and free of traffic. I came upon them suddenly.

They were struggling there in the alley. The man— stocky and bearded with a low-slouched hat—had got hold of his opponent's hair and had borne her—for it was a woman, a Negro woman—to the ground at his feet. I could see the blood streaming from her scalp—bright scarlet on her brown face. She screamed to me for help. But he, half-turning, saw instantly that I would do nothing. I stood hand to mouth, umbrella dropped at my side, frozen and useless as a stone image. The woman reared suddenly up from the ground with a knife in her hand she must have drawn from her abuser's boot. With an oath, he released her and turned his palms up in surrender, but she lunged for him, slashing. He backed away and slipped and went down heavily in the mud at my feet. She turned and ran, disappearing down the alley in the rain, like a ghost into shadow. The man glared at me wrathfully as I stood gasping for breath. They tell me that my two rescuers caught me as I fell, senseless.

Mother says I was carried into the midst of the women of the Anti-Slavery Society so pale and still she thought I was dead. The men who had come to my aid told everyone I had single-handedly prevented a slave woman from falling into the hands of a slavecatcher—holding him at bay while she escaped. I was put to bed—where I am now—urged to rest by Father before the doctor comes again to see me, though I have said many times over that I am quite well. Father has never before visited me in my bedchamber—not even when I nearly died of the influenza as a child, nor when I was so ill this summer past. And I had not the courage to tell him I did nothing as the slave woman saved herself.

Cousin Jane was an abolitionist. Temple's heart raced. A woman dedicated to the cause of freeing slaves had come to Folly Park Plantation. With the country on the brink of a vicious Civil War fought over slavery, she sat for a photo with her Southern cousins.

How could the general allow an abolitionist to stay in his home? Temple wondered. *Did he support the cause?* Suddenly, she remembered a letter from the general to a West Point class-mate describing slavery as a "maggot gnawing at the liver of the South." *What if he acted on his beliefs and betrayed the Confederacy? What would it mean for Folly Park?*

Temple looked out the window where the corner of the mansion shone bright in the morning sun. The handmade red-clay bricks were the color of the earth from which they had been formed, as if the house had grown out of the land like a living thing. At that moment, another blast rumbled in the distance, and a mug holding pens and pencils jittered across the desk. On the wall opposite, an old, framed photograph of Folly Park crashed to the floor, the glass shattering.

CHAPTER TWO

Temple hesitated in the doorway, looking down at her phone. Beau was calling again. Martha's striking, amber-colored eyes glared from behind the reception desk. Clearly, she was tired of taking down his messages.

"He probably just wants to borrow Chick again," Temple said. "He calls him 'babe bait.'"

Martha intensified the power of her glare by raising her dark brows in line with the blunt edge of her dark bangs. Defeated, Temple answered the phone.

"Temp! Why didn't you call me back?" Beau's voice boomed as if he had to make himself heard the length of a football field. "I need you to step up! I'm gonna run for mayor of Preston's Mill, and Dad says we've got to get my campaign rolling ASAP to whip that joker Poe."

Temple stepped outside so Martha wouldn't overhear. "Are you serious? You're running in the special election?"

Beau made the sharp barking noise that passed for laughter with him. "Of course I'm serious. You're the one who's always telling me I don't have a sense of humor."

"But you don't even live in Preston's Mill."

"Actually, I do. They gerrymandered the district a while back."

"You've barely started your career." Beau was only two years out of law school. *If he had a normal allotment of humility,* Temple thought, *he'd realize he's not qualified to be mayor.*

"How hard can it be? Dad says I'm ready."

"Well, I'm sorry, but I can't help you."

"Are you kidding? Come on! You don't have to babysit that run-down crapbox twenty-four/seven."

"Excuse me. I shouldn't have said I can't help when I meant I won't."

"Why the hell not?" Beau sounded hurt as well as annoyed. "You did it for Harry."

"That's why. I'll never be a part of another campaign Dad's involved in."

Beau let out a hissing breath. "Don't be so melodramatic. Harry didn't die because of Dad."

Temple said nothing.

"You might want to reconsider," Beau said coldly. "The mayor gets an automatic seat on Folly Park's board."

Temple had forgotten about that stipulation in the town's bylaws. But she said, "So what?"

"Frank's Black."

"And?"

"He won't fit in too well with the rest of your trustees. And his whole platform is about racial justice, whatever that means."

"Well, I happen to support racial justice," Temple snapped and hung up. She shoved the phone into her pocket and stalked down the brick-paved path into the park.

Temple barely noticed the decaying follies as she passed them. She dreaded what was coming after Beau reported back to their father. When stamped with the name of four very old Virginia families at birth, as she was, there were certain expectations. You were supposed to honor the lineage by conducting yourself with dignity, preserving wealth and accumulating more, successfully pursuing an acceptable career after attending an elite university, and marrying a person with a similar pedigree. Above all, you must display unwavering loyalty to your family. There would be consequences for breaking the code, especially for someone named Temple Tayloe Smith Preston. Her father, a judge by inclination as well as profession, would be seriously displeased she had refused to help her brother. She felt a familiar knot of tension settle into the pit of her stomach.

To calm her racing thoughts, Temple took a deep breath and looked around. Al had cut the grass in the park into a smooth, green fairway again. He liked to practice his golf shots after closing hours. It wasn't authentic to the historical period, but she appreciated the park's well-groomed appearance. By contrast, the kitchen garden, planted with herbs and heirloom vegetables, looked neglected. At that moment, another blast thundered in the distance and rumbled under her feet, setting the limp leaves trembling.

EVERYONE ELSE WAS ALREADY assembled in the old icehouse when Temple arrived for the staff meeting—all but Betty Jean, on duty in the ticket office. Martha, Al, and the head tour guides, Fred and Flora, sat on discarded office chairs banished to the conference room because they could no longer be adjusted. Pitching left or right or forward or backward at a variety of heights, they resembled rafters on a wild river.

Temple slid into a seat near the door, and a moment later Stuart bustled in. His round baby face turned red as he pumped the lever on the side of the chair in vain. He finally gave up and tucked his leg under himself to gain some height.

"Okay, team, let's kick this meeting off!" Stuart bawled, purposely startling Flora out of a catnap. Yawning into the back of her hand, she patted her corkscrew curls and fluffed the skirt of her antebellum gown, one of a seemingly endless supply of period clothing she insisted on wearing to work.

Stuart placed his palms on either side of his printed agenda with a habitual grimace intended to push his glasses farther up on his nose without having to use his hands. Temple mentally called it a "squinch."

"I've only got ten minutes," Stuart said. "Hunt just called and asked me to meet him at the club."

The way Stuart was always dropping the trustees' names got on Temple's nerves. The richer and more influential they were, the more Stuart shortened their names, as if to create an illusion of intimacy. Jonathan Winter, who owned a chain of hardware stores, was always "Mr. Jonathan Winter." But former state senator Thomas McCrae was "Tom McCrae," and the chairman of the board, Hunter Glass, was "Hunt."

"First bullet point," Stuart said, smoothing his tie over his small potbelly. "The kudzu infestation. Where are we on that, Gardens and Grounds?" Stuart liked to pretend his staff was larger than it was by referring to everyone by the name of their department.

Al leaned in, fingers spread wide on the table, and said dramatically, "The kudzu is completely out of control. Did you know it can grow four feet overnight?"

"Four feet a night!" Stuart's muddy brown eyes popped behind his glasses. "We can't have that! Something has to be done!"

Al winked at Temple. "I'll put up a fight. Mow where I can and try to kill it with an herbicide."

Stuart bobbed his head energetically. "Okay, good." He clapped his hands twice. "Bullet point two, Curatorial Department, has our CIP for the SHB been completed yet?"

Stuart's acronyms always confused everyone, so Temple said slowly, "The comprehensive interpretive plan for the State Historical Bureau will be submitted tomorrow. I've shown a draft to Hugh Fox, and he thinks we have a good chance of getting accredited this year."

"Hugh Fox? The director over at Cleveland Hill?" Stuart's voice rose.

"Hugh knows people on the Bureau," Temple said, realizing her mistake too late. "He's an old family friend."

"You can't go sharing confidential stuff with a rival historic home! And I don't care if your ancestors came over on the *Mayflower* together—leave the networking to me. I'm the one with the MBA!" Stuart squinched belligerently. "What happened to you anyway? What's wrong with your face?"

Before Temple could answer, the door squeaked open, and a young woman stepped into the room. "Excuse me? The lady in the ticket office directed me here. I'm the new summer intern."

In the morning's excitement, Temple had forgotten about the internship she'd arranged months ago at the behest of her adviser at the university. With everyone else, she stared in surprise. The newcomer certainly did not fit the mold of the interns Dr. Belcher usually pawned off on Folly Park—slovenly, indolent young men. White men.

The young woman had a light-brown complexion, and tight black curls framed her attractive face. Her hazel eyes were bright behind large, blue-rimmed glasses. Slender and of medium height, she was probably in her mid-twenties, dressed neatly in jeans and a printed blouse. An army-green backpack hung from one shoulder.

The silence had stretched long. "Am I in the right place?" the young woman asked.

Al snorted. "I doubt it."

Temple stood up. "Hi, I'm Temple Preston. Dr. Belcher sent you?"

"Yes. I'm Vee." She gave a small wave.

"Okay, Vee, you'll be sharing Temple's office, and she'll show you the ropes." Stuart scooped up his notepad and trotted around the table. From the doorway he called, "By the way, I've reviewed the numbers, and you all can forget about that pay increase Tate promised before he retired. Sorry!"

Stuart vanished. It was amazing that someone with his squat figure and stubby legs could move so fast, Temple thought, as everyone stared at each other in dismay. No one had gotten a raise in four years.

"You'll talk to him, won't you, Temple?" Fred asked.

The others looked at her hopefully. Because of her family connection to the house and personal relationships with the trustees, they persisted in believing Temple had some sort of pull with the new director, despite a complete lack of evidence. She doubted she could change Stuart's mind but promised to do what she could, and after briefly introducing themselves to Vee they left, their fading voices a discontented murmur.

"Sorry about that," Temple said. "It's been a strange morning."

"I thought maybe you forgot I was coming," Vee said. "But then I realized I introduced myself with my nickname. Evelyn Williams is my full name."

Relieved that Vee had come up with a plausible explanation for her awkward reception, Temple made a noncommittal noise. But her sense of relief didn't last long. She thought Vee looked a little disappointed as she scanned the dingy room. And when Vee's keen gaze returned to her, Temple felt suddenly conscious of her wrinkled khakis and faded red polo shirt with the Folly Park logo. Resisting a strong urge to fiddle with the bandage on her forehead, she cleared her throat. "Dr. Belcher seemed eager to have you here this summer. Are you studying under him?"

Vee shook her head. "Military history isn't my area. I thought Dr. Belcher would have told you I'm here to research Carolina Smith. I'm working on an article for the *American History Journal.*"

"He didn't mention it." Temple's discomfort gave way to pity. Every graduate student was working on an article for the prestigious journal. Publication guaranteed a job in a very competitive and uncertain field. But she doubted any piece about the general's wife could meet the journal's high standards. It would be kind to let Vee down gently. "Honestly, I'm surprised Dr. Belcher would support a project on Carolina. He refers to her as 'General Smith's unfortunate connection.'"

Vee shifted her backpack. "I've actually never met him. He got me this job as a favor to my adviser, Dr. Carmen Flores."

Carmen Flores was a rising star at Harvard, shaking up the field with her groundbreaking work on multidimensional identity. Temple was surprised—and impressed.

"I wanted to search your archives, and Dr. Flores fixed it

up with Dr. Belcher. They met at a conference a few months ago, and she said he owed her."

Temple could imagine exactly what kind of situation would make Dr. Belcher owe Dr. Flores—he was notorious for hitting on every woman he met. Thankfully, he'd never tried it on Temple. The fact that she was a military historian seemed to cancel out her gender.

"I see," Temple said. "I know Dr. Belcher well. He was the chair of my dissertation committee."

"He told me. He said your application of organizational behavioral theory to social and cultural aspects of military camp life during the Civil War was brilliant."

Temple wondered if Vee was flattering her. Dr. Belcher had not been enthusiastic about her dissertation, and sometimes she doubted he'd even read her drafts. "Well, welcome to Folly Park," she said. "Let me show you around."

As they walked up the drive, Temple pointed out various points of interest, such as the 150-year-old espaliered pear trees growing in the kitchen garden, the wooden-chimneyed washhouse, and the murky carp pond. One of her nineteenth-century ancestors had flung himself into it to extinguish his beard after it caught on fire from a poorly rolled cigarillo.

"What made you want to research Carolina?" Temple asked as they passed the old well. Filled in during the Civil War, it was now a grassy mound blanketed with creeping myrtle.

"I discovered something in connection with my dissertation topic."

Temple's phone buzzed with a text from Al. The structural engineer had completed his assessment and signed off on opening for visitors, but he insisted on talking to her before he left. "I've got to see somebody at the house," she said to Vee. "Why don't you come along?"

They took a shortcut through a brick tunnel running between the detached kitchen and the mansion. It was called the Whistling Walk because the slaves were required to whistle as they carried trays to the dining room so their mistress would know they weren't eating any of the White family's food. In the dim light, Temple glanced sideways at Vee. "What's your dissertation about?"

"Nineteenth-century Blacks passing as White. I've been tracing the history of a Boston family, the Stannards, who helped dozens of people cross the color line. They were prominent in the antislavery movement before the Civil War."

"That's interesting. But what's the connection to Folly Park?"

Vee hesitated for a moment. "In December 1884, one of the Stannard sons recorded in his journal that they'd taken in a biracial man named Robert Smith—they called him a mulatto. His mother owned a plantation in Virginia, and she sent him to the Stannards the day he turned twenty-one. Robert reported that his most useful skills were hunting, fishing, and mathematics. To pay his expenses until he could find a job, he'd brought a family heirloom—a gold ring carved with a two-faced head with emerald eyes."

Temple stopped abruptly. "What?"

"Robert told the Stannards he came from a place called Folly Park. I think his parents were Carolina Smith and an enslaved man."

Temple stared at her new intern in shock.

As if to forestall argument, Vee quickly laid out her theory. "Because Robert's mother was White, his father had to have been Black and probably enslaved since Robert was born during the Civil War."

"Let's continue this in the light," Temple muttered. She needed time to think.

When they reached the end of the tunnel, Temple cautiously pushed open the secret door into the dining room. Once, Al had popped carelessly into the midst of a group of seniors and nearly given them a collective heart attack. This time, the room was empty. Just beyond the doorway, Fred was giving a tour in the high-ceilinged entrance hall. "We'll just wait a minute until they pass through," Temple whispered.

Fred waved when he spotted them and continued his spiel without missing a beat. "After his entire family perished in a yellow fever epidemic, sixteen-year-old Thomas left his plantation home in Louisiana. He came to Folly Park to live with his uncle James, a widower with no children. . . ."

"Why is it called 'Folly Park'?" asked a woman. Her husband was trying to keep their squirming little boy under control.

"That's a good question." Fred beamed, as if he did not hear the same query every day. "In the eighteenth and early nineteenth centuries, it became popular for wealthy people to construct romantic ruined castles, towers, pyramids, and other whimsical or symbolic creations in their gardens. They were called follies. You will see that in the garden, or park, there are a number of these playful structures. The house takes its name from them."

"If I was rich, I wouldn't blow my money on a fake castle. I'd buy a real one," the man scoffed, looking up at Fred. Taking advantage of his father's slackened grip, the little boy twisted away and bolted into the library.

"We'll continue our tour this way," Fred called as he hurried after the boy.

"We can go now," Temple said to Vee, heading toward the back hall. "What you've told me is interesting, but Carolina never had a child."

"How can you be sure? She probably would have tried to keep an out-of-wedlock baby a secret."

"Or maybe she wasn't the mother. This Robert Smith character could have been lying, trying to slander the general." Temple's tone was sharper than she intended.

Vee looked taken aback. "But the Stannards kept everything secret in order to protect the new identities of the people they helped. Robert Smith had nothing to gain by lying."

"Look, I don't think you should try to turn Carolina into some racially progressive heroine." The conversation was making Temple very uneasy. She dragged a skeleton out of the closet to help her head Vee off. "She was addicted to laudanum—opium. And she was born and raised in the South and the mistress of a plantation. It's really hard to believe she had a child by an enslaved man." Temple chose not to mention the rumors about Carolina's infidelity, which would give credence to Vee's theory, or her discovery that very day of an abolitionist cousin.

"I understand this is hard to take in," Vee said with a strained smile. "But mixed-race children on Southern plantations weren't exactly uncommon."

"Sure, because of the men. I'm not saying that White women and Black men never had sex, but women of Carolina's class didn't have much freedom or privacy. And besides, how would she have known to send this young man to the Stannards?"

"She probably met someone who knew them. Maybe someone from Boston."

Temple wondered if Jane Elliot had told Carolina about the Stannards during her time at Folly Park. Deep in her historian's heart, curiosity stirred before anxiety crushed it with a vengeance. She wasn't ready to talk about the diary.

"What about the ring Robert brought with him?" Vee asked. "Do you know anything about a ring of that description?"

Temple did, and it bothered her. She couldn't think of an explanation for how the Folly Park ring had ended up with a biracial man in Boston. "Al's waiting," she said, avoiding Vee's question.

AL STOOD UNDER THE HOLE in the ceiling with a bored expression as the structural engineer droned on. As soon as Temple and Vee arrived, he hurried away like a kid let out for recess. But Temple saw him turn and glance back at Vee with a flat, appraising look.

The engineer greeted Temple glumly and seemed reluctant to admit the house was safe, tacking on an ominous "for now." He felt compelled, he said, to point out some issues that were likely to become serious problems. Temple already knew about those, and they depressed her, so she gave him only half her attention. Instead, she wondered if her new intern's fantastic story could possibly be true.

Glancing at Vee, Temple saw her peer closely at a framed sampler of Folly Park embroidered in the early nineteenth century. Poorly executed, it was an attempt to depict the mansion perched on its hill overlooking the river. Three misshapen figures, their faces and bodies fashioned from clumps of black thread, were laboring in a field, watched over by a white clump holding a whip. HEAVEN ON EARTH arced across the blue sky.

The sampler had hung in the back hall for so long Temple never noticed it, but she saw Vee's lip curl with disgust and realized with sudden horror how offensive it must seem to her. Face flushing, Temple quickly looked away before Vee caught her staring. The engineer was startled by her sudden attentiveness.

With a promise to email his full report, the engineer finally left. Standing under the gaping hole, Temple felt an urge to duck her head, as if something else might fall. And she wanted to get Vee away from the sampler. "You mentioned a ring," she said. "Come with me."

In the parlor, Temple pointed to a life-size portrait of the general's grandfather, Commodore J. T. Smith. It dated from 1793, soon after the mansion had been completed. In the background were the follies: a pyramid that was now a pile of rubble, a stone bridge, and a rustic mill symbolizing the virtues of country life. The castle folly was missing—it had been built later to hide the expanding slave quarters from sight of the house. Pink-cheeked and bewigged, in a blue velvet suit with a lace cravat, the commodore rested his hand on the head of an enslaved boy, whose eyes rolled up at his master in a servile expression. On that hand, the commodore wore a gold ring depicting the two-faced head of the Roman god Janus. The eyes were green emeralds.

"The ring is one of a kind," Temple said. "The commodore commissioned it after he made a fortune during the Revolutionary War. He posed as a British loyalist while running guns to the patriots. That's why it has two faces—it represents duplicity. The ring was passed on to James Smith Jr., the general's uncle, but it was stolen in the 1830s."

"How do you know it was stolen?" Vee's eyes were bright behind her glasses.

"James's wife wrote about it in a letter to her sister."

"But it must have stayed at Folly Park all along for Carolina to be able to give it to her son fifty years later."

"*If* he was her son. Please don't tell anyone else about

your theory until we can verify it. This kind of thing has to be handled carefully."

"Of course. I'm not trying to start trouble," Vee said quickly. "I don't have some hidden agenda to embarrass Folly Park."

"That never crossed my mind." Temple wondered if she'd been stupid that it hadn't. She pointed to another portrait. "That's Carolina."

Reclining on a chaise in a lavender gown, blue eyes half shut, Carolina's blond hair was piled high on her head, and a fan dangled from one slender hand. On the three-legged table by her side was a sliced lemon, supposedly representing how things that looked attractive on the outside could be bitter on the inside, and behind her a dead finch lay on its back inside a gilded cage. The motifs made Temple curious about how the artist and Carolina had gotten along.

"She looks sad," Vee said.

Temple thought Carolina looked sulky and spoiled.

Vee turned to Temple's favorite portrait of General Smith. Swarthy, dark-eyed, and handsome, he was posed amid books and scientific instruments, rather than hunting dogs and horses, like most men of his era. He held a human skull in one hand and an hourglass in the other, reminders of the fragility of human life. Temple thought Thomas looked serious and wise beyond his twenty-one years. As a kid, she'd had a crush on him. Her brothers knew it and had teased her mercilessly. It was hard to retaliate—she did indeed want to go back in time and marry him.

"He looks intimidating."

Vee seemed to be implying that Thomas had driven his wife into another man's arms. "You know, there were other women at Folly Park," Temple said. "Maybe one of the slaves got pregnant by a White man. That wasn't exactly unusual, as you pointed out."

Vee pursed her lips and looked away. *She probably thinks I don't want to learn the truth about Carolina's alleged baby,* Temple thought. Vee was right, sort of, Temple conceded. Publicity about Folly Park was exactly what she didn't need right now. She made an effort to sound reasonable. "Maybe Carolina adopted one of her ex-slaves's children after its mother died. There are other explanations you should consider."

"Sure. But can I see that letter about the ring being stolen?"

"Maybe later. I have to get some work done, and you need to be trained on the house tour. I'll take you to the ticket office, and you can shadow Flora."

Outside, the family from Fred's tour was heading toward the park. The boy looked up at Vee. "Are you a slave?"

There was a shocked silence. Then the mother hushed the boy while the father turned red and coughed.

Temple knelt in front of the child. "We don't have slaves anymore. Slavery was bad." As the family hurried away, she turned to Vee. "I'm so sorry."

Vee's face was closed and remote. "You can leave me here. I'll find my way."

CHAPTER THREE

" This is just a place to keep your things," Temple said apologetically, pointing to the corner of her office, where an old door spanned two dented file cabinets to form a makeshift desk. "You'll probably spend most of your time in the archives."

"It's fine." Vee set her backpack on the door and took out a yellow legal pad and a pen. "Can you tell me more about my duties as an intern?"

Temple appreciated how proactive Vee appeared to be on her second day of work. "You'll organize the archives, do your own research, and give the occasional tour. You need to know about the general. What did you learn from Flora yesterday?"

"That he was a rich planter who fought for the Confederacy during the Civil War, and some historians think he was a traitor, but she knows he wasn't."

Temple smiled at Vee's mild dig at Flora, but the casual distillation of the general's entire life into one sentence suggested Vee was the type of historian who saw people from the past through a purely academic lens—as evidence for a thesis, rather than human beings who had once led full lives. But she supposed it was understandable a Black scholar might not be interested in the details of a Confederate general's life. She gave Vee the abbreviated version of his biography, explaining that during the early years of the Civil War, the general was considered one of the best cavalry officers in Virginia, renowned for his strategic prowess and courage in battle. "General Smith was a hero around here—and still is to a lot of people," she concluded.

"Still? You mean like the South will rise again?"

"Not like a white supremacist thing," Temple said hastily. "But for some people, especially those whose families have lived in Preston's Mill for generations, their identity is tightly connected to the place and its past. To them, the general isn't just a historical figure. He's someone they feel they know—like a relative, a friend, or a neighbor. Do you see what I mean?"

"I'm not sure." Vee clicked her pen. "But I should probably learn more about him."

Vee looked like a child preparing to eat spinach. It made Temple self-conscious, so she spoke too fast, galloping through a recital of the Folly Park brochure she knew by heart.

"Thomas Temple Smith was born in 1837 on a backwoods plantation twenty miles from New Orleans. He was the only son and third and last child of Thomas Temple Smith Sr. and his wife, Antoinette. After a carefree childhood spent playing outdoors with an enslaved boy named Cass, Thomas was educated at home by tutors and acquired the usual accomplishments of a well-to-do Southern youth. He could read and write and do sums, parse a few Latin phrases, ride, hunt, fish, and fight. When he was sixteen, a yellow fever epidemic struck the neighborhood, killing Thomas's father, mother, and sisters, the overseer, and nearly all the enslaved people, including his boyhood companion.

Thomas liquidated the plantation, paid off his father's debts, and traveled to the family's ancestral home in Virginia with what was left of his legacy in a single trunk.

"Folly Park was owned by Thomas's uncle James, his father's elder brother, who was a childless widower," Temple continued. "James sent his nephew to West Point Military Academy, and in 1859, just before Thomas was set to graduate, James died. Thomas inherited Folly Park and shortly after married his first cousin, Carolina Gilmore. She brought him a substantial dowry in cash, land, and slaves. They'd only been married for a couple of years when Thomas went off to fight in the Civil War and was killed. They never had any children, and Carolina lived here until her death in 1934."

"And you believe she never had another relationship in seventy years?" Vee's tone was skeptical.

Although it meant condemning a young woman to a lifetime of celibacy, to Temple, the idea of Carolina remaining faithful to her heroic husband was far more romantic than that she might have found love again.

"We haven't seen evidence of another man." Again, Temple did not take the opportunity to mention the duel the general had supposedly fought over Carolina's infidelity. "After the war, she was alone out here in the country."

"Alone? Who did all the work?"

Temple was embarrassed. "You're right. There were sharecroppers working the land, and I'm sure Carolina had help in the house." She added quickly, "It's lunchtime, and I've got some errands to do. Can I give you a ride into town? There's a new café."

"I brought lunch." Vee pulled a paper bag out of her backpack.

"You'll be more comfortable at my place. It's not far."

"Thanks." Vee hoisted her backpack to her shoulder.

"That looks like a vintage bag. It's in beautiful condition."

Vee offered her first genuine smile. "It was my grandfather's. From World War II. My dad had it restored for me when I started grad school."

"He must be really proud of you."

"Well, he still tells me every other day that he hated history in high school," Vee said dryly.

"My father was so mad when I quit law school for history that he didn't speak to me for a year."

"I'm sorry. Lucky for me, one sister is a lawyer and the other's an engineer, so my dad reconciled himself to me squandering my life in academia."

"Having two sons as lawyers didn't satisfy my father."

"He sounds hard to please."

That's an understatement, Temple thought.

HALFWAY UP THE DRIVE, THEY MET AL, who was on his way back from the ticket office to give a tourist a refund for the flat tire he'd gotten from one of the sinkhole-sized potholes in the driveway. After that, Al said, he'd set up orange cones under the bridge folly, which was dropping stones from its underbelly again.

Though a daily occurrence, hearing new reports about Folly Park's decay always depressed Temple. She wished she could renovate the property herself, but she did not have access to the family wealth, which was all on the Preston side. Her father doled out only a monthly allowance designed to keep her somewhat dependent on him. Even when his wife was alive, he'd never had any interest in restoring Folly Park, where his father-in-law lived.

Renting out the mansion for weddings, like other plantation homes, had the potential to be quite lucrative, but the thought of people drinking and dancing where enslaved people had suffered bothered Temple. She had devised an alternative plan to secure Folly Park's long-term future. It involved obtaining funds from the state General Assembly to restore the plantation in return for converting the old tobacco barn, which had been her mother's art studio, into a group home for at-risk girls. She'd come up with the idea when the detention facility where she was a volunteer tutor got derailed trying to set up a program because it couldn't afford to purchase a site. Her plan had the potential to please politicians on both sides of the aisle—liberals, who would back a progressive group home, and more conservative types, who might appreciate preserving Southern heritage without having to argue for its merits. Her old schoolmate Randy Pierce, a lobbyist, thought he could interest one of the state senators in sponsoring the plan, but he hadn't been answering her texts or returning her calls lately. She planned to pressure him in person that day.

Temple stopped in front of her house, across the gravel drive only a hundred yards from the mansion's front door. "Here we are."

Vee's eyes widened. "Is this the old slave quarters?"

Temple nodded. "For the house servants. It was converted into a single home when it was renovated years ago."

Vee glanced at the water stains under the eaves, the result of a chronic leak in the sway-backed roof. "I saw another old house on the way up the drive. Does someone live there?"

"Al and Betty Jean. It's the old overseer's house."

Behind her glasses, Vee's eyes widened again. "Dr. Belcher told me that one of them is descended from Folly Park slaves?"

"Yes, Al. His last name is Smith."

Al was descended from a laundress named Phoebe, who bore ten children before she was sold at the age of fifty-seven when she failed to remove a stain from her mistress's favorite gown.

Chick darted from the back of the house and danced around Vee on his hind legs, front paws waving in the air. When Temple finally got him under control, he sat beside her panting.

"What's his name?" Vee held out her hand for the dog to sniff.

"Chick—short for Chickamauga—the battlefield. I found him abandoned there when he was a puppy." Temple rubbed Chick's head affectionately. "He's good company. It can get a little lonely here." The contrast with what things must have been like hundreds of years ago, when Folly Park was home to dozens of enslaved families as well as her ancestors, often struck Temple at night, when the only sounds came from crickets, frogs, and owls.

"I'd like a dog. We never had one when I was growing up. My dad's in the army, so we moved around a lot, and quarantine was too much of a hassle." Vee sounded wistful as she reached out to pet Chick. Lunging to lick her face, he knocked her glasses askew. Temple scolded him, but Vee laughed.

"He likes you," Temple said and was rewarded with Vee's smile. "Come on in."

As usual, the house was clean and neat, but Temple's face flushed with horror as Vee stepped over the threshold and was confronted by a large photographic portrait. Temple had put it there as a joke to greet visitors.

The subject was Captain Cadwallader "Lad" Preston, who had reportedly had the affair with Carolina and dueled the general. Dressed in his Confederate uniform, Lad had high cheekbones and waving dark hair that fell to his shoulders. Clean-shaven, his full lips smirked, and one light eye stared out from the frame—the other had been lost in a drunken brawl and was covered with a rakish patch. Lad's personal motto, LIVE TO FIGHT, FIGHT TO LIVE, was etched on the frame below the photo. By the time he was Temple's age, twenty-eight, Lad had fought four duels, been mauled by a mountain lion, survived near-fatal bouts of typhus and cholera, and fathered seven known children by four different women, both White and Black. He'd been found mysteriously murdered in his bed on Christmas Day in 1862, while home on leave from the Civil War.

Shrinking inwardly, Temple decided it might be better to deal with Lad head-on. She pointed at the portrait. "Cadwallader Preston. He was a neighbor of the general and Carolina."

Temple was surprised to see a smile curving one corner of Vee's mouth. "Why is he hanging on your wall?"

"He's an ancestor on my father's side."

"So, you're descended from him *and* General Smith *and* Carolina?"

Put that way, it sounded somehow incestuous. "Only directly from Lad."

Vee tilted her head, regarding the picture. "Your black eye actually makes you look a little like him."

Temple had often been told that with her blondish-brown hair and eyes appearing either blue or gray depending on what she wore, she didn't look anything like the Preston side of the family. Like her father and Beau, Prestons had dark hair and light gray eyes.

"Oh, great," she said. "It's well documented he was a bit of a jerk."

"I don't think that's genetic," Vee said.

NOTHING HAS CHANGED, TEMPLE thought as she entered the big, gray, government building with the three-story Corinthian pilasters and paused to go through the metal detector. She'd often visited Harry there after he was elected, but she hadn't been back since his death. His aides had cleared out his office, and now someone else had it. The passing of one idealistic young delegate had not stopped the business of politics from marching on.

An assistant told Temple that Randy was in a meeting with Senator Claiborne, and after confirming with the senator's intern, she waited in the hallway. When both men emerged, she stepped forward to give Senator Claiborne a kiss. He and her father were old friends, and she'd known him all her life.

"Oh, Senator, has Randy been telling you about my plan for the group home?" Temple glanced at Randy, whose face turned a shade of red that erased his freckles and clashed with his ginger hair.

"Temple! What a pleasant surprise!" Senator Claiborne returned the kiss. "What happened to your eye? And what's this about a plan? Randy hasn't mentioned it. I'm sure whatever it is has greater merit than more tax breaks for out-of-town developers." The senator scowled as he was summoned back into his office for a call.

Randy's eyes narrowed. "What are you doing here?"

"I didn't hear back from you, so I thought I'd stop by. Why didn't you mention my plan to the senator?"

"This meeting was about something else."

"Do you want to talk it over with him together?"

"No. I'm going to reach out to a couple of new delegates instead."

Temple was annoyed Randy would pass up an immediate chance to speak to a powerful state senator in favor of a potential meeting with a couple of junior delegates. "Great!" she said with fake enthusiasm. "Let's get started."

"There's hardly anyone around. The assembly isn't in session."

"That's good. Then whoever is here won't be too busy to talk to us."

Randy snaked his arm around Temple's waist with a patronizing smile. "I know you're excited about your idea, but you have to leave this to me. I'll call as soon as I have news." He squeezed her side.

Temple stepped out of Randy's grasp. "I'll check back in a couple of days."

"Sure, fine." Randy leaned in, but Temple turned her face, and the kiss landed wetly on her ear. Laughing shortly, Randy turned away. Temple frowned after him, scrubbing her ear.

Behind her a voice said, "Sorry it didn't work."

Temple turned and saw a tall man with dark-brown hair and hazel eyes regarding her with friendly interest. She suddenly felt conscious of the Band-Aid on her forehead and her black eye.

"What do you mean?" she asked, wondering who he was.

"Getting Randy to move on your issue. I couldn't help overhearing."

"I'll have to apply more pressure. Maybe I can blackmail him." Temple was only half joking.

"Don't bother." The man gave her a crooked smile. "It won't work. I can explain over coffee."

Temple wondered fleetingly if he were asking her on a date, and she was pleased. There was something about him that was attractive, literally—she felt drawn to him. But then he said, "You might not want to talk about it here in the hallway."

The words, which strongly suggested bad news to come, abruptly checked Temple's romantic ideas. "This is important to me. If you know something, please tell me now."

"Of course." The stranger led Temple toward a nearby alcove with a drinking fountain where they could speak more privately. "I know Randy did put out a couple of feelers. But, I have it on good authority he doesn't intend to pitch your plan to anyone who matters."

"Why not?"

"Because he believes—and he may be right—that providing state funds to restore Folly Park in return for a site for a group home is political suicide. He thinks some voters won't stand for girls who've had trouble with the law, many of whom are Black, living on the grounds of their heroes' home, and others don't want landmarks of the Confederacy preserved. And having the girls housed on an old plantation will remind Black constituents of slavery."

The summation made Temple's idea sound naïve, which she didn't much mind, and hopeless, which she did. "I wish Randy had been honest. I could have found someone willing to try, even if it is a long shot."

"I think Randy sincerely wanted to be of help to you, if that's any consolation."

"No. I don't care that he wanted to get on my good side. I wanted actual help."

"I can help," the stranger said with a warm smile. He handed her a card: Jack A. Early, Special Adviser to Senator Vance Alden.

Senator Alden was the chair of the Rehabilitation and Social Services Committee. Provided she could find a senator to sponsor it, that committee was the first place Temple's proposal would get a hearing, and the members could either kill it or send it on for a vote.

Afraid to say anything that might cause Jack Early to change his mind, Temple remarked inanely, "It's a good thing your first name isn't Jubal."

"Why is that?"

Now she was trapped into having to tell the unflattering truth. "Jubal Early was a Confederate general fired by Robert E. Lee after he managed to turn a brilliant victory into a rout."

"I see. You hope I don't prove equally inept with your plan."

"It was a joke." Temple's face burned with embarrassment.

"I'm teasing. I know about Jubal Early. If we were related, I'd regret his role as a major contributor to mythologizing the Lost Cause. But we're not."

Temple smiled broadly. He knew his history. Jack was referring to a speech Early gave on the anniversary of Robert E. Lee's death exhorting Southerners never to forget those who had died to preserve the Confederacy. "You're lucky not to have a problematic general in your family tree like I do."

Jack grinned. His teeth were white, and one was a tiny bit off-kilter. "Well, I respect that you're not shying away from the tough questions at Folly Park. And I think your proposal deserves a chance to be heard."

"Thank you." Temple held out her hand and Jack shook it. "I'll be in touch."

He strode away down the corridor. Temple saw him stop by a group of people, and someone said something that made him laugh. People passing in the hallway turned and smiled. Clearly, others found Jack as attractive as she did. He radiated confidence and optimism, which was great for her plan's prospects, of course, but she felt a sudden stab of unease. She needed to prepare for a backlash . . . just in case.

Although cities and towns across the nation were removing statues and renaming buildings and streets named after Confederates, Preston's Mill had retained its tributes to the general, not with an attitude of defiance, Temple believed, but rather with the unthinking inertia of a place lost in time. Though gentrification had come recently in the form of an organic food co-op, two boutiques, and the café she'd mentioned to Vee, scrapple was still served at the diner that had faced the general's statue since the monument was erected in the town square in 1924. The White half of Preston's Mill celebrated the general's birthday every October 14th with an enormous sheet cake, fireworks, and a reenactment of a Civil War skirmish.

Defying a tacit boycott by the other Black citizens of Preston's Mill, Al went to the party every year to sell tiny rebel flags attached to toothpicks and charge people to pose for selfies beside a wooden cutout of the general. He took pleasure in overpricing his souvenirs and enjoyed the free beer and cake. Last fall, he'd urged Temple to go with him.

"These rednecks think I'm an expert on the general because I cut his lawn," Al crowed. "They'd love to meet a real live descendant. You could sell discount passes to the house. Maybe a few of them will actually take a tour and learn something."

"I'm not a direct descendant."

"You're close enough. Come on, it'll be fun."

"I can't," Temple protested. "They're celebrating the Confederacy."

"Not really," Al said. "They're celebrating themselves. That might be worse."

PASSING THE GENERAL'S STATUE, Temple turned down a leafy side street and pulled to a stop in front of a sprawling antebellum house with a Tiffany stained-glass door.

"Hello, darling," a cool voice called from the veranda as Temple got out of her pickup. A renowned beauty in her youth, Ava Glass was the power of Preston's Mill society. She was the president of the local chapter of the Daughters of the American Confederacy and the wife of Hunter Glass, chairman of the board of Folly Park. She was also a distant relation, and since Temple's mother's death, Mrs. Glass had invited Temple to her house twice a month for "luncheon," as she called it, and a healthy serving of advice.

Settled into the chintz cushions of a wicker chair, Temple sipped a glass of chilled lemonade and watched the hummingbirds hover and dart around the hollyhocks beside the veranda. She didn't attend closely to today's lecture on how she should have her hair styled, manicure her nails, and wear more flattering clothes.

"And we'll never find you a husband if you go around with a black eye like some kind of tomboy." Mrs. Glass regarded Temple with beautiful eyes that looked like green marbles. "Darling, don't you even *want* a man?"

Temple started guiltily. At that moment, she was thinking of Jack's quick smile and warm hazel eyes, replaying their meeting in her mind.

Busy pouring out more lemonade, Mrs. Glass didn't notice. "You're only half a woman until you've been full-moon crazy about a man and only half a human being if your heart has never been broken."

"Rich. . . ."

"Don't tell me you were in love with *Rich*. I have more passion for my hairdresser than you had for him. He looks like he should be interesting, but that branch of the family has always been dull. He's a fourth cousin to me, you know."

Mrs. Glass delicately nibbled her shaved pork sandwich with teeth like cultured pearls and shook her head. "But to be your age and never in love? What would your mother say?" she sighed. "I can't believe she's been gone thirteen years already."

"Fourteen, actually, just this past April."

"Of course. She would have been so proud of you. Moving to Folly Park was a generous, loyal thing to do." Mrs. Glass touched her linen napkin to her lips. "But perhaps it's time for a change. It was a good place to write your dissertation while you kept your grandfather company, but you don't need to keep working there. Has anything come up since you had to turn down that postdoctoral fellowship?"

"I haven't really been looking for an academic position." Temple didn't feel like explaining why she wanted to stay at Folly Park. Only there did she feel truly at home, and she felt both a duty to her heritage and a desire to atone, somehow, for the stain of slaveholding that was spread like a blight through the branches of the family tree. Temple believed the house museum could help rectify that horrific heritage. In addition to her plan, she had ideas about how to share the full and true story of Folly Park's past. "I'm content where I am," she said.

"You only have one life, darling. Content is not good enough." Mrs. Glass spoke in what Temple thought of as her *Steel Magnolias* voice. "You have so much in your favor—youth, brains, an excellent education, looks. You need to use it all to your advantage. And I don't mean to find a husband—I recognize the world is different from when I was young. But you don't imagine you can make a career out of Folly Park, do you? Especially with this rumor flying around."

Mrs. Glass loved to gossip. "What rumor?" Temple asked obligingly.

"You don't know?" Mrs. Glass set her lemonade glass down so hard on the table it sounded like a gunshot. "Why, they're saying those Boston developers putting in the golf course are trying to buy Folly Park."

Temple's heart began to pound. "What do they want it for?"

"Goodness only knows. Darling, are you all right?"

Temple's face felt as if it were on fire, and her black eye throbbed. Surely, the board of trustees would not sell out to the developers. She thought of the local farm that had recently been converted into a housing development called Gone with the Wind Estates. The streets had names like Rhett Butler's Ridge and Scarlett's Circle that inspired an endless supply of crude jokes. *The trustees and the town council will want to avoid another public relations debacle,* Temple told herself. "I'm sure nothing will happen to Folly Park," she said, trying to smile.

To her surprise, Mrs. Glass nodded knowingly. "That's right. You have an ace up your sleeve."

"An ace? What do you mean?"

"Why, that Beau is running for mayor, of course."

CHAPTER FOUR

Preoccupied with worry as she hurried across the town square, Temple neglected to respond to people who greeted her. Too late, she realized she was upholding her reputation as an eccentric, a label she'd acquired at the age of fourteen, the summer she'd picketed the country club.

Shortly before the end of the eighth-grade school year, Temple's favorite teacher, an earnest young transplant from Vermont, informed her American history class that many country clubs had been established in the 1960s, when federal courts ordered the desegregation of public parks and swimming pools.

The private Horse and Hounds Club, where her father was a member, had been around since the 1920s, but Temple became fixated on its exclusivity and de facto segregation. She rode there every morning from the city with a home-made wooden sign strapped to the back of her bike that read COUNTRY CLUBS ARE RACIST. Staking the sign in the grass by the front gate, she slouched beside it in a camp chair, an awkward, gangly teenager.

Trying to ignore the stares and occasional jeers of school-mates as they drove through the gate, Temple buried herself in *Gone with the Wind*, the irony of reading a glorification of the Old South under the circumstances escaping her at the time. Her father threatened dire punishments, friends stopped talking to her, and people in Preston's Mill began to treat her with a kind of baffled caution. Temple had thought no one understood her, but years later, she learned that her grandfather had called the club manager on the first day of her campaign and convinced him to let her be. It was only six weeks since her mother's death.

Temple briefly entertained the idea of picketing the developers, but she realized this was not the time to act out her anxieties in public. She needed answers.

The Massachusetts Bay Development Company's office had once belonged to the only dentist in Preston's Mill—now retired—and the same wallpaper and purple-and-green-plaid chairs in the waiting room had been there during Dr. Buford's tenure. So had the ageless receptionist. She remarked pointedly that Temple's appointment wasn't until tomorrow, but she waved Temple to a seat and notified Mr. Starkweather he had a visitor.

From the waiting area, Temple could see into the office through a glass panel beside the door. Lounging in his chair, ankles crossed up on the desk, Mr. Starkweather was reading a book whose cover Temple recognized. Shortly before she and Rich had broken up last year, he'd given her a bestseller called *Help Yourself: Seven Secrets for Serenity and Success*. She'd found something creepy in the sibilant alliteration of the subtitle, and she didn't like the looks of the author, Dr. J. J. Dodge. In the photograph on the back cover, his smirking face looked familiar in a disturbingly intimate way—like the adult incarnation of a childhood bully. Temple suspected the book was Rich's latest attempt to get her to give up what he called her obsession with Folly Park. She hadn't read it.

After several minutes, Mr. Starkweather took his feet down, tossed the book in a drawer, and buzzed the receptionist to show Temple in.

The developer's representative was a large, solid man in his mid-forties with an oversized head carpeted by coarse, sun-bleached hair. His face was deeply tanned, and fine lines at the corners of his light blue eyes made him appear to be squinting. When he greeted her, Temple noticed braces attached to the insides of his teeth. Mr. Starkweather wrestled his features into a caricature of concern when Temple told him that the blasting for the new golf course had damaged the ceiling at Folly Park. He made a trite comment about "neighborliness" in a nasal Boston accent and carelessly scrawled a check for $1,000. Then he glanced at his expensive watch.

Temple took the check and said, "By the way, I hear your company has plans for Folly Park."

A frown pleated Mr. Starkweather's forehead. "I've been involved in a lot of new development, Temple—I can call you Temple? There are always rumors flying around, especially in small towns. People get nervous when they think things are going to change."

"You can call me Dr. Preston," Temple said, irritated by the developer's condescending tone. "And, yes, we do appreciate the past here."

"People appreciate progress too. Even in Preston's Mill." Mr. Starkweather smiled with his teeth clenched, which made him look insincere. "But there's no point in worrying about a rumor."

"So, it *is* only a rumor?"

"Look, Dr. Preston," Mr. Starkweather said after a long moment, "I know you have a personal interest. Perhaps we can work together during this . . . ah . . . interesting phase, while the rumor mill is churning."

"What do you mean?"

"People respect your family. You could reassure them nothing terrible is happening. That would be worth something to us."

"You'd pay me to keep people quiet while you tear down Folly Park?"

"That's not how I'd put it," Mr. Starkweather said blandly. "And who said anything about tearing the place down? Let's just say the company recognizes the desirability of a forward-thinking local liaison to help communicate our plans. There seems to be a bit of a leadership vacuum in Preston's Mill since your mayor resigned over those harassment allegations." He smiled expansively. "You'd be a goodwill ambassador. The job is yours if you want it."

He had not denied that Folly Park would be torn down, Temple realized, and panic set in. "I would never be such a traitor!" she hissed, leaning over the desk.

Startled, Mr. Starkweather thrust his chair back and watched her warily as she tore up his check. The tiny pieces of confetti fell as gently as ash, which ruined the effect she was going for, but Temple stalked out without looking back.

ONLY AFTER SHE HAD GALLOPED down to the family cemetery and let fly a fusillade of invective to her grandfather's headstone had Temple calmed down enough to think straight. Her plan for the girls' home had taken on a desperate urgency. Somehow, she had to thwart the developers while Jack got Senator Alden on board. There was no time to lose.

As Temple headed home to change back into her work clothes, her phone rang. Her father, she saw with dread.

The judge didn't bother with a greeting. "It's your duty to support your brother."

"I just think. . . ."

"You can stand in for Beau at some of the smaller local events. We've got to motivate our base. Poe is getting the hippies worked up about the new development. And he's got a get-out-the-vote strategy around confronting our history of racism, whatever that means." The judge snorted derisively. "You might be able to neutralize the historical stuff—you've got credibility there. Play up the heritage thing and the preservation angle."

"Dad, I can't . . . I won't. . . ." Temple said feebly.

"Yes, you will," the judge snapped, and the line went dead.

Hands trembling, Temple had trouble getting her phone into her pocket. Now her father would pretend she'd agreed to help with the campaign in the not-unrealistic expectation she'd eventually give in and actually do so. Their entire relationship consisted of these unequal battles of will in which the judge, a master of emotional abuse, nearly always came out the victor. Temple had long ago learned that standing up for herself was not worth the cost. But this time, she'd have to put up a fight. Her plan for Folly Park needed bipartisan support. She had to stay out of politics.

Temple had forgotten she'd left her new intern at her house until she walked in the door and discovered the kitchen table covered with Vee's research materials. Next to a closed laptop was a legal pad covered with handwritten notes, a stack of Xeroxed book pages, and a family tree diagram. Neither Vee nor the dog was in the house.

Some papers had fallen to the floor, and Temple picked them up just as the screen door opened and Chick bounded in.

Behind him, Vee's eyes widened. "You found those?" She snatched her notes from Temple's hand. "I'm sorry. I wanted to tell you, but I thought you wouldn't let me come. I'll go right now. This was a mistake." She began to shove the papers into her backpack.

"What are you talking about?"

Vee shook her head and picked up the backpack.

"Wait, I don't understand." Temple was dismayed she might inadvertently drive away the first Black scholar ever to be interested in Folly Park.

"It's nothing. Never mind. I should go."

"Please sit down." Temple pulled out a chair at the table. "Please."

Vee slowly sat down on the edge of the chair.

Temple felt she had very little time in which Vee might hear her out. And she realized with some surprise that despite the considerable anxiety her new intern's unsettling theories had already caused, she wanted very much for her to stay.

Temple struggled to express her half-formed thoughts. "I'm sure working on a Southern plantation wouldn't normally be your first choice for a summer job. I really respect your commitment to your research. I'm so sorry about the sampler in the back hall, and that little boy asking if you were a slave, and all the rest of it." Temple looked down at the scratched tabletop. "When I think about my ancestors and the privileges I have because they were slaveholders, I'm disgusted and ashamed. But I want to use Folly Park to make things better. It's a lot to ask, but I hope you'll help me. Please stay."

Vee was so still she may as well have been part of the chair. At her feet, Chick shifted, his toenails scraping the linoleum. The low hum of the cable modem in the next room seemed very loud, and when the icemaker in the ancient refrigerator laboriously cranked out a cube, Temple jumped. So did Vee. They caught each other's eyes and smiled awkwardly.

"I didn't mean to make you uncomfortable," Vee said. "It's not your fault your ancestor's owned people any more than it's my fault my family was enslaved. Being at Folly Park is definitely weird, but it's not that."

"What is it, then?"

"I thought it would be fair to tell you before I took the internship. But Dr. Flores said I shouldn't take the risk if I wanted the job."

"Risk telling me what?"

"Besides researching Robert Smith, I had another reason for wanting to come here. Dr. Flores thinks it's unprofessional."

"What is it?" Temple's curiosity was piqued.

"I've done some genealogy research and had a DNA test. My dad's side is from the West Indies, but my matrilineal line is about twenty percent English and Scottish and originates from this region."

"Really?" Temple was intrigued. "Have you been able to discover any surnames? If your ancestors lived anywhere nearby, I might know something about them."

"No. I found out my mother's family moved from Louisiana to Chicago in the 1880s—after Reconstruction, when all the lynching was going on in the South. I traced the genealogy to a woman named Jolie in New Orleans. She was the mistress of a White man, and they apparently lived together as if they were married. He arranged for her to receive his estate when he died. But I couldn't get any further back than the brothel where they met in the 1850s. So, I don't know anything about the Virginia connection."

"That's impressive. I've done research for people whose ancestors were enslaved, and it's really difficult. I'm not sure you'll get much further with it here, but I don't see why Dr. Flores is so concerned."

"She was already worried about my ability to be objective. I wanted to do my dissertation on Black people passing as White because of my family history."

Temple had chosen her own research focus on the Civil War because she'd grown up hearing her grandfather's stories about the general's heroics. She'd hoped learning the historical facts would help her come to terms with her family's role in upholding slavery, but it hadn't. Maybe things would be different for Vee. "So, you have ancestors who passed as White?"

"Yes. My great-grandmother on my mother's side lived in Chicago. Her twin brother lived there too, but in a different part of the city because he was passing. He'd visit once in a while and play with his niece—my grandmother. But then he married a White woman and had children, and he didn't come as often." Vee shook her head. "The last time he did was the day after he'd just visited, and he was very upset. A friend of his wife's had been in the neighborhood dropping off her housekeeper, and she'd seen him kiss his sister on the front stoop. She told his wife he was having an affair with a Negro."

Vee gave Temple a sickly smile. "He said he was going outside to smoke a cigarette. My ten-year-old grandmother found him in the backyard. He'd hanged himself."

"Oh!" Temple covered her mouth.

"My great-grandmother went to her brother's wife to tell her the truth—that her husband hadn't been cheating, she was his sister. But the wife said she would rather he'd been having an affair." Vee's tone was full of disgust. "See, Dr. Flores is right. I'm not objective."

"Anyone who thinks they are is fooling themselves. History carries into the present in all kinds of ways we can't control."

"I think so too." Vee nodded. "I've always wondered if discovering her uncle's body traumatized my grandmother. She suffered from depression all her life. I think that was hard on my mom, and so she always tried to be upbeat around me and my sisters. She didn't tell anyone when she got leukemia. She died when I was sixteen."

"I'm so sorry," Temple said. "My mom died when I was fourteen. Breast cancer."

They looked at each other, silently acknowledging their shared membership in a terrible club.

After a moment, Vee said quietly, "I don't really expect to find out anything about my family while I'm researching Robert Smith. I guess I sort of want to see if being here, in this part of Virginia, feels like home somehow." She glanced at Temple with a self-deprecating smile. "It's probably silly to think I might feel that just because my ancestors lived somewhere around here."

"It's not silly. I feel it every day." Impulsively, Temple reached out her hand. "You should stay."

Vee took it. "I think I will."

WHEN TEMPLE ARRIVED BACK at the office, Martha tilted her head and rolled her eyes toward Stuart's office. "He wants to see you."

Temple knocked and was surprised when Stuart opened the door rather than shouting from his desk. He said petulantly, "It's about time you got back from lunch."

Temple let that pass. Stuart was jealous of her occasional long lunches with the wife of Folly Park's chairman. And there was no way she was going to tell him about her visit to the city or her run-in with Mr. Starkweather.

Throwing himself into his imitation leather chair, Stuart squinched up his glasses and smoothed his tie over his potbelly. "I have something important to tell you, and I'm going to need some real teamwork. You'll be acting as my deputy on this." He narrowed his eyes and bared his teeth aggressively. It meant he didn't want any argument.

Temple stiffened automatically at the word "deputy," which implied a close working relationship, but then she noticed Stuart's face was coated with a sheen of sweat. He did not look well. "I suppose you've heard the rumor about Folly Park being sold to the developers."

Stuart nodded dejectedly, not even annoyed she already knew. "Hunt told me at our meeting this morning." He began aimlessly rearranging the items on his desk—a paperweight, a business card holder, a coffee mug proclaiming I'M THE BOSS. "But there's more."

A cannonball of dread dropped into the pit of Temple's stomach. "What?"

Pushing the paperweight around and around, Stuart squinched and said nothing. Temple waited impatiently.

Finally, Stuart spoke. "Hunt said Folly Park has to be in the black by August or the board is going to recommend the town sell it. I *told* you the low visitation would be a problem," he said spitefully.

"Hold on. You mean they're giving us a chance?"

"Yes, but we've only got two months!" Stuart nearly shouted.

"Okay, okay," Temple soothed.

Hunched miserably in his oversized chair, Stuart was now rolling up the end of his tie and straightening it compulsively. He'd had difficulty finding a job after business school, and running a floundering historic home could hardly be considered a desirable position for a newly minted MBA. The trustees were prominent, well-connected men who governed Folly Park with benign neglect. Hunter's ultimatum was unprecedented—clearly, the developers had gotten to them. Folly Park deserved better than Stuart's inept leadership, but Temple felt sorry for him. If he failed here, his career was over.

"We need a plan," she said.

"Don't you think I know that? I've got ideas."

"What have you come up with?" Temple willed herself to be patient. Stuart acted like a cranky toddler when he felt pressured, and she didn't want to deal with one of his tantrums.

Stuart opened his desk drawer, where Temple saw Dr. J. J. Dodge staring from the back of *Help Yourself*. Shoving the book aside, Stuart extracted a dozen pages of crumpled notebook paper and thrust them at her. "It's all in there."

The papers looked like the production of a madman. Half-completed flowcharts trailed off the edges of pages; cryptic calculations were scattered between little bubbles with inane mantras like TEAMWORK EQUALS SUCCESS and LEADERSHIP BUILDS LOYALTY. The last page was boldly headed ACTION PLAN in heavy marker, underlined four times. The end of the last line had soaked through the paper and made a black-rimmed hole. Temple could see Stuart through it. His glasses had slid to the end of his nose, and he was nibbling at the skin around his thumbnail. Beneath the heading, the page was blank.

"There's some stuff here we can work with," Temple said, though she couldn't make any sense of the notes.

"Really?" Stuart squinched and sat up straighter.

"Sure. Can you summarize your conclusions for me so I don't miss anything?"

"No problem. Uh . . . basically, I figure that if we cut everyone's salary in half and increase ticket prices by fifty percent, we could save enough to hold that fundraising dinner we were planning. We can get new donors there."

It was a completely unworkable strategy. Temple handed the papers back to Stuart. "The dinner would be nice. But, unfortunately, by then the rumors will have gotten around, and any potential large donors won't want to be associated with something they perceive is failing."

Stuart stared without blinking. He swallowed audibly. "Do you think we could ask some of your family friends?"

"Maybe." Temple wasn't about to give names of potential donors to Stuart, who would likely ruin their chances on first contact. She'd seen him in action. He was excessively polite to women, calling them "Ladies, Ladies"—always twice—in an oily tone, and he attempted a backslapping bonhomie with the men, the failure of which was painful to witness. She would reach out to her connections privately, though she had little hope. No doubt the developers could offer significantly more than she might raise from private funds in such a short time. Stuart interrupted her thoughts.

"Do you think *you* could—"

"No." Temple didn't care to explain her precarious financial situation. Clearly, Stuart would be no help in the current crisis. But without some kind of role, he would make

things worse. "We should keep the board apprised of everything we do. Then they'll feel invested so we can rely on their
support once we have a solid plan."

As she'd hoped, Stuart jumped at Temple's suggestion.
"Board communication is my expertise. I'll take care of it."

"Great! That's one less thing to worry about."

Stuart puffed out his chest. Then a new thought seemed
to come to him, and he deflated. "Will you. . . ? The staff. . . ."

"I'll let everyone know what's going on."

IN HER OWN OFFICE, FREED from having to manage Stuart,
Temple felt the warning signs of panic—sweaty palms, a
pounding heart, blood rushing in her ears. To distract herself,
she took the diary out of her desk drawer.

On October 27, 1859, the day John Brown was sentenced
to hang, Jane had written, "Virginia is a harsh judge. If their
slaves are so content as they claim, and Brown so insane, why
do they imagine that even a whole North filled with such
fiery old men could destroy their peculiar institution? But
he must pay for their hypocrisy with his life."

A few unremarkable entries followed, and then Temple
reached the section where she'd discovered the letter from
Carolina. There, she read, Jane's life fell apart.

November 2, 1859

*Oh, the torment of the week past! Alas, I have no one to blame
but myself. Having failed to tell Father the truth at once, I
had not the fortitude to do so after days chock-full of callers
and cards and flowers and even a writer who wanted to
interview me for the Liberator. Father let no one see me—he*

and brother William have taken it upon themselves to speak publicly about my <u>heroic deed</u>, and they are pleased I have provided this opportunity for them to promote the aims of the Society. My dear Henry is pleased too. He spoke of taking me on the lecture circuit when we are married. He kissed my forehead when he left me—the first time he has ever done so—and a rush of joy flooded my heart. But of what worth am I if all I want is to be petted and praised? And how can I deceive him, of all people? Does he not have the right to know the <u>true</u> character of the woman who will be his wife?

November 3, 1859

Henry came to call today and, before my resolve deserted me, I confessed what truly happened that day in the alley. Afterward, he was silent for a long while, staring into the fire, and then he looked at me with those eyes the color of the ocean on an autumn day. And he told me to say nothing because the story has done much good at a time when the failure of John Brown's raid has brought despair. He told me of reports that some who are suspected of helping bondsmen in the Slave States have been beaten, their lives threatened. Though he strove to hide it, I know that he was greatly disappointed in me, and I cried miserably after he had gone. I must endeavor to become what he thought I was, and what I wish to be—a woman worthy and brave in service to our great Cause.

November 9, 1859

The future, which once held so much promise, now seems but a barren wasteland. Henry—alas, no longer my fiancé!—happened upon me today at the Colored Orphans

Home. It was my first outing since that ghastly afternoon four days ago when Father told me I was <u>not</u> to be wed after all. Henry passed by with his fashionable friends—among them haughty Mrs. Fitch and her conceited daughter. Mrs. Goddard made as if to speak to me, but when he said nothing, she said nothing. And Miss Fitch smiled slyly behind her glove.

I have been poorly. I cannot catch my breath without coughing. Dr. Caldwell shakes his head and Mother watches me close. But—selfish as I am—her anxiety is nothing to me beside my broken heart.

Temple felt an ache of pity for poor Jane and turned quickly to the next entry. She read it once. Then she read it again. Vee's theory that Carolina may have learned about the Stannard family from someone who knew them in Boston was no longer a theory but a fact.

November 13, 1859

As I am not ever to become Mrs. Henry Stannard, I will find my own way to fight for the Cause. I am going into the South. I have told no one but brother Benjamin, who is to carry me to the station tomorrow before dawn. When he hears that I have gone alone into the very heart of our nation's great evil, perhaps then Henry will wonder if he might yet have loved me.

CHAPTER FIVE

The back door of the mansion burst open with a crash. Al stood on the threshold, golf club poised like a baseball bat.

"It's just me!" Temple cowered in the hallway.

"Goddamn it, I could have hurt you!" Al lowered the club. "I was hitting balls on the lawn and saw something move in the window. I thought it was a burglar. Why didn't you turn the lights on? What are you doing?"

"I came to take this down." Temple lifted the sampler she had just removed from the wall.

"Why?" Al frowned.

"I thought I'd just put it in a closet or something."

"You had to do that tonight? What's the rush?"

Temple had been driving herself crazy over her solitary dinner, her mind veering from worries over the developers and what Vee might unearth in the archives to hopes about her plan and fantasies starring Jack Early. Rinsing her dirty dishes, she'd glanced out the window at the mansion and decided on the spur of the moment to get rid of the sampler. "It seemed to make Vee uncomfortable," she said.

Al's eyebrows shot up. "You know what I'm thinking, right?"

Temple nodded, hoping he would stop there, but Al told her anyway. "After two hundred years hanging in the same spot, you realized that evil thing ought to come down because on the first day of her job an intern was offended? But it never occurred to you that me and Betty Jean and all the other Black folks who've worked here have been offended for years?"

Temple blushed. "I know. It's awful, and it's no excuse, but it was like I never really saw it before."

"Never really saw it before," Al echoed. He shook his head and turned on his heel. A moment later, his club struck a ball with a crisp thwack. Temple shoved the sampler into the coat closet and went outside.

After Al had used up his bucket of balls and returned his seven iron to his golf bag, Temple joined him at the far end of the lawn to help pick up balls. He acknowledged her with a nod, and they worked in silence until the bucket was full again. They repeated the whole process after Al went through another bucket with his five iron. By then, twilight had turned to night and they could barely see. They sat down on a bench beside a huge magnolia tree.

"I'm sorry," Temple said.

"I know."

They sat quietly, gazing out over the shadowy landscape. After a while, Temple said, "Looked good."

"Tweaked my swing a little." Al bent to untie his golf shoes.

"The board is considering selling Folly Park to those developers doing the blasting," Temple said.

"Is that right?" Al pulled on his work boots.

"You don't seem surprised."

"I'm not. We've been barely hanging on for years." Al cleared his throat. "Maybe it's time."

"What do you mean?" Temple's tone was testy.

"The place had a long run. And it could be good for you. All this pressure to restore the house and get it back into the family is too much of a burden. Your grandfather shouldn't have put it on you."

"That's not fair. He never told me to do anything."

"He didn't have to. He knew you'd kill yourself trying." Temple realized Al was right.

"You should move back to the city, be around people your own age." Al nudged her gently with his shoulder. "Get yourself out into the world."

Al sounded like Mrs. Glass. He didn't understand either. "It's my family home."

"Your mother, Harry, your grandfather—they're dead. That love is gone from here. It's time to move on."

Temple wanted to make him stop. "Where will you and Betty Jean work if the trustees sell out to the developers?"

Al snorted. "I could make more in one day cutting lawns in the city than I earn here in a week."

With his degree in horticulture from the local community college and his decades of experience, if anything, Al was downplaying his prospects, but Temple's distress made her say something she instantly regretted. "Then why don't *you* move there?"

"Maybe I will," Al snapped. "To hell with Betty Jean wanting to be near her mom, who, you know, will probably never get over that broken hip. And to hell with being able to check on my sister every day because, since the quarry shut down, they're barely scraping by. Sure, I can just pack up and move."

Temple wanted to say something, but no words came. She felt as if she were suffocating in the humid night air. Al got up, yanked his golf bag to his shoulder, and stalked off down the drive toward the old overseer's house. Temple watched until his tall form was drawn into the shadows of the ancient oaks.

IN A NEW FOLLY PARK POLO SHIRT and khaki pants, Vee somehow managed to make the unflattering uniform look neat and professional. Temple tried to smooth the wrinkles out of her own shirt as she sat down at her desk. She hadn't slept much, and she felt groggy. Although the cut on her forehead had closed nicely, her eye was now olive green, and she hadn't bothered to cover it with makeup.

"What would you like me to do today?" Vee asked.

Probably Vee was itching to get started on her research, but Temple was nervous about what she might find in the archives. "Are you ready to do a tour?"

"I think so," Vee said gamely. "I read the script in the docent guide and went through the house with Flora and Fred. She wasn't sure I was ready, but he said I was fine, and I probably won't even have to do a tour unless a big crowd arrives all at once. But it doesn't sound like that happens very often."

"Fred and Flora can usually deal with the summer rush," Temple said stiffly. She did not appreciate being reminded about Folly Park's low visitation numbers. "But sometimes we get tour buses."

"Of course," Vee said hastily.

Temple relented. "It doesn't look like it's going to be busy today, though, so you could do some research. Where would you like to start?"

"Can I see the letter you mentioned about the Folly Park ring going missing?"

Temple nodded. "It's in the archives, and I need to show you around there, anyway."

They walked up the drive, and Temple unlocked a small door on the side of the mansion. She led Vee down a steep wooden staircase into the section of the basement where the archives were located. Vee's eyebrows rose when Temple turned on a fly-specked light bulb, and she was confronted with the straining cardboard boxes, plastic bins, rusty file cabinets, sagging metal shelves, and the acrid smell of the mold retardant Al sprayed on the walls every few weeks.

"I've never seen anything like this!" Vee sounded as if she'd discovered buried treasure. "Do you think there's stuff in here no one has ever seen? I mean, no historian?"

"Sure. The collection has never been fully processed." It was a grand term for the moldering plantation correspondences, tax records, property deeds, personal letters, receipts, newspaper clippings, and scraps of notes and memoranda. Over the years, it had been ravaged by water, bugs, mice, and even a small fire. Temple's grandfather had retained ownership of the archives when he sold the house, and her predecessor, Dr. Tate, as well as Dr. Belcher's summer interns, had made very little headway processing the materials.

"I hope you can help get things organized," Temple said. The state of the archives was a nagging to-do in the back of her mind, and she dreamed of new shelving units and archival boxes. She lifted a plastic bin off the floor and set it down on an old metal desk. "For instance, anything that seemed related to slavery was just thrown in here."

"I can put things in order," Vee said with confidence. "I probably shouldn't admit this because it makes me sound obsessive, but my spices are organized by name, size, and expiration date."

"You should see my bookcase," Temple said as she went to a file cabinet, pulled out a drawer, and extracted the letter from an acid-free folder.

"This was written by James Smith's wife, Anna. She died years before Thomas—the general—came to Folly Park to live," Temple reminded Vee. Then she read the letter aloud because Anna Smith's atrocious handwriting was indecipherable for the uninitiated.

Folly Park, 21st June 1836—

My Dearest Sister—

I write to you under some distress of mind and body. My old Complaint has returned with the heat of Summer and yet James declines to say whether or not I can expect to seek relief at the Springs this Season. Indeed, he will make no decision about that or anything else. Dearest Sister, I know you will not think it a betrayal for me to tell <u>You</u> that he has not been himself since his little Pet, that spoiled and saucy Linda, was sent down to his Brother in Louisiana last month. I did insist at the last, it is true, but he himself knew she was grown too old to keep her as he did, dressed like a Doll and perched always on his lap. Even Maria, the wench's own mother, was not sorry to see her go. But his foolishness over her, My Dear Sister, has made him doubly a Fool in that he has lost his gold Ring—the one with the Janus face that has long been in his family. He puts it off in Summer, for his fingers do swell in the Heat, but now he cannot recollect when last he saw it & I fear it has been stolen. I think it likely that odious slave trader Rourke—James had him in the house when he arranged for Linda & the others' removal. I will tell you in *confidence, Sister, I had hoped to use the ring as a Means to travel, which I must for my health—& for my very Life, I fear. There is a Man in Preston's Mill who would have loaned me the funds if I could have got the Ring as surety. Alas, now I must find some other way to meet with you at the Springs. Do let me know at once if my Dear Brother Philip is to take you at the usual time.*

Affectionately,
Anna

"What do you think?" Temple asked, slipping the letter back in its folder.

"I'm not sure. We know the ring stayed at Folly Park because Carolina gave it to Robert Smith years later when she sent him to Boston. Maybe James suspected his wife planned to use the ring to finance her vacation, so he hid it and let her think it had been stolen."

"Or maybe it *was* stolen. Not by the slave trader, but by someone in the household, like a housemaid. Maybe years later *she* had a son by a White man and gave him the ring."

"That's possible," Vee conceded.

"Whatever the case, we need proof before we start telling everyone about illegitimate, biracial children."

"Any theories must be substantiated by evidence, of course. My academic career is at stake," Vee said, adjusting her glasses.

And my reputation, family, and livelihood, Temple thought. In addition to the damage it could do to her plan's chances, or how the trustees might respond, she dreaded her relatives' reactions. A formidable squad of great-aunts in particular, all named after Confederate battle victories, seemed to subsist solely on family pride.

THE MORNING PASSED SLOWLY. Temple spoke to each of the staff members individually to tell them about Folly Park's dire financial situation. They took the news calmly. Too calmly, she felt, since they all said they were sure she would come up with a solution.

If Betty Jean had already heard the news from Al, she hid it well, and when Temple had finished with everyone else, she went in search of him, hoping to make amends for the night before. She didn't find him in the park, where she thought he might be, but she did find Wanda asleep on a lichen-covered bench in the gazebo, pregnant belly bulging. Stuart referred to Wanda disparagingly as Temple and Betty Jean's "project."

Wanda was one of the girls Temple tutored, and she had been released early from the detention center because Temple had agreed to give her a job. Taking advantage of the teen's interest in social media, Temple had put her in charge of Folly Park's digital marketing, and Betty Jean had offered Wanda a home with her and Al. Like a skilled contractor, Betty Jean always had an eye out for emotional and physical fixer-uppers, eager to repair the foundations on which to build human potential. Wanda was thriving under a regimen of healthy meals and mandatory exercise, and she had inspired Temple's plan to establish a program for girls like her at Folly Park.

A GED preparation workbook had fallen from Wanda's slackened grasp and lay on the bench next to her phone. Temple was about to tiptoe away when Wanda opened her eyes.

"I'm almost finished with the book," she said, pulling herself awkwardly upright. "I didn't mean to fall asleep."

"That's okay." Temple felt bad that Wanda seemed to feel guilty about napping. She recalled Jack telling her about one of the reasons Randy thought her plan couldn't succeed. "Wanda," she said, "does working at Folly Park bother you? Since it was a plantation?"

Because she was looking for it, Temple noticed a fleeting shadow on Wanda's face before she answered. "No, ma'am. It's a good job, and I'm lucky to have it."

Wanda sounded so sincere Temple doubted what she'd seen. "Well, be sure to let me know if anything bothers you."

"I will, thank you, ma'am."

But Temple was certain that Wanda wouldn't tell her if she was bothered any more than she would stop calling her "ma'am."

"Please call me Temple," she said, as she did during every conversation with Wanda.

"Yes, Temple, ma'am."

Temple suppressed a sigh as she helped Wanda to her feet. "Could you ramp up your social media campaign?" she asked. "We need to drive more visitors to Folly Park."

"I'll get started right away." Wanda began tapping on her phone as she trundled away.

Watching her cross the park, Temple reminded herself she'd have to make sure Wanda didn't overdo things. With that thought, her responsibility to Wanda and Betty Jean, Al, Martha, Fred, Flora, and all the part-time staff who depended on Folly Park descended on her shoulders, a heavy mantle of dread.

BACK IN HER OFFICE, TEMPLE tackled the arcane instructions for another probably futile grant application. When she'd completed a decent draft, she rewarded herself with an entry from Jane Elliot's diary.

November 15, 1859

I am away. I cried the whole distance to the station, greatly distressing poor brother Benjamin. I feel sad and sick, and the air is foul, and I cough and cough. The jostling of the coach scrapes upon my nerves, and the babe opposite cries endlessly. Oh, what have I done? I will live in a household dependent on the labor of the poor benighted souls my family has been engaged in trying to free for so many years. I will be served by them while I reside with their master. Is he a despot, a tyrant? And what sort of woman is Carolina now she is grown?

My cousin and I met only once—at the White Sulfur Springs in Virginia—when I was fourteen and she twelve years old. Our mothers had not seen each other in over twenty years, and the very first night, Carolina told me the particulars of their estrangement, whispering from her bed across the room we shared.

When her father, Mr. Gilmore, wanted to marry, Carolina said, he traveled to Folly Park with a letter of introduction to our grandfather, Commodore Smith, a widower with six children, four of them daughters rumored to be both rich and beautiful. The two eldest girls—our mothers—poked fun at their suitor's bald head, and the Commodore declared in a temper that one of them must marry the man, he cared not which. The sisters put their fate in the toss of a coin, and my own mother, Charlotte, lost. But that night she fled to a neighbor's house, where the man who would be my father was visiting, and they eloped to his home in Boston. Betrayed by her elder sister, Clarissa was left to wed Mr. Gilmore. He carried her off to South Carolina, and in time they had children, three boys, and Carolina.

Our mothers' marked discomfort at meeting again did not prevent—and perhaps encouraged—a bond between myself and Carolina. Embracing me impulsively when we were introduced, she declared we would be great friends, and she followed me everywhere, a charming, vivacious child. When we parted at the end of our stay, she said fervently, with many tears, that we would meet again, but we both knew our mothers' attempted reconciliation had been a sad failure. Shortly after the visit, Mother dedicated herself wholeheartedly to Abolition. My correspondence with Carolina fell off after a time. And now, six years later, we are to be reunited. What will she think of me?

Temple admired Jane's courage in leaving her home and venturing alone into the South—enemy territory for an abolitionist. It gave her the uncomfortable feeling she wasn't doing nearly enough for her own cause. She left a message for Jack, although it was probably too soon to expect any progress, and then turned doggedly back to the grant application. In his office, Stuart began calling supporters and soliciting them for donations—never a pleasant task at the best of times. His efforts were painful to hear, and by lunchtime, Temple had to get away.

LEAVING THE SOUTHERN COMFORT CAFÉ, Temple noticed red, white, and blue bunting lining the windows of the long-vacant storefront that had once housed her grandfather's favorite bookshop. It was now, according to the banner over the door, campaign headquarters for Beau Preston. Ducking her head, she picked up her pace, but it was too late.

"Temple Tayloe Smith Preston! Don't you sneak on by!" shrilled a voice behind her. Temple slowly turned. Her cousin Pixie—a nickname for Patricia—stood on the side-walk, hands on hips. With skin as smooth as an old-fashioned china doll's and eyes nearly as vacant, Pixie had two expressions: perky and pained. "Aren't you going to come in and see what we've done?" she asked, pouting.

"Sorry, Pixie, I don't have time. I'm on my lunch break."

Bobbed hair bobbing, Pixie shook her finger. "Don't be a doodle! You can come in just for a minute." Clutching Temple's arm, she dragged her into the building.

At a dozen desks crowded into the space, a dozen young White men with fresh haircuts and button-down shirts were tapping on laptops or making calls. Temple noticed a stack of *Help Yourself* books on a table. "What are those for?" she asked.

"Beau says that book will help us win the election. It explains how to uncover people's deepest fears so we can reassure them."

Or more likely scare them, Temple thought.

"We'll have so much fun canvassing together," Pixie gushed. She smiled so wide, Temple could see where the bleach strip she'd used to whiten her top teeth had ended.

"I'm not getting involved with the campaign," Temple said.

"What?"

"Beau and my dad know."

Pixie shook her head. "I don't think they do."

"Well, they should. I told them."

"But why?" A tiny line appeared on Pixie's smooth brow.

"Because of Harry, for one thing."

"Oh, *Temple*, I'm *so* sorry!" Pixie looked stricken.

Between Al last night and Pixie today, Temple thought she'd had just about enough reminders of the losses in her life. She said quickly, "Just give me a copy of Beau's plat-form. I'll look at it later."

Instantly, Pixie was all smiles. "Of course! Our slogan is 'Beau Preston for Building Progress.'"

Temple felt a chill. "Building progress" sounded like a euphemism for development.

"Stay *right* there!" Pixie ordered and ran to her desk. She returned a moment later with a glossy brochure. Temple shoved it into her back pocket and headed to the door.

"Say, Temple," Pixie called, "you *are* going to the recep-tion, aren't you?"

Temple nodded reluctantly. Her father had endowed the new wing of the city's art gallery in memory of her mother, and the black-tie opening gala was that night. Judge Preston had never been supportive of his wife's interest in art, but he was a master strategist. He'd announced the gift two years ago during Harry's run for Congress, and now construction had conveniently finished in time for an open-ing during Beau's campaign.

Pixie stepped closer, her expression switching doubt-fully between perky and pained. She fingered the tiny, embroidered cats on her skirt. Finally, she said in a strident whisper, "I just thought you should know that *Julia* is back. She'll be there." When Temple did not reply, Pixie added, "With an *engagement* ring."

That was news. Temple took a moment to digest it while Pixie watched her anxiously. Julia, who had outgrown the nickname "Jujie," was Pixie's older sister. Temple had assumed she would stay in Los Angeles, where Rich had moved last month for a new job. To Temple's surprise, they had started dating shortly after she and Rich had broken up. She imagined both the triumph and resentment that would color her already strained relationship with her cousin now that Julia was engaged to Rich.

"Thanks for the warning," she said as she turned away. She had more important things to worry about.

TEMPLE PARKED HER TRUCK AND went into the office to find Stuart haranguing Martha. She quickly veered away and went to check on Vee in the archives.

When she opened the basement door, Temple heard Vee down below talking on her phone. ". . . family that's been inbreeding for centuries in a town that's still basically segregated. The whole place is like a shrine to this Confederate general. One of the tour guides even dresses up like a plantation mistress. My boss is all White guilt and kind of defensive, but I think it will be okay." There was a pause, and then Vee said sharply, "No, Dad wasn't right. You can tell him I'm still glad I came."

For some reason, Vee's comments didn't bother Temple. She was actually relieved to hear Vee's honest opinions of Folly Park and Preston's Mill. It validated what she always suspected outsiders thought. She didn't disagree with Vee's assessment of herself, and she was happy to hear Vee intended to stay, despite her father's apparent disapproval. As she tiptoed slowly backward, her phone rang in her pocket. She quickly shut the door behind her and answered without checking the caller ID.

"Temp!" Beau bawled. "Pixie tells me you picked up my brochure! Good deal. You'll be able to talk turkey at the party tonight."

"You misunderstood. I just happened to walk by your office. I'm still not helping with your campaign."

"What the hell? What's your problem?"

"You know exactly what my problem is. Even if you want to pretend it didn't happen."

"Watch it," Beau warned.

Temple didn't listen. "You know Dad accepted contributions for Harry's campaign from your girlfriend's father and promised to grease the wheels on his permits. You remember, that was the same night our brother died! Because he got in a fight with Dad when Mr. Rengstorff thanked him at the party and stormed out and got in his car and—" The line went dead.

Behind her, the basement door opened. "I found something," Vee said. "It's evidence about the baby."

Turning, Temple frowned. "Really?"

"It was in the bin you pulled out. An interview by the WPA Virginia Writers' Project."

Temple knew about the New Deal program that had sent unemployed writers into rural areas of the South during the Great Depression to capture the recollections of ex-slaves. She wasn't aware that anyone from the program had come to Folly Park.

Temple followed Vee down to the basement, where Vee handed over a packet of papers held together by a tarnished brass fastener. The cover sheet was dated March 12, 1936, and the interview had been conducted with a woman named Louella Halliday Moore, who was eighty-one years old. That made her roughly twelve when the Civil War ended.

"Did you read this whole thing?" Temple asked. It was nearly a hundred pages long.

Vee nodded.

Skimming through the narrative, Temple noticed the interviewer had made a clumsy effort, offensive to modern sensibilities, to reproduce the dialect of the woman he was interviewing. She scanned through the parts where Louella related her duties on the plantation, "feedin' the chickins" and watching after the "younger chillun," and her recollections of what the enslaved families had been given to eat: "pork and molasses and corn pone, but Mama was the cook, so we ate better than most." The interviewer must have asked Louella to tell him more about her mother, for many pages described the meals the cook had prepared during slavery times with the help of her assistant, "po' pretty Jewel, who kilt herself over a broken heart."

Jewel! That was the name of the girl in the photograph, Temple remembered. She was curious to learn more about her, but Jewel's name did not appear again. At the end of the long narrative, Vee had marked a passage with a Post-it note.

After the War, Miz Carolina kept Mama and me on. I stayed at Folly Park until I got married and went North with Jimmie in September of '68. I helped in the kitchen, and I watched the Missus' baby. Robbie was a cute little thing. I was sorry to leave him, he was barely five years ole, and he didn't have no one else to pay him any mind 'cept King. There weren't hardly nobody left on the place by then. Miz Carolina had to work in the fields herself in those hard years.

"I worked out that the baby was probably born in August or September of 1863," Vee said, "given how old Louella says she was when she left home and the boy's age then. The Robert who came to the Stannards with the Folly Park ring in December 1884 said he was twenty-one years old. Robbie would have been twenty-one in 1884 if he was born in 1863. The names and dates match up."

"But it doesn't prove Carolina gave birth to the baby. We need conclusive evidence she hadn't adopted him or taken responsibility for someone else's child. We need to know about the father."

Temple had no idea where all this would lead, but Louella's narrative was compelling. Interestingly, the enslaved man from the photograph, King, was still living at Folly Park after emancipation, and she wondered what had prompted the girl, Jewel, to take her own life. No matter how much she dreaded the consequences, Temple was intensely curious about what else Vee might discover.

"I've got a chronology of the general's movements during the war," Temple said. "You might be able to rule him out as the father."

Vee nodded and said carefully, "Are you really okay with me pursuing the idea that Carolina may have been the mother?"

"Yes," Temple said firmly.

Vee looked down at the floor. "I'm sorry about what I said earlier. On the phone with my sister. I think maybe you overheard me."

"It's okay. It's all true, I guess."

Vee shook her head. "I didn't need to say it like that. It wasn't kind. I'm sorry."

Temple smiled. "Thanks."

CHAPTER SIX

The zipper on her little black dress had snagged, and Temple couldn't get it loose. She tugged it one last time and gave up. Despite not yet making up with Al, she had to stop at the overseer's house for help or she would be late.

"Why, look at you!" Betty Jean exclaimed when she opened her front door. "All dressed up, with lovely waves in your hair."

Temple laughed because the waves were caused by the ponytail she'd been wearing all day. She explained her predicament, and Betty Jean quickly fixed the problem and zipped her up.

"What a beautiful necklace," she said when Temple turned around. "Are those real?"

Temple touched the diamonds at her throat. "It was my mother's." She remembered the day her mother had given her the necklace shortly before she died. Temple had expected a sentimental speech, but her mother just handed her the jewelry case and said, "It's important for a woman to have something to fall back on. You can sell this in an emergency."

Al looked up from a baseball game on television. "That must be some party you're going to."

"I'd rather be home eating takeout."

"And cleaning your guns," Al said with a grin, and Temple understood everything was fine between them again.

Al was referring to a brace of antique dueling pistols that had once belonged to General Smith. Temple kept them in perfect condition, like everything her grandfather had bequeathed to her. Beau often suggested she sell it all and give him half the proceeds, but Temple prized the heirlooms for their association with their grandfather.

"Hold still," Betty Jean commanded as Temple turned toward Al. "Let me brush off the dog hairs."

"These kinds of parties aren't any fun," Temple said. "Just the same people standing around drinking too much and congratulating themselves on being rich." She yanked at the hem of her dress.

Betty Jean batted her hand away. "It's perfect. Leave it alone." She gave Temple a little push toward the door. "You try and have a nice time."

THE VALET GRIMACED AT THE SIGHT of Temple's dusty truck and took the key between his thumb and forefinger. She thought he looked familiar from other events, and when she entered the lobby of the art museum, she recognized some of the catering staff weaving through the crowd with silver-plated trays of Virginia ham on miniature biscuits. Numerous relatives were sprinkled about, including her father's two cheerfully indolent younger brothers and their cookie-cutter wives. It was going to be a long night.

As Temple waved to acknowledge a couple of women she'd known in high school, she saw her mother's name gleaming in foot-high letters along the wall behind them.

Her stomach lurched. Looking away, she spotted an elderly guard watching her.

"Hi, Lamar, how've you been?"

"Can't complain," Lamar said, smiling. "It's nice to see you. I'm real glad they're honoring your mother."

"Me too. Do you know if her piece is still hanging in the Shaw Gallery?"

"Sure is. Do you want to see it after the reception? The Shaw Gallery is closed tonight, but we can make an exception for you."

Just then Temple saw Pixie across the room. At her side was the top of an auburn up-do. Under it, she knew, were slate-gray eyes and a thin-lipped mouth. Julia. Temple turned back to the guard. "Can we do it now?"

Lamar looked surprised, but he nodded. "I'll get someone to cover for me. Meet you there."

Temple needed a little time alone. And although she'd avoided seeing her mother's artwork in the years since her death, she wanted to tonight. She missed her with an ever-present dull ache that was stronger than usual lately. It probably had something to do with fearing that the home she loved—where her mother had grown up and where she had died—might be snatched away at any moment. Temple hurried down the corridor.

"I remember when you used to come here with your mom," Lamar said, unlocking the metal gate to the gallery. "You look just like she did."

"No one's ever told me that," Temple said skeptically. Her beautiful mother was always impeccably dressed and flawlessly made up.

When Temple was young, her mother had spent nearly every Wednesday morning at the art museum, copying the paintings. She'd intended to become a professional artist but had given it up when she married. Temple often accompanied her mother, and when Lamar was on duty, he'd helped her set up her miniature easel. She loved the white plastic tray with its oval pools of color. Her mother would critique her paintings, referring to her as "the artist" and using impressive-sounding words to describe her work. Temple took the paintings home and presented them proudly to her father. Until, hiding under his desk one rainy afternoon while Harry hunted her in a game of hide-and-seek, she found her latest creation crumpled in the wastepaper basket.

"You take your time." Lamar turned away, keys jingling.

Temple walked slowly through the gallery. She could hear faint jazz music and the buzz of voices and laughter. Her mother's piece was in the post-modernist section. It was an eight-by-ten-inch collage of faces that formed a woman gazing into a mirror. The indistinct reflection was washed in a thin sheen of red that looked like blood. The label read, "*Self-Portrait*. Margaret Smith Preston, New York, 1989." Temple looked again. *The museum must have made a mistake,* she thought. Her mother had not been in New York in 1989. That was the year she was born.

"YOU'RE LATE," SAID BEAU.

Temple was surprised he'd approached her, given how their last phone call had ended, but ignoring inconvenient disagreements was a family trademark. "Actually, I've been here for a while. I was looking—"

"Why didn't you get your hair done?"

Beau's own hair had been shorn into a bristly cap. Along with his broad shoulders and the aggressive glitter in his eyes, he looked like the bullying ex-football player that he was. "Betty Jean thinks I have lovely waves." Temple batted her eyelashes.

Beau snapped his tongue against the plate that had held his false front teeth in place since a vicious helmet-to-helmet tackle his senior year in high school. "You're wearing the same dress you wore to the Jefferson Davis birthday dinner."

"I had it dry cleaned."

"And you've got a black eye. My *sister* has a black eye. Listen to me, goddammit. I've just about got this election in the bag. You'd better not screw it up." Somehow Beau managed to flash a congenial smile around the room while he lectured her. "You can hide out in that moldy mansion for the rest of your life, for all I care. But, for the next six weeks, when you show your face in the real world, you'd better be wearing nice clothes and—"

"Temple! So nice to see you!"

Temple turned with relief toward the cultured voice of her mentor, the retired director of Folly Park, Dr. Montgomery Tate. A distinguished, fit-looking gentleman with a smooth, pink head, pointed incisors, and an air of vaguely hostile reserve, Temple had always found him a bit intimidating.

"Hi, Dr. Tate," she said. "You know my brother Beau."

"Certainly, certainly." Dr. Tate floated his hand before Beau's face in a kind of royal wave. In the year she'd worked with him, Temple had never seen Dr. Tate voluntarily touch another human being, though he would scrabble barehanded through dirt in pursuit of a nineteenth-century toothpick.

"Now, Temple," Dr. Tate said, ignoring Beau's outstretched hand. "I hear Stuart Sprigg met with Hunter Glass yesterday."

"Yes." Temple didn't want to talk about Folly Park in front of Beau. To change the subject, she told Dr. Tate she thought her new intern may have found mention of the lost Janus ring in a Boston archive related to a family named Stannard. Predictably, Beau turned away. He had no interest in history.

"I've never come across any Stannards linked with Folly Park," Dr. Tate said, "but you know the general's paternal aunt Charlotte married a John Elliot of Boston." He transfixed Temple with shrewd dark eyes. "What is it your intern is after?"

"I'm not sure she knows," Temple said, evasively.

"Well, I do recall mention of a Jane Elliot, who would have been a cousin, of course. It was in a letter written—if one can use that word to describe an illiterate scrawl—by Carolina when she was a youngster. I transcribed it when I was preparing that insipid exhibit on Southern girlhood a few years before you joined us." Dr. Tate touched his wine glass to his lips for a moment before lowering it without taking a sip. "The exhibit was the brainchild—now there's an oxymoron—of that silly cow over at the university, Dr. Constance Morecott. Poor deluded thing, she never did make tenure."

"But, Jane Elliot, sir," Temple said. If Dr. Tate became distracted talking about his enemies at the university, he would never return to the original subject.

"Yes, of course, I digress. As I recall, Carolina was writing to her father from the White Sulfur Springs. She'd fallen off her horse when riding with her cousin Jane. Carolina insisted she was a much better rider than Jane, but, after all, she was the one who fell off!" Dr. Tate snorted. He was capable of despising long-dead people as well as those still living.

Temple was excited to hear there was evidence to back up the diary. The box of materials from the *Southern Girlhood* exhibit was stowed in the far corner of the basement, she knew, near the wall that sprouted white beards of mold during wet summers.

Dr. Tate swirled his wine. "Frankly, I don't know why you're focusing on such trivialities when these scandalous rumors about Folly Park are being bruited about."

"You've heard them too?"

"It's revolting. What do you plan to do?"

"I have an idea."

"You've got to act boldly, my dear."

"Act boldly about what?" Beau asked, rejoining them.

Before either could reply, Judge Preston appeared with Mrs. Glass, who wore an elegant, champagne-colored gown. Hunter Glass was nowhere in sight, for which Temple was grateful.

Mrs. Glass's smile was a little loose. "There's that adorable dress again!"

Beau laughed nastily. Temple kissed Mrs. Glass on the cheek. "Good evening, Mrs. Glass. Hello, Dad."

Flicking the inevitable breath mint around inside his mouth, Temple's father let his critical gaze travel from her worn shoes to her recycled dress and up to her face, skating over her mother's diamonds. "You should put on lipstick and cover up that black eye." He frowned. "Incidentally, how did you get a black eye? You're not protesting again, are you? I didn't get a call about bailing you out of jail." He laughed humorlessly and crunched down on the breath mint.

Pixie and Julia joined the group just in time to hear the judge's remark. Julia tilted her face up from her diminutive height and called out, "On the West Coast, people live in trees to protest logging. You could give it a try, Temple. It would be a nice change from a roof."

The others laughed at Julia's gibe, no one heartier than the judge, as Julia was a favorite. Last year, Temple had camped on the roof of a dilapidated building with two other volunteers for a few days to raise awareness about a drive to renovate low-income housing. She was relieved when Mrs. Glass turned everyone's attention by inquiring about Julia's visit to Rich.

Julia thrust out her left hand to show off her engagement ring and began talking about her wedding plans in the hyperanimated manner she affected at parties. Temple listened with only half her attention. Julia's face looked different somehow. Turning to Pixie she whispered, "Has something happened to her mouth?"

"Shh," Pixie hissed. "She'll hear you. Yes, she had some work done."

"Work?"

"She had her lips plumped up. Stop staring, she'll notice."

"Isn't that what she wants?"

Pixie giggled and slapped her hand over her mouth.

Julia rounded on Temple, legs wide, feet planted firmly on her four-inch heels. "Is there something you want to say?"

Out of the corner of her eye, Temple saw the others drift away. Her father looked back and shook his head. He was probably still annoyed she'd "lost" Rich, as he put it, who was the son of one of his oldest friends. No doubt Julia's engagement had scored her more points with the judge.

"I'm happy for you," Temple said.

Julia's eyes were like pebbles in a cold creek. "Really? Because you seem put out. Can't you at least *try* to be gracious about Rich breaking up with you?"

Obviously, Rich had not told Julia the truth. "I'm happy for you both," Temple said, pinning on a smile. Julia stared at her suspiciously before she turned on her heel and clicked away.

JUDGE PRESTON POSITIONED BEAU and Temple on either side of him on the dais set up in the new gallery. He delivered a patronizing speech about the importance of contributing one's "mite" to the nurturance of culture, made a few shameless plugs for Beau's candidacy—fabricating Temple's enthusiastic support—and barely mentioned his deceased wife.

Temple was disgusted with her father's pressure tactics and embarrassed being on stage. She had a nagging urge to tug at the hem of her dress and moved her hand to do it half a dozen times before she caught herself. She must have looked like a broken mechanical doll, she thought, glancing over at her brother.

Beau stood at his ease under the hot lights, nodding frequently with a self-satisfied smile. In the audience, Julia twisted her engagement ring, and a facet caught the light, briefly blinding Temple. Behind Julia, Randy Pierce stood glaring with his arms crossed. When her father finally finished, Temple escaped from the stage and hurried over to him.

"Is there something wrong?"

"You went behind my back." Randy's tone was deeply aggrieved. "You didn't even give me a chance to find a sponsor for your plan before you ran to someone else."

"You mean Jack Early? I didn't run to him. He offered to help."

Randy thrust his lower lip into a pout. "I was helping first."

"I didn't think it could hurt to have another person involved."

"Early isn't even a real legislative aide. He works for the district attorney in New York. He only got the job because he's related to Senator Alden."

"In my experience," Temple said dryly, "family connections can be very useful."

"He's just going to use your plan to rehabilitate Senator Alden's image because he's up for reelection this year."

"Why does Senator Alden's image need to be rehabilitated?"

Randy shook his head with a pitying smile. "I swear, sometimes it seems like you live in another century. Don't you pay attention to the news?"

Temple hadn't been able to get to the news much lately, but she did vaguely recall that Senator Alden had been in the headlines not long ago. She thought it was about something he'd said. Something racist, she remembered with a chill.

Just then Jack himself strode up with a glass in each hand, looking handsome in a well-cut tuxedo.

Jack handed one of the glasses to Temple. "Gin and tonic?" To Randy, he said, "I'm sorry, I don't know what you drink."

As Randy mumbled something incoherent, Temple asked, "How did you know this is what I like?"

"Lucky guess," Jack said with a smile.

Temple almost smiled back, but she noticed Randy staring at her. "We were just talking about you," she said hastily.

"Oh?"

"Randy thinks you're using me."

Jack raised his eyebrows at Randy, who stammered a disclaimer and quickly excused himself.

Jack turned to Temple. "Would you like to talk?"

Passing Mrs. Glass, who beamed approvingly at Temple with a suggestive nod at Jack, they carried their drinks to the far corner of the room. A bench behind a row of potted palms offered relative privacy. As soon as they sat down, Temple said, "Are you going to use my plan to help Senator Alden not look racist?"

"I hope so," Jack said frankly. "I'm sorry. I assumed you were aware of the senator's optics issue, but it sounds like you've just learned about it."

Optics issue? The phrase seemed disingenuous to Temple. "*Is* he a racist?"

"I'll tell you his side of the story, and then you decide if you want us involved in your plan. No hard feelings if you decide to pass, okay?"

Temple nodded. The thought of relinquishing hope for her plan was too depressing to think about.

Jack regarded her attentively as he spoke. "Senator Alden is my uncle by marriage. I would do anything for my aunt Claire, but that doesn't include helping someone committed to racist policies win reelection, even if he is her husband. The senator is a moderate Republican, but he's been getting a lot of pressure to vote with the more extreme wing of his party. At the same time, the left is treating him like a reactionary. My aunt hoped I might be able to help with the campaign. Remind people about his record of working across the aisle."

"Why is he being called a racist?"

Jack spun the ice cubes in his glass. "He was due to speak to a community group in the Meadow Gardens public housing project about their complaints that the property wasn't being maintained. It was raining that night, traffic was bad, and his driver got lost. When he arrived late, an organizer accused him of not thinking the meeting was important. The senator apologized and made an unfortunate remark about the neighborhood being 'like a jungle.' He was referring to the confusing roads. I don't know if you've ever driven around down there?"

Temple nodded. The detention center was in that part of the city.

"Then, after taking questions for three hours, the senator unfortunately said, 'Wait just a cotton-picking minute' when a journalist—who was Black—suggested he had no intention of following through on the residents' concerns."

"I think I remember seeing that in the paper."

Jack nodded. "He used words with racist meanings, and it's certainly no excuse that he comes from a different generation. But he understands bad policies and systemic racism are at the root of problems like housing and jobs, and he wants to make things better. He feels terrible about this rift with his constituents. He's reached out to community leaders, and for the most part they've accepted his apologies, but things are still sensitive."

Temple thought about Wanda, arrested when her boyfriend hid an eighth of an ounce of marijuana in her backpack before entering the security checkpoint at a concert. Although underage, pregnant, and a first-time offender, she'd been sent to the detention center. If Wanda were White, she likely would have been let off with a warning.

"You think if Senator Alden sponsors legislation to create a home to help Black teens, it'll redeem him with Black voters?"

"Yes," Jack said simply.

"Well, I hope he can help. The girls deserve a chance."

"I look forward to working with you." Jack clinked Temple's glass and smiled. She wished she'd made a better effort to cover her black eye.

On the other side of the palms, in the salacious tone used for particularly good gossip, a woman said, "Harry Preston was the older brother. You know, the state assemblyman? He died a couple of years ago."

Unable to stand up without being seen, Temple was trapped behind the palms. It was futile to try to talk over that strident voice. Staring down at the tiny white veins in the slice of lime in her drink, she winced as the voice told how, driving home from a fundraising event, Harry slid out of control on an icy bridge, and the car plummeted through the guardrail, down the embankment, and into the river.

Temple would go miles out of her way to avoid the bridge. The section of metal guardrail that had been replaced was still shinier than the rest of it. And even on a bright summer day, she imagined she could see the shiver of black ice.

Mercilessly the voice continued, saying it looked like Judge Preston was grooming Beau to take his brother's place in politics. He hadn't bothered with the middle child, the girl—Temple. She was smart but eccentric, nothing like her mother. So sad, poor thing. The new gallery was a wonderful memorial to her, wasn't it?

After what seemed like a lifetime, the voice moved away.

Temple stood up on feet that felt like cinder blocks. Jack said something she didn't hear as she searched for an escape route. She needed to get away from these people, with their smooth faces and false smiles, who never stopped gossiping, gossiping, gossiping. . . .

"There you are, Temple!" Julia squeaked triumphantly. "What are you doing hiding back here?" Her voice took on a flirty lilt. "Jack! Has she tied you up with her hopeless causes? She's made you miss all the fun!"

Temple wondered when Julia had met Jack.

"I don't feel I've missed anything." Jack smiled gently at Temple, his eyes troubled. With an effort of will, she smiled weakly back. Jack's smile broadened to a grin, and he nodded at her in a wordless conversation.

Julia's head swiveled back and forth between them. Then she took Jack's arm. "Come on, there are people here you should meet."

As Julia dragged Jack away, Temple scanned the room. She was disconcerted to see Mr. Starkweather talking with Beau, a town councilman, and another man she didn't recognize. Pixie was nearby, and Temple tapped her shoulder. "Who's the guy in the plaid shirt?"

Pixie looked pained. "You'd think he'd know enough to dress up for a black-tie event. But what can you expect from the vice president of New World Estates? *So* tacky."

CHAPTER SEVEN

New World Estates! The words ricocheted inside Temple's head as she paced around the park in the moonlight. She had no recollection of retrieving her keys from the valet or driving home from the party. All she could think about was losing Folly Park—the place she loved most in the world—to a New World Estates development!

The gated communities concentrated in the Northeast had recently begun to spread to other regions of the country. Luxury houses came in three Native American-themed models—Pueblo Adobe, Chumash Grass, and Algonquian Bark—that purported to be environmentally sustainable. The fourth model, Pilgrim Stone, was a nod to the company's Plymouth headquarters. The streets were named after famous chiefs, and clusters of houses were organized into separate "villages." Temple couldn't believe such a place might be built on the grounds of Folly Park.

Stalking past the castle folly, whose lowest tower was just a foot above her head, made Temple feel larger-than-life. With a kind of visceral knowledge, she understood that this was how Lad Preston, a man who reportedly lost his temper quicker than a lightning strike, must have felt before a fight.

She was enjoying a fantasy about verbally flaying Mr. Stark-weather with rapier wit when the heel of her shoe caught in a gopher hole.

Finding herself suddenly sprawled on the ground, Temple's anger flickered out. When she gingerly rose, she realized she was on the edge of the front lawn. The battlefield below was very still. Moonlight frosted the meadow grasses, silver tendrils of ground fog scalloped the tree line, and a fox skimmed silently toward cover. It was eerily, achingly beautiful.

Anger, no matter how righteous, would not serve her ends. If she indulged in it, sooner or later she would do something impetuous and probably stupid. Lad Preston couldn't be her model. Her inspiration must come instead from her mother's ancestry. Like General Thomas Temple Smith, she would be patient and controlled and quietly but relentlessly push her plan forward. Temple was certain if Jack and Senator Alden could come up with a deal that passed muster with the Rehabilitation and Social Services Committee, the board would also accept it. The development threat might even help her cause. Though the group home might offend those who saw Folly Park as a shrine to the Confederacy, how could anyone disagree that it was far better than a New World Estates?

IT RAINED HEAVILY DURING THE NIGHT, and when Temple opened her front door the next morning, the air was thick with the odor of damp earth. The early sun glinted off mineral chips in the wet gravel, birds trilled, and drops of water fell from the softly rustling trees. Everything looked fresh and bright and clean.

Just then, the roaring farts of a dying muffler assaulted her ears, and Temple turned to see a battered yellow Honda Civic struggling to round the bend in the tree-lined drive. The small car slewed side-to-side in the muddy ruts, lurched into a pothole opposite the overseer's house, and came to an abrupt halt. The driver hit the gas, and red clay sprayed from the tires as the engine squealed, but the car didn't budge. After another try the engine stalled. Temple started down the drive and arrived at the car just as Al and Betty Jean emerged from their house.

"Something must have broken," Vee said as she got out of the Honda.

Al popped the hood. "You might have burned out the carburetor."

Betty Jean patted Vee's arm sympathetically. Temple noticed a new VOTE POE button pinned on her electric-blue blouse, and she looked quickly away. She and Betty Jean were carefully avoiding talking about the election. Though Temple wanted Frank Poe to win, it was too much of a betrayal to openly root for her brother's opponent.

"How much will it cost to fix?" Vee asked apprehensively.

The situation was ripe for Al to escalate with melodrama, but he took pity on Vee. "It might not be so bad. We need to tow it off the drive and get a good look at it."

Vee stared glumly at the car. "My dad is going to be so mad."

"He'll understand," said Betty Jean. "These things happen."

"Not to him. And he warned me not to get a used car."

Betty Jean put her arm around Vee. "Come inside for a cup of coffee while Al takes care of things, honey."

"We need a tractor. I'll call Bill Edderly," Al said. "We can't have that thing sitting there or Sprigg will blow a gasket." Snickering at his own joke, he pulled out his cell phone.

Temple did not hear the smooth purr of an approaching engine until another car rounded the bend, and by then it was too late. Right in front of her, Flora's vintage El Dorado convertible rammed into the back of the stalled Civic.

Temple helped Flora, who was unhurt, out of the driver's seat. "My, my. . . ." Flora clutched at the throat of her white muslin gown and surveyed the damage. Despite crushing in the backside of the Civic, the bigger car had suffered nothing but a broken headlight. "Who's car is that?"

"Vee's," Temple said.

"Maybe get those new glasses now?" Al suggested sarcastically, as he headed off to meet Bill.

Flora needed bifocals, but she'd said many times she would not be pushed down that slippery slope by an ophthalmologist younger than some of her horses.

"It was an accident," Flora said. "Who expects a car to be sitting in the middle of the drive? That gal shouldn't have left it there."

"She didn't mean to. It got stuck and stalled."

"It's very inconvenient. I must take my car in right away and get it fixed before Ward sees it."

"Sure, okay," Temple said, nodding. Flora's husband was a brash, fleshy man from Alabama who spoke like his molars were glued together. What he did for a living was unclear, and it was rumored he had "partners" in Chicago. Temple wanted to avoid having Ward come to inquire about compensating him for the damage to the car. She watched Flora gun the El Dorado in reverse, wrestle it through a five-point turn, flattening a bush in the process, and rocket back up the drive.

Betty Jean came out of the house and surveyed the crushed Honda. "I thought I heard a crash. What happened?"

"Flora hit it. Hopefully insurance will pay for the damage."

Betty Jean shook her head. "Vee can't report it. She's insured under her father, and she doesn't want him to know. And I don't think she has the money for repairs."

"I'll talk to Flora."

"Don't bother. Al can work on it in his spare time, but it could be a while. That'll be tough for Vee."

"She can borrow my truck when she needs to."

Betty Jean waved to Bill Edderly, who had just arrived on his tractor. "Vee's renting a room near the university. On the west side, near the train tracks. It's probably a dump."

"That part of town isn't so great," Temple agreed. She watched Al attach a chain to the Honda's bumper.

"There's no way to get from there to here without a car. It's not on the bus line."

"That's true." Now Temple could see where this was going, and although living by herself was definitely lonely, and she liked Vee, she wasn't thrilled by the prospect of a roommate.

The tractor drew Vee's car slowly out of what could legitimately be called a sinkhole. Temple glanced at Betty Jean in her Sprigg-defying blouse and cheetah-print leggings. Her large hoop earrings seemed to be vibrating with purpose. "Seems to me like it makes sense for Vee to stay somewhere closer to work," Betty Jean said. "She could get along without a car for the summer if she didn't have to commute."

Bill towed the Honda to the one-car garage, where Al had been restoring a 1956 Chevy for years. Al set traffic cones around the hole.

"I've got Wanda, you know, or she could have our spare room." Betty Jean faced Temple and crossed her arms under the VOTE POE button.

"Okay, okay." Temple surrendered. "She can use the extra bedroom at my place if she wants to."

"Perfect!" Betty Jean smiled broadly. "It'll be good for you."

"You think I need company?"

"Sure, that too," Betty Jean said and went back into the house.

A few minutes later, Vee caught up with Temple on the drive. "Betty Jean told me about the room," she said breathlessly. "Thanks."

"No problem."

"How much is the rent?"

"There's no rent. The board lets me live there for free," Temple lied. Her own anemic graduate student budget was still fresh in her mind.

IT WAS MADDENING TO WATCH Stuart whipsaw between anxiety and willful denial as they worked through the details of his so-called action plan for Folly Park. Hypersensitive to imagined criticism, he challenged Temple's every suggestion. The only real hope lay with Senator Alden, but she couldn't tell Stuart about her plan until it was too late for him to ruin it.

When Stuart's phone rang, Temple grabbed her work bag and escaped to the archives. He would never follow her there.

The vinegary scent of deteriorating film had overpowered the basement's usual musty aroma, and Temple saw Vee hunched over the secondhand microfilm reader. Funds from a preservation grant a number of years ago had paid to photograph some of the deteriorating plantation records.

Settling at a desk in the corner, Temple casually turned her back and took Jane's diary out of her bag. She wasn't ready to share it with Vee yet.

November 22, 1859

I am homesick. This land is so foreign to me—so dusty and barren, the red roads riddled with holes. The town is small and mean, and nothing is to be got there that is not too dear to purchase because it all must come from the North! Houses and barns and fences are shoddily built, and many have never seen a lick of paint. There are no schools anywhere. This is the result of a system of unfree labor! The fieldhands look like paupers—roughly clothed, unkempt, and terrified to meet my eye. In the house, Carolina directs the servants to adjust the curtains so I might not suffer the glare, to bring cushions for my back, a shawl for the drafts, treats from the kitchen. But she only makes it worse, for I loathe to have them serve me!

November 23, 1859

The slaves are everywhere—in every room, around every corner, in the outbuildings and gardens and fields. I am awkward with them, and they seem indifferent to my sympathy. Carolina treats them with easy familiarity and appears not to notice their hands upon her, their quiet forms coming and going, their eyes downcast but always watching. This morning, she brought her maid, Sukey, to help me dress, and I drew back without thinking. Carolina laughed and said she supposed I needed no help for I was a Yankee lady. Sukey curtsied, and I blushed for having startled at her touch like a nervous filly. "Do you not have servants at home in Boston?" Carolina asked. "Of course," replied I. "But our servants only clean and cook. We look after ourselves." Carolina laughed and said, "Is not cooking and cleaning looking after you? I daresay those who haven't any servants at all would make no such distinction between you and me, Cousin." Someday I must explain the economics of wages to her, but I fear I am proving a poor champion of our cause.

It was beautifully warm today, and we went riding. Previously, my exercise was confined to a few short walks through the park to see the follies and the family cemetery, where our ancestors are buried with their favorite hunting dogs nearby. A boy came from the stables with a lovely, spirited bay for me. Though her own riding is much improved since we were young, Carolina herself rode a placid gray mare.

We were accompanied around the plantation by a slave named King. Carolina says that when she came to Folly Park, he was called by a nickname "not fit for a dog," and she demanded his birthname be restored. Though he carries himself with dignity, his face is terribly marred by scars. Carolina told me he was born twin to a beautiful sister named Linda, who was sent South as a girl. King's wife died in a fire, from which he tried to rescue her, leaving him with the scars and a young daughter. Carolina related this intimate history within yards of the man. When I whispered that King might not like to hear himself spoken of, she replied, "What of it? He knows my secrets." Then she said, all in a rush, as if she could keep it to herself not a moment longer, "When I first came here, I took laudanum. Was a very slave to it." She proceeded to tell me a most harrowing tale of how she'd resolved to break herself of the habit to begin her new life afresh. When Mr. Smith was away, she locked herself in her room, and put King to guard the door to prevent anyone from succumbing to her threats and entreaties. She was told she'd screamed for five days and nights. When it was over, Carolina dragged herself to the window and saw all the people on their knees in the moonlight, praying for her. Mr. Lamb—the overseer—said they had done so every night, and that King had asked them to do it.

I was terribly shocked by this astonishing confession, but I pitied Carolina, and looked to distract her. When King rode out of earshot, I said I was surprised to see him permitted to carry a gun. "But how would he hunt without a gun?" Carolina asked and told me that, notwithstanding the gentry's boasting, King is the best marksman in four counties. I wonder she does not fear her servant might one day incite the others to rise against their master rather than pray for their mistress! And although I told her of my commitment to abolition, Carolina clearly sees no threat in me. Of course, that may reflect doubts about my insurrectionary skills! But I rather think it must be a willful blindness. Or perhaps it is this pastoral land that makes one complacent. There is a quality to the air, a softness to the rolling hills, that already I love. Carolina says I must remember I am only half a Yankee, and this country is in my blood too.

Temple was impressed by Carolina's battle to break her addiction—a woman she had often dismissed as unworthy of serious attention. She continued reading.

November 24, 1859

Today I inquired if I might see the slave quarters. Carolina exclaimed, "Good heavens, whatever for?" then shrugged and said I might do as I liked. The quarters were windowless, with dirt floors, but sturdy enough, I suppose. There are garden plots between them, and the slaves tell me they sell some of their produce, as well as eggs and game, to their mistress. I have learned that King is a redoubtable fisherman as well as hunter, and Old Bet assures me she can conjure charms to make the hens lay or to make a man fall in love!

Carolina desires me to teach her how to keep the household accounts. She has a little book for that purpose. She is a dunce at such matters, she says, and though she does not mind her mistakes shorting Mr. Smith, she does not want the people to lose by them.

November 25, 1859

Carolina insisted again today that she must improve her management of the household. It is not the custom, she says, to relinquish such matters to the servants, who will cheat and steal and not think it wrong. When still I demurred, she said that as I am an Abolitionist, she would consent to keep mum if I wished to teach the servants as well as her. I was astonished by her maneuver, but I saw she was in earnest, and so I went to the kitchen this morning. It is a brick building separated some little distance from the main house. The cook, Etta, is a slight woman of perhaps thirty-five with a shy child named Louella, who runs errands for her mother. King's daughter, a pretty girl of about fifteen named Jewel, works under Etta. I felt her bright eyes upon me, though every time I looked at her, they were trained upon the floor.

I told Etta I had no wish to interfere with her arrangements. Neither Carolina nor I could manage the kitchen half as well as she, and well she knows it. I do not see how I will help these people. Mother would find a way—she would not be deterred by their closed faces or shamed into inaction by their servantly attentions. I appear only capable of being a small help to my cousin—a woman who would seem to want for nothing!

But we have made a beginning. I hold Carolina's keys and unlock the pantry and storerooms when Etta requires it. These are stocked full with hams hanging on beams, tubs of pickled pork and corned beef, loaves of white sugar, barrels of flour, casks of oil and wine and brandy. Carolina will keep a record of the provisions she purchases from the people. I have been teaching her simple arithmetic. She is hard upon herself for what she terms her "abominable ignorance" and is determined to prove herself a capable mistress.

Here again were King and Jewel, the enslaved people in the photo from the box. Jewel was apparently King's daughter. And King was the brother of the girl Linda, James Smith's favorite, who was sent south when the Folly Park ring disappeared. Here also was Louella, who, more than half a century later, would recount memories of these very days in the kitchen for a WPA interviewer. Temple eagerly turned the page.

The basement door creaked open, and Martha peered down from the top of the stairs. "We've got a situation, Temple. Flora left early to pick up her car, and Betty Jean's got two busloads of guests. Fred needs help."

"Two *busloads*?"

"A group of retired history teachers. There was a gas leak at Cleveland Hill, so they were diverted here. What do you want to do?"

"Well, Vee," Temple said, "I guess this is your chance to do a tour."

"What?" Vee looked up, blinking.

"We need you to do a tour."

"Oh. Okay." Vee stood and smoothed her shirt. "I'm ready."

"Come with me," said Martha. She stared at Temple as Vee gathered her things, her glasses, brows, and bangs merged into one dark band of disapproval.

Temple guessed Martha thought it was too soon for Vee to conduct a tour on her own and suspected she might be right. "You'll be great!" she called, as Vee headed up the stairs.

Once she was alone, Temple dug the tin box from her bag and took out the photograph. Now that she was looking for them, she could discern a faint network of scars on King's face. Staring at Jewel, she wondered what had compelled the girl to take her life, but Jewel's expression held no clue. Another detail, however, caught Temple's eye.

There was an odd blurring of the general's hand where it rested on Jane's shoulder. *Maybe he moved while the negative was setting*, Temple thought. Unearthing a magnifying glass from the desk drawer, she dragged a chair beneath one of the high, small windows and stood on it to get closer to the light. She looked through the magnifying glass at the photograph and a chill shivered down her spine. On the general's hand, reflecting the sunlight, was the Janus ring. The same ring that had supposedly disappeared from Folly Park years before the general had come to live there.

JUST AS TEMPLE OPENED THE basement door, squinting
in the bright daylight, a large tour group passed by. Usually,
people looked a bit tired by the end of the Folly Park tour,
but these visitors, despite their age, walked briskly, talking
excitedly. Temple hurried to the front of the house, where
she found Vee alone on the veranda.

"You must have given the teachers a great tour. They
looked really pleased."

"Did they?" Vee's voice was flat, her shoulders slumped.

Temple sat down beside her. "Are you okay? I know
giving a tour can be exhausting."

"I was terrible. They knew everything about the general
and Folly Park. They knew about Carolina. They even knew
about the general's valet, Titus."

"Don't worry. This was your first time. You'll get better."

"They thought it was weird I was giving a tour. Because
I'm Black. They wanted to know why I'm working at Folly
Park." Vee twitched her shoulder. "A lady asked if I'm angry
about slavery."

Temple was dismayed. "I'm so sorry."

"When we got to the music room, I blanked on what I
was supposed to say. They were all staring at me, waiting.
This one old man was the worst. He wore wraparound sunglasses—even inside the house—and he kept correcting me.
And when I froze, he crossed his arms and shook his head."

"There's always someone—"

"I didn't mean to. It was totally unintentional, I swear.
But the old guy was smirking at me, and one lady yawned,
and the others were getting impatient. I forgot everything
in the tour about the Beethoven bust, the pianoforte, and
Carolina's favorite piece of music." Vee sighed. "I can
remember it now—Schumann's 'Vanitas Vanitatum'—but

I couldn't then, so I pointed out her portrait instead, and I told them about the baby."

"You what?"

"I told them Carolina may have given birth to a baby during the Civil War while the general was away—a biracial baby."

Vee put her head in her hands.

Temple's heart began to race. She took a deep breath to force back her panic. "I guess the cat's out of the bag." She patted Vee's shoulder. "Don't feel bad."

Vee plucked at a splinter of wood on the step. "I know you didn't want me to say anything until we had some evidence."

"We do."

"Not really. Louella's interview won't hold up. I told the teachers about it, but the old guy said those interviews are problematic because ex-slaves just told White interviewers what they thought they wanted to hear. I don't know who the father of the baby was, and I have to explain how the missing Folly Park ring got to Boston."

"We have evidence Thomas Temple Smith had the ring at Folly Park years after it was supposed to have been stolen from his uncle." Despite the enormity of what had happened, and which some part of her understood she was not yet fully grasping, Temple felt pleased about being able to surprise Vee. "I also discovered that a cousin of Thomas and Carolina's came to visit before the war—a Boston abolitionist who had been engaged to Henry Stannard."

Vee stared at Temple like she'd lost her mind. Temple took the box from her work bag and showed Vee the photograph and the diary. She explained how the box had fallen out of the ceiling and pointed out Jane, King, and Jewel. She mentioned Carolina was rumored to have been unfaithful. And she drew Vee's attention to the ring on the general's hand.

"This is amazing," Vee said. "I wish I could have used it on my tour."

"No doubt we'll soon have a chance to share it with an even larger audience," Temple said dryly.

Vee grimaced. "Is there any chance people won't mention what I said?"

Temple's cell phone buzzed, sparing her from having to tell Vee there was no way the story wouldn't spread. It was Jack. Vee turned back to the photo as Temple walked out of earshot.

Jack told Temple that Senator Alden was intrigued by her plan.

"That's great news."

"You don't sound like you just got great news." There was a smile in Jack's voice. "I can't make any promises, but this is a good start."

"I know. I appreciate what you've done, of course, and I'm really glad to hear about the senator."

"So, what's up?"

With that invitation, Temple told Jack everything. Everything she'd just told Vee, along with Vee's theory that Carolina had given birth to an illegitimate baby and what she'd just done during her tour.

When she finished, Jack was silent.

"It's okay," Temple said. "I understand if the senator can't support my plan now. This will upset a lot of people. We'll be called traitors, accused of politicizing the house, you can't even imagine."

"Hold on. Don't give up just yet. You're being transparent about confronting issues around race. It works for Monticello."

"The general isn't Jefferson. He wasn't a Founding Father who established the country. He tried to destroy it."

"Still, besides being the right thing to do, telling the truth puts you in a stronger position."

They talked a bit longer, and when she hung up, Temple felt better. "Let's go pick up your things and get you moved in," she said, helping Vee to her feet. "I'll meet you by my truck. I have to run into the office for a minute."

CHAPTER EIGHT

"What's all this about a bastard kid?" Stuart burst into Temple's office. "I just got a call from Hunt. Some old duffer who took a tour yesterday called him at home last night blathering about the general's wife giving birth to a Black man's baby during the Civil War. Who told him that nonsense? Someone is going to get fired!"

"Hold on a minute. It was my fault."

"*You* said it?" Stuart's eyes popped behind his glasses.

"No, Vee did, but I made her give a tour before she was ready. She added some stuff from her research when she couldn't remember the script."

Stuart threw his hands in the air, treating Temple to a close-up of the wet patches under his arms. "Darn it, Temple! Hunt is mad. He gave me hell about blindsiding him. I think he might shut us down right now!"

Before Temple could respond, Martha appeared in the doorway. Though it was not yet ten o'clock, she appeared ready to speak.

"What is it?" Stuart barked.

"You should come outside."

"We're busy here!"

"You need to see this."

Stuart let out an exasperated snort. "Come on, Temple. I'm not through with you." He jerked his head toward the door.

Outside was a scene of bustling activity. The parking lot was packed full of cars, and more vehicles lined the drive, making it difficult for a tour bus crawling toward the mansion to pass. Al was directing overflow traffic into the fallow wheat field. A line of guests waiting outside the ticket office stretched beyond the washhouse nearly to the old well. Those who had already purchased tickets jockeyed for position in front of the veranda, eager to be included in the first tour when the mansion opened.

Stuart gasped. "What the. . . ?" His glasses slid to the end of his nose.

"Apparently we were mentioned on the late-night news," Martha said, a gleam in her amber eyes.

"What? Why?"

"The newscaster said he would have something exciting to report about the history of Folly Park."

The turnout was better than Temple could have imagined. "Should I call our volunteer guides to help out?" she asked.

Stuart didn't answer. He seemed completely overwhelmed.

"I'll brief Fred and Flora about what's going on," Temple said. "And Martha should open the other register in the ticket office." Martha nodded and left.

Stuart wheeled to face Temple. "Tell Vee to shut up and don't say anything else about a baby. We'll just keep quiet until it all dies down."

"I don't think that will be possible." Temple pointed.

A white news van with a giant aerial tower sprouting from the roof worked its way up the drive.

Stuart yelped and dove back through the door. "Oh no! How did *they* find out?"

"Martha said—"

"Quiet! Let me think, will you?"

Temple realized Stuart was too panicked to see the opportunity Vee's slipup had provided. She would have to lay it out clearly. "Being on the news will increase ticket sales and could buy us some time. We might have a real chance to save Folly Park."

Stuart squinched. "Can we prove there was an illegitimate kid?"

"We've got some archival evidence, but it's fairly circumstantial."

"Can you find out if it's definitely true?"

"I don't know."

"But what are the chances?"

"It's impossible to say. Vee's trying to see what else she can discover."

"Keep on her. Make her earn her paycheck or her credits or whatever she's getting. And work on it yourself too. This is big." Stuart shoved his glasses back up to the bridge of his nose. "When the trustees want to shut us down for blasting the general's reputation, I might be able to convince them we were pursuing bona fide scholarship."

"It really is legitimate research," Temple said, but her boss wasn't listening.

The news van had gotten stuck behind a slow-moving RV. While Stuart yanked a comb from his breast pocket and fussed with his hair, Temple went up the drive to the ticket office.

Betty Jean and Martha were working the cash registers, and when her fingers weren't flying over her phone posting to social media, Wanda handed out brochures and directed guests to the house. There was a palpable energy in the air, and Temple noticed the crowd was different— younger and more diverse—than their usual visitors. Someone in the back of the line called out to ask if the rumor about Carolina's baby was true, and everyone quieted to hear Betty Jean's answer. "I'm not going to give it away! You enjoy the tour."

While Martha waited for a woman to locate her wallet inside a cavernous handbag, Temple leaned over and said, "There's a news van here."

"Oh?"

"It's WTRU."

"What a coincidence. That's where my brother-in-law works."

"Thanks."

Martha did not reply, but Temple glimpsed a fleeting smile before she turned back to the visitor saying, "Yes, ma'am, we'd be happy to take a check."

STUART STOOD ON THE LAWN in front of the mansion next to a broad-shouldered young man in a suit with hay-colored hair tinged slightly green, as if he swam regularly in a chlorinated pool. Temple recognized Chip Davenport from the evening news. When she walked up to them, Stuart ignored her. Chip did not. "Do you work here?"

Temple introduced herself.

"Preston? As in Beau Preston? You're his sister?" When Temple nodded reluctantly, Chip motioned peremptorily to Stuart. "Move over. I want her in it too."

"But I'm the *director* of Folly Park."

"Look, Stanley, she doesn't have to talk. She'll just be in the background to give the story some pizzazz."

Stuart squinched. "Stuart," he said.

"What?"

"My name is Stuart. Not Stanley."

"Right. Okay." Chip turned away. "Come on, people, let's go!" he snarled at his crew, and then turned to the camera and said enthusiastically, "Tonight, something new about a very old place! Who says you can't change the past? With me here is Temple Preston—sister of mayoral candidate Beau Preston—and Stanley Twig, the director of historic Folly Park. . . ."

It was over in a few minutes. A few minutes in which Temple discovered that her desire to save Folly Park had blinded her to the danger of Stuart talking about history in public.

"Why did you tell him we'll reveal the identity of the baby's father in two days?" Temple asked bleakly, as the TV van crunched away over the gravel.

"You have to build suspense to keep them interested. You don't understand the media."

"This isn't a soap opera. I can't promise we'll know anything so soon."

"Just tell them *something*. It doesn't matter what."

"But we've got to do the research. We're professional historians."

Stuart's eyes narrowed behind his glasses. "I don't care about that or your precious PhD. I have an MBA, you know!" He stomped off toward the administration building.

TEMPLE MET FRED AND FLORA in the docents' breakroom, a closet-sized room at the back of the house that had once served as the butler's pantry. She briefed them about the biracial baby and asked them to revise their tours. Flora immediately collapsed onto the ratty couch in a flurry of petticoats.

"No! It can't be true," she wailed, clutching her chest. Fred sighed. Temple crossed her arms.

Getting no reaction, Flora sat up, comforting herself by remarking that they still didn't know the truth about "that new intern's nasty ideas." Temple rolled her eyes at Fred and hurried down to the archives to help Vee.

Last night, after retrieving Vee's few belongings from her rented room, the two of them had stayed up late strategizing on a research plan. They discovered a shared passion for thoroughness and details, and Temple was grateful to have such an ally. She told Vee about the trustees' ultimatum, the development threat, and the daily deterioration of Folly Park. She even told her about her plan.

"That's a nice idea," Vee said.

But Temple was becoming attuned to the nuances of Vee's tone. "You don't think it will work, do you?"

"I really hope it does."

"Why don't you think it will?"

"Look how worried you are about the reaction to a baby born over one hundred and fifty years ago. For your plan to work, an awful lot of people have to behave better than even you seem to expect."

Temple was thinking about that conversation when Vee called out, "I think I've got something!" as soon as she appeared on the basement stairs.

"About the baby?" Temple asked, ashamed she was relieved when Vee shook her head.

"No. I was skimming through the microfilm, and I found some letters between the general and Carolina's father. I know why Thomas and Carolina married although they'd never met."

"They were cousins. They were trying to keep the wealth in the family."

"They were trying to keep more than that in the family." Vee herded Temple to the microfilm reader. "Look at this."

Lancaster County, 4th May 1859

Dear Sir,

I hope, My Dear Nephew, that this letter finds you well and prospering. We have but recently learned of the death of my wife's brother James, and of your succession to his place as Master of Folly Park. I offer you such of our condolences and congratulations as it may please you to accept.

Now I come to the subject of my Letter, which is to make you an offer of my daughter's hand in marriage. This may be too prosaic an approach to such a Romantic subject, but I am a practical man with no inclination to Poetry, and therefore you must excuse me. I desire to strengthen the alliance between our two families. In these uncertain times, one can never be too careful. My business takes me often to the North, and I do not underestimate these cursed Abolitionists as many of my neighbors do. Zealotry can move mountains as well as faith. Carolina, though she has been a headstrong girl ~~which led her to ruin~~ and somewhat prone to error —but of this I will be silent until we meet—is now eighteen years old. Of her charms you must judge for yourself—I am a businessman and no Lothario! She brings with her $72,000 cash money, 22 prime hands—including 12 bucks & 5 *breeding wenches—and 800 wooded acres in this County, suitable for lumbering. There is a mill in good condition upon the land operated by a respectable man named Ross, who would be willing to serve your pleasure.*

My wife insists that some of the People, who came with her upon her marriage, are eager to return to Folly Park with my daughter, though I do not believe they can have any real attachment to the place after the lapse of 25 years. Be that as it may, they have multiplied prodigiously under my care and, in consequence, Carolina's dowry is many souls larger than her good Mother's.

If you find my proposal of interest, advise when we may expect you as our most welcome guest in Lancaster.

Yours,
William Gilmore

"See?" Vee said.

"See what? Marriages were arranged all the time back then."

"Not that part." Vee shook her head. "There was something in Carolina's past. He blotted out 'which led to her ruin'—look, I turned up the light on the microfilm reader so you can read it through the ink blotch."

"But what—"

"Just wait!" Vee flipped through her notes. "There's another letter from Carolina's father in July—that's two months after Thomas and Carolina were married. Mr. Gilmore says he wants to be sure Thomas understands that 'Carolina's continued treatment is necessary to ensure her respectability.' He goes on to say that when she was at home, she had been administered one hundred drops of laudanum a day."

"But we already knew Carolina was addicted to laudanum."

"Yes, but why did she became an addict in the first place? Don't you wonder why her father thought keeping her drugged was necessary for her respectability? That was a code word for sexual behavior."

"You can't be sure about that. He could have meant anything."

"This was clearly about sex. I found something else."

Temple thought it might take her all summer to get used to Vee's habit of dropping bombshells.

Referring again to her pad, Vee said, "Carolina's mother called her an 'indefatigable flirt.' There's a series of letters from Clarissa to her husband when he was away on business. She gets more and more worried about Carolina's relationship with the music teacher, Gregory Steele, who's giving her lessons on the pianoforte. Clarissa tells her husband she's considered ending the lessons, but it would put Carolina at a disadvantage with the other girls in the neighborhood." Vee dropped her voice. "Then, in the last letter, Clarissa begs her husband to return home at once. She says that Carolina has behaved outrageously."

"What did she do?"

"Clarissa surprised her and the music teacher in a compromising position."

"Seriously?"

Vee nodded. "Between fainting fits, Clarissa manages to confront Carolina, who declares her passionate love for Gregory. Her mother locks her in her bedroom, and Carolina tries to run away—she's caught climbing out the window into a magnolia tree. In her last letter, Clarissa tells her husband that Gregory Steele has left town, but she's keeping Carolina locked in a storeroom as a precaution. I think that when Mr. Gilmore came home, he kept his daughter drugged until he could make arrangements to marry her off—to Thomas Temple Smith."

Poor Carolina, Temple thought. Abandoned by her lover, locked up by her mother, drugged by her father, and married off to a man she'd never met.

"Given what she'd been through, Thomas's eagerness to marry Carolina for her dowry seems pretty heartless," Vee said.

Temple nodded. She was disappointed in her childhood hero.

Just then, Betty Jean texted to say they were both needed to conduct tours. Even with the additional help, the guides couldn't keep up.

Vee dropped her yellow pad, eyes wide. "It worked?"

"It looks that way."

The night before, Temple had confessed to Vee that she'd enlisted Martha to tip off station WTRU about the biracial baby.

IT WAS A LONG DAY. AT THE END of it, Al, Betty Jean, Vee, and Temple sat exhausted on the veranda as dusk gently fell over Folly Park. Flora and Martha had left as soon as the last car pulled away, and Fred had just headed home, his perpetual smile sagging at the edges. No one knew when Stuart had disappeared.

"I didn't get a chance to tell Mr. Sprigg how much we made," Betty Jean said.

"How much did we make?" Temple asked.

"Six thousand, three hundred and sixty-eight dollars. That's about four thousand more than we ever made in one day before."

Al whistled.

"My feet ache." Vee winced as she rubbed her instep. "I did five tours."

"You'll probably never have to do another one," said Al. "When the trustees realize why we had so many guests, we'll all be fired."

"But I was careful to say we're not sure yet if the story is true. And I know the other guides used the same language."

"Everyone except Flora," said Temple. "Fred told me she wouldn't even mention the baby because she won't believe Carolina cheated on the general."

Betty Jean shook her head. "I always give Flora the guests who don't seem like they want to hear about slavery. But people who came today were really interested, even some I wouldn't have expected."

"One lady hugged me and apologized for slavery," Vee said. "And a few others said they never learned in school about how enslaved people had families and celebrated weddings and birthday and funerals. They didn't realize that selling slaves separated people who loved each other."

Al snorted. "They didn't realize they were human beings?"

Vee shrugged. "At least they're trying."

"If this keeps up, hopefully the trustees will honor their pledge to keep us open since we're paying our own way—at least for now," Temple said. "But they might not want to deal with the scandal. It's touch-and-go."

"In that case, let's have takeout in the parlor," Al joked.

"Sure, why not? I'll order pizza. My treat."

Temple had just taken out her phone when a silver sedan pulled up in front of her house. Spotting her as he got out of the car, Temple's father made his way purposefully toward the veranda. Al stood and tucked in his shirt.

Betty Jean patted her hair, and Vee sat up straighter. Judge Preston had that effect on people.

The judge's lips were pressed into a thin line. There was a flake of dried blood in the corner of his mouth, Temple saw, and his cheeks were slightly swollen. He'd obviously been to the dentist again for his chronic periodontitis, and that always put him in a foul mood.

"You know Betty Jean and Al, Dad," Temple said. "And this is Vee, our summer intern."

The judge nodded curtly in Vee's direction. Al he acknowledged only with a nod as well, but he reached forward and shook Betty Jean's hand. Her people had belonged to his ancestors and worked for the Preston family after emancipation. At her request, Temple had traced Betty Jean's lineage back to a West African girl named Tana, purchased by a Tayloe in 1704.

"I'd like a word with you, Temple," the judge said. "A private word."

Clearly, her father didn't want witnesses while he bullied her, and Temple steeled herself as they crossed the drive to her house. Inside, the judge scanned the living room with cold eyes. He squinted into the cabinet where Temple kept her Civil War memorabilia and family mementos. These included Lad Preston's leather eye patch, the bullet dug out of his shoulder after a duel, the table fork that had been used to do it, an engraved locket that had belonged to the first mistress of Folly Park, and a nearly intact, three-hundred-year-old china tea service. Turning away with a scowl, the judge sat down on the corner of the couch, and as usual, did not speak until he was ready. By then Temple's nerves were stretched taut. "You need to campaign for your brother."

Temple sank onto the bent wood rocking chair Al had made for her twenty-first birthday. She was relieved that her father either didn't know about or wasn't interested in what was going on at Folly Park, but this subject was hardly more pleasant. "I told you I don't want to get involved."

The judge acted as if she hadn't spoken. "The first thing you'll do is nip that stupid story about a baby in the bud. It's upsetting Beau's base."

So, he did know about the baby. "I'm sorry, Dad, but I happen to agree with Frank Poe that it's time to talk about race. And I don't think Beau's politics are right for Preston's Mill."

"No one asked what you think," Judge Preston snapped. "You worked on Harry's campaign, and you'll work on Beau's."

"I won't. Please stop asking." Temple despised herself for pleading. "You know I don't like what you did during Harry's campaign."

"Get off your high horse. You don't understand what it takes to win an election."

"Maybe not, but I know that dangling political favors in return for campaign contributions is wrong."

"My God, we've been over this!" The judge pounded the arm of the couch. He winced and blotted his mouth with a bloody handkerchief. "I've told you before I never promised anything. I had a casual conversation on the golf course. That's how things get done."

The judge glared at Temple while sweat crawled down her back. Finally, he spoke. "Are you going to help your brother, or aren't you?"

"No, Dad, I'm not."

"You're so self-righteous. You never were a team player."

Temple felt as if all the oxygen had been sucked from the room.

"After that nonsense with the picketing and getting arrested in college at a protest, I thought when you enrolled in law school you'd finally grown up." He rose abruptly and stared at the dueling pistols in the cabinet. "But you decided you didn't want a real profession. You'd rather make up stories and call it studying history. After that stunt on the roof last year, I finally knew for sure."

"Knew what?" Temple got up from the rocking chair. There was something different in his tone.

"Never mind."

"Knew what, Dad?"

Temple's father turned to look at her, his gray eyes like concrete. "Do you really think a child of mine would have turned out like you?"

Temple stared, wondering what he meant. Suddenly, with an icy clutch at her heart, she remembered her mother's self-portrait in the art gallery. The label saying she'd been in New York the year Temple was born. She said slowly, "What exactly are you driving at?"

The judge ignored her question. "Pixie will email you a schedule of Beau's upcoming fundraising events, where I expect you to make an appearance. If you remain unwilling to do your duty, you will no longer receive a quarterly allowance."

Crossing the room in three long strides, the judge passed through the kitchen and wrenched the screen door open with such force it hit the wall and a chunk of plaster fell. He took the time to grind it to powder under his heel before he stalked out to his car. Gravel spit up from the tires and sprayed the house like birdshot.

Temple sank heavily on to the couch. She couldn't believe her mother had been unfaithful. She had many memories of her handsome tuxedoed father and beautiful begowned mother heading off to some social event, where they would effortlessly command attention. Her father was probably just disappointed in her, as usual. He'd always treated his children as underdeveloped versions of himself, pushing them into his own interests, where he would monitor their every move. Unmarried at twenty-eight, in a job with no prospects, in a field that promised only modest returns, Temple had never fit into his mold. His threat to withhold her allowance would not alter her course. Knowing he begrudged every cent, the prospect of no longer receiving checks from him felt more like a relief than a hardship.

Temple slowly dug her phone out of her pocket and ordered the pizza. When she hung up, Vee spoke tentatively from the doorway. "Are you okay?"

"I'm fine."

"Jack Early is here. Betty Jean invited him to stay for pizza, and he says he'll drive you into town to pick it up."

Temple scrambled to her feet, raking distractedly at her hair.

"You look fine," Vee said, grinning.

Outside, Jack was leaning against one of the pillars on the veranda. Tie removed and sleeves rolled up, he'd apparently come straight from work. When he saw Temple, he smiled and straightened up from the pillar.

"Congratulations! Betty Jean says you've had quite a day. Can I give you a lift into town?"

A weathered, dark-green MG convertible older than Temple was parked on the drive. Al crouched beside it, peering at the tires with the avidity of a connoisseur. "Thanks, but we can take my truck."

Jack laughed. "You're a historian, you're supposed to like antiques." He opened the passenger door, which emitted a prolonged squeal. "I restored it myself, but I think it's safe."

"Seriously?"

Jack nodded. "A mechanic checked it over."

Al looked up. "You went with the one-inch band. Looks good."

"Thanks. Are you going with whitewalls for your '56 Chevy?"

"Yup, thick-band," Al responded, slapping the hood with a rare smile.

Jack closed Temple's door and climbed into the driver's seat. "I hope you don't mind I stopped by. I texted earlier."

"I didn't see it."

"You were busy. Anyway, I thought I'd take my chances. I wanted to do my due diligence and see Folly Park."

"I'm glad you came. You seem to have gotten to know everyone pretty quickly. Al doesn't smile for just anyone."

"Car talk."

"Maybe later I can show you the tobacco barn. My grandfather converted it to an art studio as a birthday surprise for my mother in the late '90s, and I think it could easily be retrofitted. It's got electricity, running water, and even a kitchenette."

"That sounds great," Jack said, changing gears as the car approached the bend in the drive.

They passed the overseer's house, a large VOTE POE sign propped in the window. Temple realized her father couldn't possibly have missed it.

As if he had read her mind, Jack said, "I have to ask. Is your father on board with your plan?"

"I doubt he would be if he knew about it. He doesn't care about Folly Park. It belonged to my mother's side of the family."

As the fields and fences flashed by, Temple told Jack she was certain that if Beau won the election and became mayor of Preston's Mill, he wouldn't stand in the way of the developers.

"I've heard rumors about potential development. Senator Alden knows your father slightly and wondered about his position, but don't worry."

Temple's mood lightened, and she relaxed in her seat. "Has working with the senator been rewarding?"

"Is that a diplomatic way of asking why I would take a job in politics?"

Temple laughed. "Maybe."

"Well, I wasn't interested when my aunt Claire first proposed it. But I needed a change, and the senator wanted my help. He remembers when people on opposite sides of the aisle would actually talk to each other, not to mention cosponsor legislation. He'd like to restore that kind of respectful disagreement."

"Is that even possible? It feels like those days are gone."

"I've met some well-meaning people in the last few weeks who want to make things better."

Temple thought of Harry. He and Jack would have liked each other.

"But I'm not naive," Jack continued. "I'm not above doing deals with the kinds of politicians who are attracted to office because they like power. And I don't mind fighting when necessary." He turned his head briefly to give Temple a wry smile. "I hope for the best but prepare for the worst. I'm not sure if that's idealistic or cynical."

"I'd say it's pragmatic," Temple said, as they turned down a side street around the corner from Beau's campaign headquarters and pulled up in front of the pizza parlor. "I'll be right back."

When Temple returned a few minutes later, Julia was standing beside the car, chatting with Jack. She flashed her wide smile and tilted her head flirtatiously when she laughed, trademark techniques she'd used to capture admirers since they were teens.

Temple felt a sharp stab of irritation. She slowed her steps, but Jack saw her and jumped up to stow the pizza boxes in the trunk.

"See you later, Jack," Julia called as she turned away, waggling her fingers. "Bye-bye, Temple!"

"I didn't realize you knew Julia so well," Temple said, as they pulled away from the curb.

"I don't, really. The senator asked her to introduce me around, and she's been very helpful."

"Julia does know everyone," Temple agreed, gloomily.

"That she does. And she doesn't mind telling me every detail about everyone she knows. Except for one person."

Glancing sideways, Temple found Jack grinning at her. She smiled as they drove slowly past the statue of the general in the town square, the lowering sun setting his bronzed face aglow.

VEE HAD COVERED THE DROPLEAF table in the parlor with paper towels, and they sat gingerly on the antique Chippendale chairs. Betty Jean told stories about the strange things visitors asked her to watch for them while they were on the tour, including dry cleaning, a canary in a cage, and a priceless cello. Al and Jack found common ground talking about cars and sports, and Vee teased them for it. Temple discovered she liked the way a twist of dark hair curled on Jack's forehead, and she noticed a small scar on the edge of his chin and wondered if it came from a childhood fall. After the pizza was gone, Betty Jean and Al offered to make ice cream sundaes at their house for dessert. Vee accepted. Jack and Temple declined.

After the others had left, Temple asked, "Do you have time to see the barn?"

"Sure," Jack said, crushing the pizza boxes. "I'm intrigued."

Strolling through the park in the twilight, Temple pointed out landmarks and told Jack some of the more amusing family stories associated with them. He was easy to talk to and laughed readily. Getting to know him seemed more worthwhile than anything else in her life. That careless thought, which slithered into her mind like a snake into a henhouse, scared Temple back to herself. She hurried the last fifty yards toward the looming bulk of the barn.

"Here we are," Temple announced unnecessarily as she unlocked the door and flicked on the lights. She could almost smell the long-gone paint, linseed oil, and turpentine that always reminded her of her mother. Trying to stave off the familiar pinch of loss, she began to point out areas that could be modified to accommodate the girls.

Temple's mouth suddenly went dry and abruptly she stopped talking. A few paintings were propped against the wall under the stairs to the loft. Though wrapped tightly with plastic, the images were clearly visible. One depicted a seven-year-old Temple gazing solemnly from the canvas. Perched in the middle of an oversized wicker chair on a flagstone patio, thin arms hugging knobby-kneed legs, she looked like a baby bird abandoned in its nest.

Her mother had not said a word while she painted, Temple remembered. And she wiped away tears with a tissue she had tucked in her smock. At the dinner table the previous evening, Temple's father had told her mother that if she insisted on "dab-dabbing," she would have to do it outside. He couldn't invite important people to a house that smelled like a construction site, he had said, to meet a wife covered in paint like a kindergartener. Just before dinner, he'd discovered Beau scribbling on the oak-paneled wall in his office "like Mommy." The judge's wedding ring cut open Beau's cheek when he had hit him. But, at the table, while Harry and Temple hung their heads over their uneaten food, Beau sat up straighter in his booster seat. Blood showing pink through the white bandage, his piping voice scolded, "Bad Mommy! Bad Mommy!"

The judge had tousled Beau's hair and laughed. "Yes, she is, isn't she?"

Looking at the painting now, Temple felt sick. Not long after it was finished, her grandfather had converted the barn. Her mother often asked her to model, but it was dull and tiring. The few times she did agree, her mother provided cushions and cold root beer and set an egg timer for frequent breaks. Embarrassed by her mother's deference to her petty tyrannies, after the age of ten, Temple never modeled again. Now, as she stared at the painting, her own child's eyes seemed to accuse her of betrayal.

"She captured you well. I've seen that expression on your face," Jack said. "As if you're off exploring the past in your mind."

Suddenly, the lonely years of missing her mother melded into a tight band around Temple's heart. Looking away from the painting, it seemed as if her bones had turned as fragile as glass.

Jack was very still, and Temple felt him watching her. Then he began to speak in a matter-of-fact tone, filling the silence with stories about growing up in a small town on the Hudson River. He described a big, old house and earnest, distracted parents who filled it with pets and rescued wildlife, foster children and foreign exchange students. He talked about his brother and sister, and their neighborhood chases over backyard fences. And the ghosts in the barn, and in Temple's heart, silently retreated.

CHAPTER NINE

L eading her fourth tour of the day into the parlor, Temple pointed out the deep scratches in the parquet floor that family lore attributed to an eccentric bachelor bringing his favorite horse to a dance as his date. Looking up, she saw Vee beckoning outside the window, and she hurried the tourists through the last few rooms. Vee waited on a bench by the kitchen garden, shielding her face from the sun with her ubiquitous yellow pad.

"Did you find something?" Temple asked hopefully. The deadline to reveal the father of Carolina's baby was quickly approaching. Last night, on the Sunday evening news, Chip Davenport had put his viewers on notice that a big announcement was imminent, and the *Preston's Mill Progress* had picked up the story in the morning's paper.

"I think so. There's a box of letters from the mid-eighteen-hundreds between two sisters—aunts of Thomas, Carolina, and Jane. What do you know about them?"

"They were the youngest of the six children from that generation. James was the oldest, followed by the general's father, Thomas Sr. Then came the four girls. Jane's mother, Charlotte, was the oldest; then Carolina's mother, Clarissa;

and then the two sisters you're talking about. Harriet—my direct ancestor—lived on a plantation five miles from here, and Lavinia was married to a lawyer in Preston's Mill. They wrote each other notes pretty often, as I recall, about arranging visits or sending a Folly Park ham or whatever."

"They also wrote letters, especially when one of the sisters wanted to share some gossip." Vee flipped through her pad. "I put the letters in chronological order and checked to see if there were any between the time when we know the general last visited home and nine months after he was killed. The military history you gave me helped to map the only time he was gone long enough so we can rule him out as the baby's father if he impregnated an enslaved woman."

"Good thinking," Temple said. Vee waved her hand dismissively, but she looked pleased.

Temple felt a sting of misgiving. She was doing her best to protect Vee from the nasty calls and emails from people who felt they were tarnishing the general's legacy, but Temple worried what she'd gotten Vee into. Just that morning a message on her office voicemail warned there would be "hell to pay" if they didn't stop. It had made her edgy and distracted. She dragged her attention back to what Vee was saying.

"Lavinia called on Carolina in April 1863, almost a year after the general was last home," Vee said. "She'd been hearing rumors the Folly Park slaves were getting 'more uppity than ever,' and she wanted to check on Carolina. Guess what she found?"

"What?"

Vee glanced at a clutch of women admiring the irises in a nearby flowerbed. "We need to go somewhere more private," she whispered and stood up, holding her yellow pad close to her chest.

Curiosity piqued, Temple led Vee to the gazebo in the park. As soon as they sat down on the lichen-covered benches, she asked, "So, what did Lavinia find?"

"Carolina serving tea to—and I quote—'a great dirty buck in the parlor.'"

"An enslaved man in the parlor? Drinking tea?" Temple was stunned. She wondered what possible reason Carolina could have had to invite a slave to tea—and a male slave at that. Temple could concoct a scenario where the plantation mistress might have had a tea party with a housemaid if she was bored or lonely or something, but not this.

Vee continued. "Like he was a 'sable gentleman caller,' as Lavinia put it. She wrote that Carolina introduced him as her new driver with 'unpardonable impertinence.'"

Temple laughed, a little hysterically. "This is incredible. You may have found plausible evidence of Carolina's relationship with a slave. Did Lavinia mention his name?"

"No, and I found a tax list from 1860 with all the slaves and their occupations, but there isn't any mention of a coachman. Maybe he came on later."

"I wonder. . . ." Temple frowned as her thoughts took shape. "I suppose Lavinia may have been so disgusted she would have referred to any enslaved person sitting in the parlor as dirty, but maybe he wasn't a coach driver. Maybe he was a slave driver. He wouldn't have been dressed in livery like a coachman, but in work clothes, which Lavinia would probably see as dirty, even if they weren't literally."

"You mean he was in charge of the field hands? Like an overseer?"

"Yes. The White overseer, Edgar Lamb, joined the army early in 1863. Carolina would have had to find a replacement, and it wasn't uncommon to use an older, well-respected enslaved man. It seems unlikely she would have acquired a new coachman—the army would have confiscated the best horses."

"I'll look for older men in the records."

"He'd probably be receiving more rations or cash or special privileges than the others. Carolina had to be careful to treat him well since he was in a position to influence the other slaves."

They had reached the mansion, and Vee was about to veer off to the basement when Temple stopped her. "There's another source you might want to look at—a couple of journals. They're in the top drawer of the file cabinet in my office."

"Whose were they?"

"My great-great-great-grandmother, Agatha, Lad Preston's wife. They lived a few miles away on a plantation called Wild Oaks. Agatha mentions Carolina in her journal once or twice, but I don't remember the details. I only skimmed them looking for military stuff."

"This whole area is really in your blood."

"For better or worse." Temple laughed ruefully.

"Is Wild Oaks still standing?"

"No. It was ransacked near the end of the war—Agatha and her children escaped to Richmond. The main house stood vacant until the late nineteenth century. My father's grandfather fixed things up a bit but abandoned the property during the Depression. When my grandmother died, my father sold it. The house was torn down sixteen years ago—the Food Emporium stands where it used to be."

The roof had caved in and part of the back wall collapsed by the time Temple and her brothers had sneaked over to the ruin during visits to Folly Park. They'd been forbidden to play there, but Harry and Temple hunted for Beau—cast as a Yankee spy—in the echoing bedchambers. Once, Temple had crashed through the rotten floorboards in the dining room and sprained her ankle, but they told their parents she'd fallen out of a tree. When she was twelve years old, Temple and Harry rode their bikes all the way from the city to witness the house being dismantled, the wood and bricks harvested for reuse. When the demolition crew ripped the nails out of the porch, the old boards squealed like an animal in pain.

"Your family couldn't have kept the house and restored it?" Vee asked.

"My father said it would be a waste of money." Temple believed the main reason why the Prestons had been able to retain their fortune when so many other families had lost theirs over time was because of their hard-hearted focus on money at the expense of everything else.

AT THE OFFICE, MARTHA TRANSFIXED Temple with a glare. "Your voicemail is full. And I'm getting a lot of calls to the main number. People want to know what's going on."

Temple spent the next two hours on the phone, patiently listening to the complaints of various concerned citizens, local organizations, and irritated relatives, including Great-Aunt Manassas, who likened her to a turkey buzzard picking over the carcass of the past. Other people were angry that Temple was "politicizing" Folly Park by "highlighting" race. A longtime supporter canceled his lifetime membership.

"The general was a hero," he explained in an aggrieved tone. "His house should be the one place where people don't try to convince me he was a bad guy because he owned slaves back in the old days."

A few callers were supportive and curious, but Temple had to be cautious about what she said to them, too, and she was exhausted by the time she finished. She made one more call—to Jack. She wanted to hear a friendly voice, particularly his, and she wanted to be reassured that any new revelations about Carolina wouldn't derail their plan.

Jack said that Senator Alden was curious about the mystery baby's father. He didn't seem any more eager than she was to get off the phone, and when they finally hung up, Temple felt energized. She got out the diary, interested to see how Jane was faring.

November 26, 1859

Mr. Smith has been away for many weeks, and his return is imminent. I suspect Carolina has no particular fondness for her husband. Though I have told her all about Henry, she has shared nothing about Mr. Smith. I do not welcome the disruption to our routine that his arrival must entail.

Carolina retires earlier than I—she needs as much sleep as a child—and then I go to the library to read or write. There is a wealth of books, evidencing a catholic taste. I have a treasure trove all to myself, for no one comes here save the housemaids who venture in to dust.

Temple was intrigued by this mention of the library, which her grandfather had treated as something of a shrine, the shelves packed full of old books that were never touched. She suspected the room had remained essentially unchanged since Carolina's death.

November 28, 1859

Carolina's spirits are low. When I asked if she was quite well, it seemed a relief to her to confess that she had been, as she termed it, "a stupid, silly creature." She sighed and told me that a week before she had written entreating me to come to Folly Park, their neighbors, the Prestons, had given a party at Wild Oaks—the first she had attended since her marriage.

Carolina said she made a fool of herself at the party, flirting with Mr. Preston. She did not spare herself in the telling, and my heart did ache for her. It became clear to me that ever since Carolina has been married, there has been nothing but disinterest, even neglect, on the part of her husband. I was indignant on her behalf when she told me that at the end of the evening Mr. Preston—quite the worse for drink—had insulted her. When she told Mr. Smith, he asked her before all the company, what she wished him to do. She cried that he must fight Mr. Preston to preserve her honor. But Mr. Smith said he would have better success, and more cause, to fight a duel with <u>her</u> if the object was to preserve her honor, and he would not punish a drunken man for teasing a woman who flirted so shamelessly. And then he called the carriage for her and later walked home himself. He left early the next morning for his business, and she has not seen him since.

Carolina had heard people were saying her husband and Mr. Preston fought a duel, but she discovered it was not so. They had indeed had words that night after she had gone, but it was about Mr. Preston's interference with one of her husband's female slaves. She declared she did not mind her husband caring less for her than a servant, for their marriage was only a business arrangement. But she said she has truly tried to mend her ways, and she dreads his return. She wrote to him only once, she said, to tell him of my coming, but she had no answer until this week past.

I am now more apprehensive than ever about meeting the Master of Folly Park. He sounded awful enough in prospect even before I had decided to teach his slaves to read and write—despite the abominable laws of this land. I wonder if he will banish me from his house.

Temple was amazed by Jane's audacity. Virginia laws of the time not only outlawed educating slaves but also forbade people associated with antislavery organizations from even entering the state. She also realized this was the first evidence she'd seen to directly refute reports of a duel. It seemed to disprove the rumors of Carolina's infidelity—with Lad Preston at least. Since it was well known Lad had fathered multiple children out of wedlock, it seemed plausible that Thomas might have confronted him about one of his enslaved women. Temple was eager to read more, but Martha notified her that Jerry Hoyle was waiting outside.

While most of the residents of the Park Crest subdivision, which had been built just outside the Folly Park grounds thirty years ago, occasionally found artifacts when they turned over their gardens in the spring, Jerry was the only one who manufactured fake ones and tried to pass them off as real, hoping Temple would buy them for the collection.

That afternoon, it was an old nail Jerry claimed he had dug up when setting a posthole for his new deck. He talked nonstop, bouncing from heel to heel, while Temple examined the nail. People in his neighborhood were annoyed that the increased traffic to Folly Park was making it difficult to get in and out of the subdivision, he reported. And some people thought the idea of Carolina cheating on the general with a slave was ridiculous, but it sure looked like the story was good for business.

Offended, Temple told him she wasn't making up fake stories to sell more tickets, but Jerry clearly didn't believe her. He rambled on until she interrupted him.

"Look, this is a steel-wire nail. They weren't manufactured until the 1890s, long after any building had stopped at Folly Park. What did you use to rust it—saltwater and vinegar?"

"That's right," Jerry admitted with a grin, not at all ashamed by his subterfuge. "And I sanded it first so the rust would take better."

"Well, obviously we don't want it."

"Can't you just think of it as a very young artifact?" Jerry asked hopefully.

Temple handed the nail back. "Better luck next time."

"And good luck to you." Jerry winked as he went out the door.

DESPITE MORE PHONE CALLS interrupting her throughout the day, Temple managed to verify Vee's timeline of the general's movements. There was no evidence he had returned to Folly Park in the entire year prior to his death. It would hardly have escaped notice by the family, neighbors, or business associates. But the lack of evidence could not be considered conclusive proof. The past only surrendered a tiny fraction of its moments to the present.

Aside from family photographs, there wouldn't be much evidence of her own existence for future generations, Temple reflected. A couple of journal articles coauthored with Dr. Belcher, her dissertation, a few lines in the news-paper related to protest activities. A story from the time when she and her grandfather had found the remains of a Confederate soldier's haversack in the battlefield one memorable day when she was eight. Her mother's obituary. Some campaign coverage for Harry, and those terrible articles after his accident. All the countless small moments of Harry's life had died along with him—as had those of her mother and grandfather and the innumerable ancestors buried in the family graveyard.

Temple looked down at the last date on Vee's timeline: September 5, 1863. The day the general was killed. Her thoughts shifted to the strange events on the night of his death. Pulling a book off her shelf published in 1923 by military historian Hannibal Butts, she looked up his account.

The usual preparations were made to ready for battle at dawn. As General Smith reviewed orders with his staff, a captured federal dispatch carrier was brought to his tent. Captain Evans handed the dispatch pouch to the general, who looked in it and, in the captain's color-ful phrase, "blanched as pale as the alabaster brow of Michelangelo's David." Shortly afterward, the general ordered his subordinates to leave him and called for his trusty Negro servant, Titus. Presumably, it was at this time that the general executed his quickly conceived plan to disguise himself in his servant's clothes to spy upon the enemy and ascertain their battle plans, of which he had no doubt been alerted by the contents of the pouch. While some creative chroniclers have suggested that the general instead undertook to treat with his foe and make a bargain to preserve his plantation home from destruction by the federal marauders, there is no evidence, other than the coincident survival of Folly Park, to lend credence to such half-baked theories.

Temple smiled at Dr. Butts's blatant lapse from objectivity, but there was something about the passage that bothered her. The quotation Butts attributed to the captain was jarring. Evans had kept a journal of his wartime experiences, and as she recalled, he had not been a particularly well-educated man. The reference to Michelangelo didn't feel right. She wondered if Dr. Butts had transcribed the passage accurately from the original journal entry, and she headed to the archives to check.

Down in the basement, Vee was hunched over Agatha Preston's diary, lips silently moving. Tiptoeing past her, Temple located the reel containing Captain Evans's journal, threaded the microfilm through the machine, and easily found the entry.

"Spt. 4. Cloudy & Warm. Men restless. . . ." Temple skipped through a monotonous litany of camp duties to the section dealing with the events of the evening. There was indeed a reference to Michelangelo. Butts seemed to have transcribed the passage correctly, although he had not retained the captain's appalling spelling, odd syntax, and unorthodox abbreviations. Evans had written, "Browt rider to Gnls tent. Gnl look the powch and went pale as allybaster brow of Michel Angellos David. Tole us to go but leve prisner. Gnl calld 10 minuts later for Titus."

Temple banged her forehead on the machine as she bent closer. She twisted the dial to magnify the image. What she'd initially thought read "look" was actually the word "took"—the cross to the "t" was very faint and floating a bit high, but it was definitely there. She had thought the line was a scratch on the film, but now, with the page magnified, she could see the faint blot of ink at the end of the mark. The diary actually said that the general *took* the pouch, went pale, and told everyone to leave—except for the captured rider.

A pulse throbbed in Temple's forehead, where her cut was just about healed. Changing that one word could alter the whole interpretation of the crucial events on that mysterious night. Unlike what Dr. Butts had written, the general had not yet seen what was in the dispatch pouch when the color drained from his face. *What shocked him so badly if it wasn't the papers in the pouch?* Temple wondered. *Could it have been the dispatch carrier? Did the general recognize the captured rider?*

Temple hurried to the collection of dusty reference books stacked on a rusting metal shelving unit in the middle of the basement. The regiment that had engaged the general's troops on September 5 was the 8th Ohio. Feverishly, she pawed through the book for the muster rolls, seeking anyone identified as a dispatch carrier. After a few minutes, she discovered them: George Bowen, Archibald Cunningham, Benjamin Elliot . . . "Elliot!" Temple shrieked.

Vee jumped up, wildly looking around. "What is it? What's the matter?"

"Jane Elliot had a brother named Benjamin! I think he was the captured dispatch rider brought to the general on the night he was killed." Temple quickly explained what she'd discovered.

"Do you think the general recognized Benjamin because he looked like Jane?" Vee asked. "Do you think he sneaked through the lines to go back to Folly Park to tell Jane they'd captured her brother?"

"Maybe. But he could have sent his servant to do that.

He didn't need to go himself. And we don't even know for sure if Jane was still at Folly Park."

Their speculations were interrupted by Stuart trumpeting Temple's name from the top of the stairs. She appreciated his poor timing even less than usual.

"COME WITH ME!" STUART HUSTLED Temple into the golf cart Al used to transport his tools around the grounds and zipped down the drive toward the road.

"What's up?" Temple asked.

Stuart didn't reply. He stopped the cart with a jerk at the end of the drive and pointed.

Across the street from the entrance to Folly Park, two dozen men dressed as Confederate soldiers were setting up a camp. They had already erected a couple of tents and begun clearing ground for a fire pit, and some of the men were weaving a screen out of brush and branches to conceal a portable toilet. Others were busy securing a homemade banner between two trees. It read: LOYAL REBS FOR GENERAL SMITH. Hand-lettered signs posted on tree trunks accused Folly Park's management of being traitors. One of the signs advocated "bushwhacking" the director.

"What do you think of that?" Stuart squinched convulsively as he climbed out of the golf cart. "What does it mean?"

Temple didn't think it would be wise to explain to Stuart that bushwhacking was a sudden attack by enlisted men on unpopular superiors. They needed to be careful with the reenactors. Though some groups would probably have been just as happy swapping a fishing trip for a battle reenactment, others might have white nationalists in their ranks. Last fall, a push by the university to rename buildings named for prominent Confederates had resulted in an ugly protest by a small group of neo-Nazis and a confrontation with a larger group of counter-protestors. Two people had been hospitalized.

Temple spotted Colonel Townsend handing out flyers to tourists as they slowed down to turn into Folly Park's driveway. She'd only met him once, a couple of years ago, and she had no idea if he sympathized with the extremists, or even if he was really a colonel. He'd written a letter to the local paper correctly pointing out that a Union soldier's canteen in one of the displays at Folly Park had been mislabeled as a Confederate artifact. Appeased by Dr. Tate's personal apology, he had accepted an invitation to take a special tour through parts of the house not open to the public, which Temple conducted. The colonel had been charming, but like the South's vaunted hospitality, she knew, you could never be really sure what lay beneath the surface.

"Let's go talk to Colonel Townsend," Temple said. "He's a big fan of the general."

It looked like the colonel hadn't shaved in a very long time, and his ragged uniform was dirty and stained. "Nice beard," she complimented as she and Stuart approached. "It looks really authentic."

The colonel tipped his hat. "Hi there, Temple, thanks. Haven't touched it since last fall."

"This is Stuart Sprigg, the director of Folly Park."

The colonel smiled and held out his hand.

"What do you think you people are doing?" Stuart barked, ignoring the proffered hand.

Temple winced as Colonel Townsend raised his eyebrows and treated Stuart to a long stare before silently handing him a flyer. Turning to her, he said, "I see your brother is running for mayor. I used to enjoy watching him play football. He was quite a defensive tackle. You tell him he's got my vote."

"You can't distribute these!" Stuart crumpled the flyer into a ball.

Temple started to speak, but the colonel held up his hand. He worked his jaw meditatively for a long moment and then abruptly spat. Stuart flinched away, although the dark stream of tobacco juice went nowhere near him. "The flyers summarize our feelings about what y'all have been saying about the general up at his house," the colonel said. "Implying he was a cuckold and such."

Stuart shrugged impatiently. "All that happened a long time ago. I don't understand why you people even care."

Colonel Townsend narrowed his eyes. "I don't reckon you would. We're defending the general's honor because he can't do it for himself."

"Cuckold? Honor? You can't be serious. I'll have you people arrested if you keep this up."

"I don't think so," replied the colonel. "A little thing called freedom of speech, protected by the Constitution of the United States of America, gives us the right to pass out our flyers."

Stuart's face flushed. "You'll scare our guests away coming up to their cars like that! You look like you haven't bathed in weeks, and you smell like it too!"

The colonel seemed pleased. "You think so? Temple, do *you* think so?"

Temple nodded. "Months even."

"Well, now, that's great!" Colonel Townsend beamed. "I paid my nephew to roll around on the floor of my brother-in-law's cow barn with my uniform on, but you never can tell if the odor will take or how long it'll last. And I stopped using modern-day soap—"

"You can't camp here!" Stuart stamped his foot like a child in a temper. "This is private land. It belongs to Mr. Edward Gordon, who is a very prominent attorney. When he hears what's going on, he'll have you arrested for trespassing!"

The colonel's face hardened. He pulled a paper out of his knapsack and handed it to Stuart. "This gives us permission to trespass here." The colonel made air quotes with his fingers when he said the word "trespass." He continued. "Ed Gordon—or Lieutenant Gordon, I should say—will be bivouacking with us as soon as he can clear his schedule."

Reading over the paper, Stuart's shoulders slumped. He shoved his glasses up his nose with the heel of his hand, leaving sweaty smudges on the lenses. "How long are you staying?"

The colonel popped another plug of tobacco into his mouth and chewed reflectively. "Well, now, let me see . . . I suppose we'll stay as long as y'all keep telling stories, let's call them, about the general's family." He turned to Temple and grinned, revealing authentically tobacco-stained teeth. "You might consider us a kind of counter-narrative, as it were."

AT THE END OF THE DAY, TEMPLE went to the smoke-house to get the gate receipts from Betty Jean. She'd offered to drop the money at the bank for Martha on her way to pick up some groceries. To placate Stuart, Temple had given him some carefully scripted remarks about Carolina's possible involvement with an enslaved overseer for release to the media. He was briefing the board members, and she hoped the reports of high visitation would keep them satisfied until she could present them with a concrete offer from the legislature about her plan.

The deposit bag was bursting at the seams, and Betty Jean smiled broadly as she handed it to Temple. "It's still mostly White folks, but it was a different crowd again today," she said, nodding toward where Wanda sat behind the other register. "They're finding us on social media."

"That's great! Thanks, Wanda." Temple smiled as the girl stood up and put her hands to her back.

"No problem!" Wanda launched into an enthusiastic and detailed rundown of the response to her social media campaign. Temple tried to follow along while Betty Jean grinned at her. She knew Temple had no idea what Wanda was talking about. But Temple did manage to understand that it was good news if one counted the sheer volume of responses— both positive and negative. Temple was shocked by the vitriol in some of the posts and comments, but Wanda was unfazed.

"That's normal," she said, shrugging at a post whose writer wished Temple could be "found guilty by military tribunal and executed by hanging." Temple escaped as soon as she could, wondering why she seemed to be the only person of her generation who lacked a natural affinity for technology.

Catching up with Fred in the parking lot, Temple noticed that, like Betty Jean and Wanda, he too exuded a glow of satisfaction. He told her he hadn't had so much fun in years. On the short drive into Preston's Mill, she realized her fears about the trustees selling out to the developers had subsided a little. No one could argue, in the last couple of days at least, that Folly Park wasn't earning its keep.

When she pulled into the Food Emporium parking lot, Temple's sense of well-being quickly evaporated. A large sign proclaiming BEAU PRESTON FOR BUILDING PROGRESS was posted near the entrance of the store, and she saw her brother shaking hands with customers. Pixie and Julia stood beside him, passing out campaign buttons. It was too late to turn around. Pixie was waving.

"Taking a break from trash-talking our ancestor to grocery shop?" Beau asked as soon as Temple was in earshot.

"It's historical research, Beau, not trash-talk."

"Not to my constituents."

"Well, maybe their side of the story has been the only side long enough."

"So, it's an equity thing? Voices of the powerless and all that?"

"It's actually a truth thing."

Beau wrestled a bag of cat litter more securely onto the bottom of an elderly woman's cart. "Whose truth?" he said over his shoulder. "Don't kid yourself. Truth is a choice."

Beau had always been a cynic. Temple refused to have this conversation with him. She turned away to find Julia blocking her path.

"What do you think you're doing with Jack Early?"

Julia was the last person Temple wanted to know about her plan. "Isn't he great?" she raved, hoping to distract her cousin. "He's smart and nice, and he really *gets* me. I feel like I've known him all my life." Though she tossed out the clichés mockingly, Temple realized with a little shock, that they did actually reflect how she felt. She supposed there was a reason that a cliché becomes a cliché.

"Very funny," Julia said. "I can tell you really do like him. But you should pick another guy for a rebound fling. After the election is over, he'll go back to New York and forget all about you. I recognize his type, and I've heard some things."

"His type? You've heard some things? I don't care about gossip." Temple had, in fact, googled Jack and learned little other than that there was a deceased artist of the same name.

Julia raised her eyebrows. "Oh, come on, I know you're dying to hear the gossip."

Temple suddenly had a very strong desire to know what people were saying about Jack. Julia smiled smugly, waiting for her to ask. Temple said nothing. They didn't move for a ridiculously long time, as if engaged in one of their childhood staring contests. Julia's new lips were a little uneven, and when she finally spoke, it appeared as if only one side of her mouth moved. The lopsided effect reminded Temple of an actor in an old detective movie, and what Julia said next sounded like a bad line from the movie.

"It was a friendly warning, Temple. You'll be sorry."

CHAPTER TEN

"Thomas and Carolina attended a party at Wild Oaks in October 1859," Vee said, reading from her notes on Agatha Preston's journal while Temple fixed dinner.

"Yes," Temple said, "Carolina told Jane she'd made a fool of herself flirting with Lad Preston. What did Agatha say about it? I've always had the impression she was a bit stuck-up and judgmental."

"That sounds about right. Agatha was annoyed the gentlemen didn't share her disgust with Carolina's 'indecorous laughter and scandalous exposure of her bosom.' She wrote, 'studious, skeptical Thomas must certainly fail to achieve conjugal felicity with his featherbrained bride.'"

Vee quoted Agatha in a simpering, nasally whine that made Temple laugh. "Was there anything else about Carolina?"

"Just one entry from the spring of 1863, during the war, about the 'two pert misses' at Folly Park sending her a side of pork. Agatha seemed to resent having to thank them."

"*Two* pert misses?"

Vee nodded. "I think she meant Carolina and Jane. Later in the diary, after she's worked out that she'll send them some asparagus from her garden so *they* will have to thank *her*, Agatha refers to them as 'that overdressed filly and her Yankee drudge.'"

"Nice." Temple shook her head.

"Isn't it strange Jane didn't go back to Boston when the war started? I mean, she was an abolitionist. And didn't she want to be with her family? What does her diary say?"

"I don't know, I'm still in 1859." Setting a plate of pasta with olive oil and herbs in front of Vee, Temple sat down at the table. "But I think I'm starting to understand Jane. She was well-educated and intelligent, and her life in Boston was pretty dull. I think she liked it here. Helping Carolina run the household was probably fulfilling, and she was intrigued by her cousins. I'll show you what I mean." Temple retrieved the diary from her bag, pushed her plate aside, and read an entry to Vee.

November 30, 1859

I have met Mr. Smith, and I must confess I am surprised. He was not cold and unkind as I had anticipated. In fact, quite the reverse. But perhaps tomorrow he will not be so easy and friendly as I have seen him tonight. Used as they are to power and indulgence, these slave masters doubtless have mercurial tempers!

As usual, I saw Carolina to bed and then went to the library. I was startled to see a man there and drew back to observe him from the doorway. Mr. Smith is very like his portrait—tall, even-featured, with dark curling hair and a swarthy complexion. He was standing over the books I had laid out on a little table. He took up this diary, and my heart caught in my throat, but he put it aside immediately and looked about, frowning. And all at once I saw the room anew. Saw how worn the spines of the books were and how they were organized according to a purpose. I saw the leather of the chairs rubbed smooth, the ink-marked blotter on the desk, the mending tools for the pens, the heavy ledgers close to hand. Feeling a fool, I understood for the first time that this was no neglected room but rather the beating heart of the plantation, the sanctuary of its Master!

Just then, Cousin Thomas saw me. Oddly, I felt as if I looked on the face of an old friend with whom I had just been reunited rather than a stranger I was meeting for the first time. He said, without introduction, "And how persuasive do you find Wollstonecraft's claim for the rights of women—it is a passionate plea, though perhaps not as tightly reasoned as it might be, would you agree?" And he indicated one of the books on the table. Though later I marveled at his having read <u>A Vindication of the Rights of Women</u>, then I did not reply to his question as I came forward with apologies for intruding upon his privacy. He waved away my words and said, "Anyone who wishes to savor the pleasures of this room is welcome. We are few enough, indeed, under this roof." I was dismayed by this slight of Carolina, but he invited me to sit, and I could not refuse. He lounged in his chair, quite at his ease, and asked me how I liked Folly Park.

I gathered my courage and prepared to have it out at once. But on that instant, I had to cough, which delay annoyed me. Finally, I said, all in a rush, "Sir, I feel I must tell you I am not in sympathy with the practice of slavery, and I intend, while I am here, to do what I can to educate your servants. You may put me out at once, of course, and indeed I have every expectation that you will." He raised his brows at this speech, but his dark eyes were amused,

I saw with astonishment, when he said, "Intellect is an inconvenient accoutrement for those who labor for life. And I do not see how teaching a few slaves their A-B-Cs will make any difference. It is but a tiny drop in a vast ocean of ignorance." I retorted that it might make a great deal of difference to the few slaves. He shook his head but said, "Very well, I give you leave, Cousin, to bring us all enlightenment." After that he bid me go, though he told me that his being at home must not prevent my using the library.

I do believe my cousins must surely be two of the most confounding characters I have ever met with!

"She told him she wanted to educate his slaves?" Vee said. "And he gave her permission?"

"Seems like it. Listen."

December 1, 1859

When Mr. Smith and Carolina met at dinner today, they were stiff as two strangers. Carolina was much subdued and laughed only once, at some silly remark of mine, and Mr. Smith glanced quickly at her. She immediately sobered, though I saw no condemnation in his look. And when he spoke with me of my studies and my plans for instructing the servants, she stared at him wonderingly. When he noticed her looking at him, he turned his attention to his plate and did not speak again.

But he came to us this evening in the parlor. Carolina was chattering away with one of her stories, and I could not breathe for alternately laughing and coughing. Mr. Smith walked into the room, appearing expectant and eager to me, but Carolina stopped abruptly when she saw him. I urged

her on in her tale, and she winked drolly at me and rolled
her eyes toward him, as if he might not catch the humor. But
at the conclusion of her story, he burst into a laugh, and she
could not help herself and joined him. I think perhaps they
might yet learn to love each other as a man and wife should.

"Thomas and Carolina didn't seem to know each other very well," said Vee. "Jane is like a bridge between them."

"Right. And the next entry explains more about the relationships at Folly Park, including the enslaved people." Temple read on.

December 8, 1859

We gather, the three of us, in the parlor in the evenings, and
Thomas reads aloud, or Carolina performs imitations—
Thomas insists her mimicry of sour Agatha Preston is
uncanny. Sometimes Thomas and I play chess while
Carolina plays her pianoforte. But we are not engaged
in amusements alone—the days pass in a blur of activity.
Thomas has complimented us on the smooth order in which
the household is run.

I have not written at length to my family. I do not
like to confess that, as yet, I have done nothing for the
slaves. Instead, Carolina is educating them! Or rather, I
am tutoring her, and she in turn teaches the servants in
a roundabout way. It began with Jewel, King's daughter.
She brought our tea one day during our lessons, and
Carolina asked her what was such-and-such divided by
such-and-such—teasing and not expecting a reply—
but Jewel answered prompt and correct. We were
astonished, and the girl confessed she had learned her

sums to understand cooking receipts. She has become quite a favorite with us. Carolina gave her ribbon for her hair and some cast-off clothes. She really is a lovely little thing—with smooth brown skin and dimples and the whitest teeth. Thomas says her aunt, Linda, was his nursemaid, and she was uncommonly intelligent. Certainly, Jewel is smart as a whip. I have undertaken to instruct her regularly, and I have high hopes for her continued rapid progress.

Now, the house servants find work to do in the room where Carolina has her lessons, and she calls out to them for help when I quiz her. The servants delight in showing they have learned what she has not—although I know her ignorance is largely feigned—and she praises them and calls herself a dolt. She has no fear they will become disobedient as a result, and indeed they seem rather to take some pleasure in serving her favorite cakes and hearing her shrieks of delight. Yesterday, Carolina gave Etta, the sober cook, a great smacking kiss on the cheek, and the woman actually smiled! My cousin is so free with "the people" as she calls them. I know not what to make of her behavior sometimes, but I do love her and wish that I myself did not feel so ill at ease when they are near.

"I'm not sure what to think," Vee said, when Temple had finished. "For an abolitionist, Jane seems clueless."

"Yes," Temple agreed, "but this is probably the first time she's interacting with slaveholders as an adult. Carolina looks up to her, which must have been flattering, and she has interests in common with Thomas. She's related to them, and a guest in their house. I think she's inclined not to be too critical of their lifestyle. Even though she believes slaves should be freed, Jane doesn't actually connect very well with them in person. I think she's disappointed in herself and a little envious of Carolina."

"I understand, I guess. You're more comfortable with Al than I am, for instance. You've known him a long time, but it's more than that. I feel like he judges me."

"He judges everyone."

Vee shook her head. "This is different. It's like he has all this hard-earned knowledge about how his corner of the world works, and he's afraid I'll mess it up for him. Maybe he's right. I've been back from overseas for six years, and I'm still sometimes blindsided and not sure how to respond to the racism. And the South feels harder to navigate than a foreign country."

"You're not the first person to think so, unfortunately."

"I'm sorry about it. My mother used to tell us how much fun she had when she went to Louisiana for the summers when she was young. She and her cousins played outside all day and ate homemade biscuits with fish her uncle had caught in the creek. The kids all slept in the same room and would stay up late talking." Vee's voice was wistful. "My dad said she was glorifying poverty and oppression. She didn't see her family much after they got married, so my sisters and I never got to know them. If I had, I might not feel like a stranger in the South now."

"You know, I'm uncomfortable with people from the North," Temple said. "When they learn I'm from an old Southern family, I assume they all think I must be racist."

Vee wrinkled her nose, brows raised. "Well. . . ."

"I know, I know." Temple sighed. "I've benefited my whole life because of my heritage. So have all my relatives and ancestors. For generations. That's not a small thing."

"No, it's not," Vee agreed. "But we aren't going to solve white supremacy in America tonight. The news is starting, and we're on it."

CHIP DAVENPORT TOOK A NEW ANGLE on the events at Folly Park by interviewing Colonel Townsend. Throughout the segment, the newsman appeared to be repelled by the rugged living conditions in the reenactors' camp, and by the colonel's hygiene in particular. Grimacing, Chip kept leaning farther and farther away, taking the microphone with him, so that the ends of the colonel's sentences were inaudible. Chip's eyes watered from the smoking campfire, and he sneezed often. After only a few minutes, he violently dispatched a mosquito, which left a bloody smear on his cheek, and wrapped up the segment.

Temple turned off the television. Stuart would have a fit that the reenactors had gotten airtime, but at least the colonel hadn't had a chance to air his grievances about the management of Folly Park.

Chick picked up his tennis ball and pushed it into Temple's thigh. She wiped her leg and said to Vee, "Do you want to come for a walk?"

"I don't know if I can." Vee looked embarrassed. "Wanda just texted about a meeting. Betty Jean asked me to volunteer with Frank Poe's campaign. But it might be weird now that we live together, since your brother's running."

Temple shook her head. "No, go ahead. I don't agree with Beau's politics, anyway."

"Is that hard for you?"

"I'm used to it. I told Beau and my dad I'm not working on the campaign, but they still expect me to show up

at events. There's a barbecue fundraiser tomorrow night."
Temple yanked at a burr on Chick's neck, and he yelped
and shied away.

"Frank Poe could use a spy in the enemy camp," Vee
said jokingly.

Maybe there's something in that, Temple thought. *But not to
find out about Beau's campaign strategy. It could be a chance to learn
if he has anything to do with the developer's plans for Folly Park.*

THE SKY WAS DARKENING INTO NIGHT as Chick ranged
back and forth across the lawn tracking deer, and fireflies
sparked under the trees. It was easy to imagine ghosts in
every shadowy corner of the plantation. Temple shivered as
she passed the old well. Al's grandmother had told him it was
haunted by a slave girl who had thrown herself in it when
her lover rejected her. Temple's grandfather had known
the story too. He'd never seen any sign of a ghost, he said,
but it was true the old well had been abandoned and a new
one dug during the Civil War.

Louella's WPA narrative mentioned that Jewel had
committed suicide because of a broken heart, Temple
remembered suddenly. Did Jewel throw herself down the
well? Did the ghost story have some basis in real events? She
glanced uneasily back at the grassy mound. It looked very
much like a grave.

A bit spooked, Temple peered down the drive. A dusky
tunnel formed by the canopy of trees, it looked as if it led
back into the past. She imagined the master of the house
returning home for his supper at a slow trot, surveying his
realm and those over whom he held dominion—the women,
children, the enslaved workers. He was a king in his narrow

world. Like some kind of vestigial organ in the body politic, a plantation master was a despot in a nation that had renounced a monarchy.

Unsettled by her thoughts, Temple hurried into the park, craving the tonic of open air. Despite a fresh pile of stones on the damp ground beneath the crumbling bridge folly, she climbed to the top of the arch to watch the sunset. *It's ironic*, she thought, *to be concerned about signs of deterioration in a bridge built to look like a ruin.*

"IT WAS KING," VEE ANNOUNCED as soon as Temple arrived in the basement, summoned by a text.

"What do you mean?"

"King was the enslaved man having tea with Carolina. You told me to look for someone who was getting special treatment. The records for 1862 and 1863 show that he was given twice the food and clothing rations as the other slaves and some cash payments."

"Great work! That should give us some breathing room with the media."

"There's more. But I'm not sure you'll want to hear it."

"What is it?"

Vee consulted her yellow pad, but Temple could tell she was just using her notes to avoid looking at her.

"King and his twin sister Linda were born at Folly Park in 1821. Their mother was described as a bright, or light-complexioned, slave named Maria. The tax lists group slaves by family unit, and it looks like Maria didn't have a slave husband." Vee adjusted her glasses. "But she had thirteen children before she died in childbirth."

"That's a lot of children."

"Yes. It's . . . interesting." Vee's voice was oddly toneless. "I was going through the plantation documents in those unprocessed boxes, and I found a series of letters dating from the eighteen-twenties and 'thirties. They were from the general's father in Louisiana, Thomas Smith Sr., to his brother James, here at Folly Park."

"I know about those. They talk about how James occasionally sent slaves to his brother's plantation, right?"

"Yes, but Thomas Sr. didn't keep the slaves. He sold them as soon as he got them."

"Prime field hands were lucrative in the Deep South."

"They weren't field hands," Vee said. "And he sold all of them to the same New Orleans slave trader, T. R. Vincente. Well, all but one," she added.

"So what? I'm not following."

"T. R. Vincente only dealt in girls. There's a whole chapter on him in a book I read for my family research called *Sex and Skin: Gender and Power in the New Orleans Slave Market*. I compiled the names and ages of slaves sent from Folly Park to Louisiana over a fifteen-year period. They were all girls between the ages of ten and sixteen. Nine of them, including King's sister Linda, were Maria's daughters."

Vee looked at Temple expectantly.

Temple frowned. "What exactly are you saying?"

"I think James Smith sent his brother slave girls from Folly Park to be sold into prostitution. Remember his wife's letter about the lost ring? She mentioned selling Linda and 'the others.' James would have gotten thousands of dollars for the girls, especially if they were light-skinned." Vee glanced down at her pad again. "I think he may have been the father of some, if not all, of them."

Temple couldn't speak. She felt numb.

"I'm sorry, but there's more."

Temple's voice came out in a croak, "What?"

"It's in the last few letters. Thomas Sr. kept Linda for himself. Apparently, he never paid James for her, and it doesn't look like James sent any more girls to Louisiana after that." Vee handed Temple a folder. Inside was a letter.

Marais Parish, Louisiana
February 25th, 1836

My Dear Brother—

You write to me in an uncharitable Spirit. I have remitted to you every dime that Vincente gave me for the last lot of pickaninnies you sent down. True, the Sum is something short, unaccounted for even by the deduction of my share, as you have so sharply noted. As you suspect, they were not all sold. None was lost to Disease or Accident during the Journey as you fear, however. Certainly not Linda, in whom you take such Particular Interest as to single her out in your Enquiries. It will shock you to learn, I am sure, that she is fair along in a breeding way, and as Vicente would not have her, useless as she now is for his business, I have retained her as a nursemaid. Antoinette is again in a Delicate State of Expectation and nearly overcome by the care of the Two Screaming Infants already in Residence. I will give you fair price for Linda when I have Funds, which I frankly confess may be delayed, as I do—you so charitably point out—suffer from the Vice of Gambling. Your other aspersion upon my Character brings to mind the idea of the Pot calling the Kettle Black. You need not remind me of the impropriety of retaining any of Maria's girls to sport with, *dear Brother, <u>particularly</u> the lovely Linda. Whether such a relationship as you imply exists between Myself and Herself is as unnatural between Uncle and Niece as between Father and Daughter, I leave to your Superior Moral Sense. <u>Our</u> Linda, indeed, has become an indispensable addition to the <u>Family</u> circle, and her new <u>Master</u>, no less than her new Mistress, finds her eager <u>desire to please</u> a most refreshing quality, for such Training of which we are deeply grateful to her Previous Master. I remain,*

Your Most Appreciative Brother,
Thomas T. Smith

Temple's stomach turned over as she handed the letter back to Vee. She sat limply on a chair and put her head in her hands. One of her ancestors had been fathering slave children to sell and likely made a mistress of his own daughter. Another had perhaps carried on where his brother left off.

"I think James's wife found out Linda was pregnant and made him get rid of her," Vee said.

Temple's mind churned. "Whether such a relationship as you imply exists between Myself and Herself is as unnatural between Uncle and Niece as between Father and Daughter, I leave to your Superior Moral Sense." These two powerful men had been respected and admired, considered upstanding citizens in their communities. But at home, on their plantations, where they had no one to answer to, they behaved worse than animals. Temple raised her head and cleared her throat. "I think you're probably right."

EVEN IF SHE HADN'T KNOWN SHE WAS over an hour late, Temple would have been able to guess as much from the volume of the alcohol-laden laughter as she made her way through the crowd. The caterers were dressed in barbecue-themed overalls and red-and-white-checked shirts, but they looked like the same staff that had been at the museum opening. Everywhere she looked, Temple saw people she knew. Relatives accosted her, concerned about Folly Park and the family name. With Vee's new revelations fresh in her mind, Temple evaded their questions. Pixie reported in an aggrieved tone that the United Daughters of the Confederacy had overruled Mrs. Glass and were threatening to censure her and Julia if they couldn't stop Temple from saying terrible things about Carolina.

Mumbling an apology, Temple turned away and was relieved to see Jack coming toward her. He, at least, wouldn't badger her about Folly Park. "I was hoping you would be here," she said. "Maybe we can find a potted palm to talk behind."

"Let's get a drink and find one," Jack said, smiling, and Temple's heart skipped a beat.

Before they could get anywhere near the bar, they were accosted by Trevor Bacon, the florid, overbearing host of the party, who sported a mullet haircut he'd been declaring was "business in the front, party in the back" since the '80s.

"Temple! Sweetheart! Do me a favor! Find your brother in the house and get him out here. The natives are getting restless." Trevor sketched a salute and hurried away, calling back over his shoulder, "Thanks darlin'!"

It took them quite a few minutes to locate Beau. The house was one of the larger models in an expensive new development. There didn't seem to be any logical layout to the floor plan. Every time they turned a corner, they were

confronted by a set of Doric columns or an elaborate archway framing a closet. Then, as they stood hesitating outside
the last room to look in, the door opened a crack.

". . . this little meeting, Beau, Judge Preston," a voice
with a nasal Northern accent declared just on the other side
of the door. "I'm pleased we've got your support."

"And we're glad we've got yours!" Beau's blaring voice
responded.

The man by the door laughed. "I'll get that check to you
first thing tomorrow."

The door opened wide, and Temple found herself face-
to-face with Mr. Starkweather of the Massachusetts Bay
Development Company. He stopped short.

"This is my daughter, Temple," Judge Preston said, coming
quickly forward. "Come on, Beau, it's time we got outside."

"Mr. Starkweather and I have met." Temple tried to
sound haughty.

"You've met?" The judge frowned.

"Yes. We've discussed his company's plans to buy Folly
Park, where I believe he hopes to build a New World Estates
development."

Jack made a disgusted noise.

"As I explained to Dr. Preston the other day," Starkweather
said smoothly, "at this stage, there are always rumors floating
around." He bared his teeth in a parody of a smile, revealing
invisible braces, and left.

It was very quiet in the hall. The judge busied himself
with extracting a breath mint from its wrapper.

"You and Beau are in bed with the developers," Temple
said.

"Come on, Temp—" Beau stopped when she stared
coldly at him.

"I hope you lose."

Temple turned to her father. "Go ahead and cut off my allowance. You can stop worrying about whether or not you're giving away your precious money to someone who might not even be your daughter."

The judge crunched down on the mint in his mouth and said nothing.

Beau's eyes widened. "What?"

"Ask him," Temple said sharply. "Jack, do you mind if we go? I need some air."

In front of the house, Temple scrabbled around in her handbag for her keys. Jack gently took the bag from her and retrieved her key from the valet along with his own. Soon, they were in the MG, navigating the maze of roads that led out of the development. Temple concentrated on watching the mailboxes flash by until she could breathe again.

"I'm sorry," Jack said. "Is there anything I can do?"

"No," Temple said. "Don't be sorry. I'm not."

Jack reached over and briefly touched her hand. "Let's go get that drink."

CHAPTER ELEVEN

The reenactors' daily bugle call woke Temple early, and she completed her rounds in record time. She was eager to get to the university library to research the dispatch carrier captured by General Smith's men, who she was convinced was Jane's brother Benjamin. She wanted to escape any more appalling revelations that Vee might turn up, and she needed to get away.

On Friday night, after leaving Beau's barbecue, Temple and Jack had gone to a bistro in the city and talked until midnight. When Jack brought up his life in New York, Temple quickly steered the conversation to less personal topics, suspecting he was trying to encourage her to talk about her rift with Beau and her father. But that wasn't what he was doing. When the waiter brought the check to signal closing time, Jack mentioned that he and his wife had separated just before he came to Virginia.

Temple's heart seized at the word *wife*, but Jack continued in a normal tone. She hoped her responses sounded just as casual, while her brain fixated on the wife, imagining an intimidating paragon of beauty and intelligence who—incredibly—did not appreciate Jack. *What is the matter with her?* Temple wondered.

Jack had driven Temple home without asking if she wanted to retrieve her truck at Trevor Bacon's, and she hadn't brought it up. They both knew she'd had a little too much to drink. By the time they reached Folly Park, she was fuzzy-headed and sleepy.

Tucking Temple firmly against his side, Jack walked her to her house. When he let her go to open the screen door, she leaned into him without thinking, resting her head against his chest. She became aware of his heart hammering against her cheek just as she realized with a jolt of foggy shock what she was doing and jerked herself upright. Mumbling an apology, she escaped into the house and shut the front door in Jack's face.

Temple's blundering entrance had wakened Vee. She came out of her bedroom to ask how the party was, and Temple blurted out a confusion of half-remembered conversations, random impressions, and uncensored feelings about her father, Beau, Mr. Starkweather, and Jack. Vee listened sympathetically, plied Temple with water and aspirin, and helped her to bed.

For a good part of the night, Temple lay awake, dismayed she'd let herself drink so much and embarrassed about her behavior. Dragging herself out of bed Saturday morning, she found that Vee had prepared a light breakfast of toast and coffee. After they'd eaten, Vee borrowed Betty Jean's car and drove Temple to pick up her truck.

Temple's was not the only vehicle still parked along the street. Trevor's place had the bedraggled look of a fraternity house after a night of hard partying. Red plastic Solo cups and napkins soggy with dew littered the lawn. The flowerbeds had been trampled, and one tattered curtain hung out of a wide-open upstairs window, its mate draping a rhododendron bush below. The place looked as rough as Temple felt.

By Saturday evening, after ten hours of yard work, Temple felt more like herself. The fresh air fortified her for the rash of phone calls, texts, and emails she received on Sunday from people who had read in the *Preston's Mill Progress* that the general's cousin Jane was an abolitionist. But nothing could prepare Temple for the bombshell that hit on the evening news when Chip Davenport interviewed the candidates for mayor.

In a powerful, two-minute pitch, Frank Poe made it clear that he was a strong and relentless advocate for "progressive action to correct historical inequities." He described the South's 150-year track record of dispossessing Black farmers as the "largest transfer of assets from Black people to White people in American history, unless you counted their bodies in slavery times."

"Is Frank Poe talking about reparations?" Temple asked Vee, who was also watching.

"He's considering a plan to pay a basic monthly income to local descendants of enslaved people. It would be funded initially by selling city-owned property."

Temple's skin went cold. The city of Preston's Mill owned Folly Park Plantation. *What could be more fitting than to sell it off to pay the descendants of slaves who had labored there, unpaid, for generations?* she thought.

Chip turned to Beau, who promised to "aggressively promote economic development." To Temple, that was alarming enough, but then Beau went on to say he was "extremely concerned about a growing disrespect for Southern heritage." When Chip asked him what he meant, Beau said,

"Take the crazy stories about Folly Park flying around. The place belonged to my ancestors, and I don't appreciate that some Harvard student can come down here and make all these accusations against a Civil War hero's wife just because she's Black. The management is so worried about being politically correct, they're letting themselves be used to push a liberal agenda. And, frankly, Chip, that's the way everything is these days. They can say whatever they want about things I care about, but if I stick up for my own heritage, they'll call me a racist. They want me to agree that my ancestors were monsters."

They were, Temple thought. *They were pedophiles and rapists—monsters.*

Beau turned away from Chip to look directly at the camera. "I've had enough, and I know I'm not alone. Anyone else who's sick and tired of it, too, should stand by."

"Does he really think I'm using you?" Vee asked.

"No. He's the one using you to push his agenda. And he seems to be reaching out to neo-Confederates and white nationalists." Temple shook her head. "He has no conscience."

"Should I stop my research? Or wait until after the election?"

"No," Temple said firmly. But she wondered if Beau had just painted a target on Vee's back. Or if she had.

VEE OFFERED TO DROP TEMPLE OFF at the university on her way to the historical society in the city, but Temple elected to ride her bike. It was not a coincidence that she'd chosen to do research at the Special Collections Library, which did not permit cell phones. She wanted to drag out the time she would be away from more ugly phone calls, but she was also avoiding Jack. He'd called Saturday morning to check on her, which she learned from her voicemail because she was too cowardly to answer her phone. She was afraid she'd made things permanently awkward with him. But worrying about Vee's safety, the upcoming election, and Folly Park was more than enough without adding that to the mix.

At the end of the driveway was a new banner: JOHN BROWN WAS A TERRORIST. Presumably the reenactors had put it up in response to the story about Jane. Stuart would be livid, Temple thought. Across the street, where the backyards of the houses in the Park Crest subdivision met the road, she was surprised to see a plastic table with an umbrella. A hand-lettered sign read: GENUINE HISTORICAL ARTIFACTS—MADE WHILE U WAIT. Jerry Hoyle was sitting at the table, and he waved as she pedaled by.

The library had an extensive collection of Civil War materials Temple had buried herself in for years when she was working on her dissertation, and the librarians greeted her enthusiastically. Laureen was a petite woman with pale skin, rosy cheeks, bristling gray hair, and a lively sense of humor. Clayborne, an imposing dark-skinned man who was never without an unusually patterned bow tie, was always setting off Laureen's wild cackling with his dry wit. They had been keeping up with the events at Folly Park, and they peppered Temple with questions. Did she think there was something in Special Collections that would reveal more about Carolina's alleged child?

Evading a direct answer, Temple explained that she was interested in records related to soldiers in the 8th Ohio regiment, particularly during September 1863, and any other regiments in the area around that time. Laureen bobbed her head up and down and darted off to her computer.

Clayborne stowed Temple's backpack beside his desk instead of sending her over to the lockers where other researchers stored their personal items. He jammed a couple of pencils into the electric sharpener and handed them to her with a fresh pad of paper. Then he escorted her into the reading room and over to her favorite table in a corner near the fireplace. Pulling out the heavy wooden chair with a flourish, he said, "Laureen and I can help with whatever you need, since there's no one else working here today."

Temple glanced around at the other people in the room hunched over archival folders and manuscript boxes. A few were looking at her resentfully, no doubt wondering why she merited special treatment.

"Genealogy buffs. They're not *working*," Clayborne said, not bothering to lower his voice.

Avoiding eye contact with the other researchers while she waited, Temple gazed into the glass-fronted cases of rare books. In this room she always felt removed from present time, cocooned in the past. The floor was covered with a forest-green carpet, so thick it hushed all sound. The mahogany tables and rows of bookcases absorbed the soft light of the old-fashioned reading lamps. The vast fireplace had not been used for a century, but it lent an air of antique elegance to the room with its eighteenth-century andirons and carved mantel. She felt a thrill of anticipation as Laureen's metal cart whispered toward her, archival boxes stacked on top.

Temple worked her way methodically through the boxes, her spirits flagging as each hour passed. By noon, she began to fear that she wouldn't find anything about the dispatch rider. She took a quick break for lunch at the campus café and returned to her research. Almost immediately, she came across the small leather-bound diary of Hiram C. Tinsley, a soldier in Benjamin Elliot's regiment—and in the same company.

The diary revealed Tinsley to be a discontented Ohio schoolteacher who had joined the army "to escape the futile drudgery of hammering sums into the thick skulls of farmers' offspring." He would, he explained on the first page of the little book, take pains to make the account of his time in the army "faithful to life for the edification of posterity." Hiram had hoped to relate his experiences in letters to a certain Adeline Cavanaugh, but she, "being a cruel, faithless girl," had broken his heart when she became engaged to Gil Wheeler on the very day that both young men enlisted.

Highly entertained by Tinsley's writing style, Temple read on, discovering he had spent much of his time keeping jealous watch over his rival. Tinsley gleefully recorded the details of Gil Wheeler's rare mishaps and gloomily reported his frequent commendations. It was clear, despite the negative bias of the diary, that Private Wheeler, soon Corporal Wheeler, was a popular and competent man. One of Tinsley's entries in early January 1863 complained: "G.W. currying favor with the others <u>again</u>, having volunteered for the sentry shift of Alex Marsden who <u>claims</u> he has contracted the dysentery." And the next day: "G.W. has taken in the new dispatch carrier as if he is a lost puppy. Though his story of falling ill and being left behind by his regiment—the 32nd Massachusetts—seems thin indeed, the captain is so impatient to replace Will Featherstone, who left this life when his horse planted its hoof between his eyes, that he does not question if this malingerer might serve us ill. Credulous as ever, G.W. does not suspect the fellow, bringing him round—a slight, sickly-looking boy—and introducing him as, 'My Young Friend, Ben Elliot.'"

Temple snapped to attention in her chair. This was likely the very soldier captured five months later and brought to the general's tent on the battlefield near Folly Park. He was originally from a Massachusetts regiment, and Jane Elliot's family had lived in Boston—he must be Jane's brother. She hurried to the reference desk and asked Clayborne to bring her anything he could find on the 32nd Massachusetts.

Returning to her table, Temple fervently resumed reading. She learned that a month after his arrival, Benjamin Elliot's masterful horsemanship forestalled capture by a rebel patrol and earned him the respect of the entire company. Tinsley wrote, "I suppose the beardless boy has some gumption after all." A few pages later, Temple was appalled to find that Tinsley had received a letter from his mother informing him of Adeline Cavanaugh's death of a fever "sudden and strong." Tinsley's own grief was tempered with some compassion for his rival, Gil Wheeler, who had received the news from his fiancée's father in the same mail delivery. According to Tinsley, Gil had passed a hand over his eyes, then promptly put on a brave face, saying, "Well, Hi, she's in a better place than I ever could have given her in this life. But it goes hard with me to lose her."

Shortly after this devastating news, Ben Elliot fell sick. Tinsley reported, "Gil tends to the boy as if he was our own dear Adeline." A telltale water stain had smudged the ink at the end of entry. Temple stared down at it.

"Are you all right?" Laureen gently pressed Temple's shoulder.

Temple looked up. "What?"

Laureen glanced at the other researchers, who were openly staring, and leaned in close. "You're crying," she whispered.

"I'm fine." Temple tried to smile as she looked away from Hiram Tinsley's tear mark. Laureen nodded skeptically and handed her a folder containing the muster rolls.

Temple checked twice, but there was no Benjamin Elliot listed in the 32nd Massachusetts. Perhaps he had lied. Maybe he was a deserter afraid of being tracked down. Or maybe Tinsley had recorded the wrong regiment. She supposed it didn't really matter, but she hated loose ends.

Turning back to the diary, Temple found that it ended abruptly on June 14, 1863, the remaining yellowed pages blank. In the official battle reports, she discovered that Hiram Tinsley had been killed the next day. He had been trapped with a handful of men, cut off from the rest of the regiment. They fought fiercely before their redoubt was overcome, leaving no survivors.

Depressed and drained, Temple slowly returned the materials to the boxes and packed up her notes. She asked Laureen to see if she could find any records for Hiram Tinsley, Gilbert Wheeler, or Benjamin Elliot. She also included Adeline Cavanaugh, just in case.

Temple had retrieved her bike helmet and backpack and was headed out the door when Clayborne called to her, ignoring the startled glares of the patrons in the reading room. "Temple, come back! Laureen found something."

"Already?"

Clayborne straightened his bow tie with a pitying smile.

Peering through her bifocals at her computer screen, Laureen said, "Adeline Cavanaugh's papers are at the Alliance Historical Society in Ohio." She tapped a few keys. "There's one box of correspondence. I'll ask if they'll scan the contents and send it to you."

TAKING THE LONG WAY HOME through Preston's Mill, Temple spotted Mrs. Glass among the potted ferns on her veranda and pulled up her bike.

Mrs. Glass shook her head at the sight of Temple's face, shining from heat and exertion, and rang a little silver bell. When a young Filipina woman appeared, immaculate in her white uniform, Mrs. Glass requested her to bring lemonade.

"There's something I wanted to ask you," Temple said when the young woman had gone. "Something personal."

"Oh, that's nice." Mrs. Glass nestled into the chintz cushions. "Is it about your handsome Jack Early?"

"No. It isn't about Jack." Temple was annoyed with herself for blushing and worried that Mrs. Glass may have heard about her plan for Folly Park, which would mean Hunter Glass had also. "I just met him."

Mrs. Glass's green marble eyes narrowed. "I've known you since you were born. Are you going to sit there and tell me you aren't in love with that gorgeous man? It's written all over your face."

Temple was relieved Mrs. Glass didn't seem to know about her plan. "I hardly know Jack. And I don't have time for a relationship right now."

"Temple Preston, you listen to me," Mrs. Glass said in her *Steel Magnolia* voice. "You can't choose who you fall in love with or when. Forget how you think things should happen—all that will get you is a man like Rich."

Temple shook her head. "Folly Park is in trouble. I have to think about other people."

"What people? Dead people? Dredging up old scandals? You need to start living, darling. In the present."

The young woman returned with the lemonade and poured it into two crystal glasses, sparing Temple from a reply. After she'd left, Mrs. Glass sighed and said, "I'm sorry about Folly Park. I wish I could influence Hunter, but I know better. What is it you actually came to talk to me about?"

"I saw my mother's piece at the museum opening the other night."

"Her self-portrait!" Mrs. Glass exclaimed. "The one with the blood? I remember. Margaret hoped the gallery would take it because your father didn't want it at home."

"That's the one. I hadn't seen it since I was a kid. I never read the label back then, but I did the other night, and I noticed something strange. It said the piece was done in New York in 1989. But that was the year I was born. I know Mom went to art school in New York, but I never knew she went back after she and my dad got married."

She let the question hang in the air, but Mrs. Glass had looked away and was running an elegant forefinger through the condensation on the lemonade pitcher.

Temple asked bluntly, "Did she?"

Mrs. Glass folded her hands in her lap. "Your mother went back to New York when Harry was two years old—she left him at home with the nanny. She stayed about two or three months with an artist friend. Then your father went up there, and she came back with him, and later that year you were born."

"An artist friend? You mean a man?"

"Yes."

Temple felt as if she couldn't breathe. "Was he my real father?"

"I never thought so. I knew Margaret. But I think your father always wondered."

Temple had been holding her breath, and she let it out slowly. "Why did she go?"

"Oh, darling, it was so long ago."

"Why won't you tell me?"

"It's not my story to tell."

"But she's dead. And you know."

Mrs. Glass pursed her lips and shook her head. "Gossip drove her away."

Gossip in their social circle usually involved a few standard topics: suicide, abuse, infidelity. Temple ruled out the first possibility, considered the second, and then said, "My father? He had an affair?"

Mrs. Glass's green marble eyes clouded. "I'm so sorry."

RIDING SLOWLY BACK TO FOLLY PARK, Temple thought about what Mrs. Glass had told her. She wasn't exactly surprised. Her father had been something of a ladies' man before he met her mother when he was nearly forty. Margaret Temple Smith was beautiful, reserved, and sixteen years younger. An only child, she'd led a sheltered life at Folly Park, and the family's genteel poverty had prevented her from attending the private schools and social events girls with her background usually experienced. Despite going to art school in New York, she retained a certain naivete, and she didn't have a chance against Harrison Preston's practiced charm. They became engaged in six weeks and were married three months later. After a honeymoon in Paris, they settled into a privileged social circle in the city.

Temple understood from the time she was quite young that her mother's public poise masked a private unhappiness. She never saw her parents touch. Though Temple and her brothers were subjected daily to their father's hectoring lectures, his interactions with his wife rarely extended beyond household decisions and plans for social engagements. Their disagreements centered on Temple's grandfather, who had lost his wife to breast cancer, leaving him selfish and demanding, her father claimed.

Harry had told Temple he'd overheard their parents talking about divorce once, but it had never happened, maybe because their mother—in a grim reprise of family history—was also diagnosed with advanced breast cancer that resisted treatment. She insisted on going to live at Folly Park until she died. At the time, Temple had thought, along with everyone else, that her mother didn't want her children to witness her decline. Now, after speaking with Mrs. Glass, Temple wondered, with a painful squeeze of her heart, if her mother had instead sought some peace from her husband.

Passing the reenactors' camp, Temple saw Colonel Townsend and his men cooking anachronistic hot dogs over their campfire. They smelled delicious. Jerry Hoyle had packed up his fake artifacts and gone home but left the table in place. She turned up the drive and rode slowly beneath the green canopy of trees.

Closed for the day, Folly Park was quiet and peaceful. At times like this, the plantation seemed like it could be any aging family estate, the sins of its youth long past. Temple felt a rush of gratitude. Folly Park had been a refuge for her mother, and it provided her with a home where she felt she belonged. Only here did she feel the abiding presence of her mother, her grandfather, and Harry—as if they still walked on the grounds and through the rooms, and she had only just missed them.

CHAPTER TWELVE

"I found a very interesting entry in Dr. Burrough's case book from October 1863," Vee said. "Do you want to hear about it now or after dinner?"

"Very funny." Holding Chick's food bowl high, Temple waited for him to sit. "Tell me now."

"Carolina sent King to town to bring the doctor back to Folly Park instead of sending a boy with a message, which Dr. Burroughs thought was unusual. He also said King was 'excessively agitated' and insisted he come at once."

"Go on," Temple prompted, setting Chick's bowl down.

"When the doctor got to Folly Park, he found Carolina in the house tending 'a very sick mulatto infant.'"

"What?"

Vee's eyes were bright behind her glasses. "Doctor Burroughs diagnosed cholera and wanted to treat the baby with laudanum, but Carolina wouldn't let him. His exact words were, 'Mrs. Smith snarled at me like a madwoman. She said that if *that poison* was all I could recommend, I was no better than a horse doctor.'" Vee turned a page. "Dr. Burroughs asked why the infant wasn't being nursed in the quarters, and Carolina said its mother was dead and there was no wet nurse. Dr. Burroughs told her the baby probably wouldn't live without laudanum, but she could try giving him cow's milk with molasses."

"I suppose as a recovered addict, Carolina's reaction is understandable," Temple said. "Especially if the baby was hers and King's, and she made up the story about his mother dying."

Vee's phone chirped with a text before she could reply. "Sorry, I have to go. Frank Poe's called a meeting." She was out the door before Temple had a chance to tell her what she'd found out at the library.

Anticipating a quiet evening by herself, Temple retrieved Jane's diary. She was frustrated that she hadn't been able to devote much time to it lately.

December 16, 1859

Feigning headache, I begged off tea to recover myself. A Mr. Hudspeth arrived without warning an hour ago. Carolina told me he is a commissioner appointed by the Circuit Court and wondered what business he had here. We had not long to wait, for Thomas brought him to us directly. "Jane," he said, "Mr. Hudspeth believes you to be a dangerous insurrectionary." I stared, astonished, as the visitor, an unremarkable looking man with a soiled cravat, turned red in the face. A neighbor—who wished to remain anonymous, Thomas said scornfully—had reported me to be a member of an Abolition society and thus barred from entering the state under an 1836 statute. Carolina began to protest, but Thomas stopped her. "Show Miss Elliot the so-called evidence brought against her," he said. Mr. Hudspeth, sweating profusely, produced a tattered clipping that proved to be the story about me in the Liberator.

"Now, Jane," said Thomas, "Is it true that you interfered in the recovery of an escaped slave woman?" Of course, I had done nothing to aid her escape—to my great regret. I said, "No, I did not save any woman." "There, you see?" said Thomas, tossing the clipping at Mr. Hudspeth. It floated to the floor, and the man lowered himself laboriously to one knee to retrieve it. When he stood again, I was seized with a coughing fit, and Carolina bade me lie on the chaise. She glared fiercely at our visitor, who knew not how to look, and cried, "Oh, see what you have done!"

When I could finally draw breath again, Thomas said coldly, "We will have nothing more to say of this matter while Miss Elliot resides at Folly Park. I would deem it outrageous impudence for you to interfere with my private affairs a second time." At this, Mr. Hudspeth tendered his profuse apologies and beat a speedy retreat. I myself was not far behind, to hide away here in my bedchamber, sorry beyond words that I have brought trouble to this house.

Temple was delighted with Thomas's bold defense of Jane. But she was both appalled and amazed at his arrogance in contending that within the bounds of Folly Park, even the law must bow to his authority. Eagerly, she read on.

December 23, 1859

The holiday season has been a whirl of excitement. There were nightly dances around a bonfire while the slaves husked the corn, and the past fortnight my cousins and I have attended <u>six</u> parties in the neighborhood. I have *never been so gay—or so weary! The night before last, we went to a party at the Prestons. I was surprised by the invitation, given that the last time they had been to Wild Oaks, Lad Preston had accosted Carolina, and Thomas refused to come to her defense. But Carolina only looked quizzical when I asked her pointedly if she was not feeling too fatigued to go. Thomas smiled at my maneuver and said sardonically that I might safely assume Lad Preston had forgotten the matter quite as thoroughly as Carolina, and there would be no scenes. And, though once she might have been annoyed at being teased, Carolina laughed merrily—a sign, I felt, of the greatly improved relations between them.*

The big house at Wild Oaks was decorated with evergreen boughs and mistletoe, and there were wonderful things to eat—nuts, fruitcakes, puddings, mincemeat, and candy set out in silver bowls. But the party was the strangest I have ever attended, and that not disregarding the wedding feast poor Miss Baxter gave herself in Boston when she had given up all hope of marriage. The Prestons keep an old Southern custom of turning the Christmas season into a kind of Saturnalia, where the servants are treated as masters, and the masters serve the servants. We were all made to greet an elderly uncle and a bent old crone—both tricked out in finery—where they sat in chairs decorated like thrones. The old uncle laughed at everything with a shadow of fear in his rheumy eyes, but the old woman remained stone-faced. I was distressed by the antics of the young men trying to make her smile. A man I later learned was a neighbor called Poole, saw my discomposure and said sneeringly, "The disapproving cousin ought to take her sensitive notions back North where she belongs."

Thomas asked Mr. Poole in a dangerous tone if he wished to "elaborate upon his concerns outside," and Mr.

Poole blanched and claimed he meant no offense. Thomas took me away to another room and sat me by the fire with a glass of syllabub. I felt as out of place as a duck in a room full of peacocks until a young Englishman—Mr. Emory— was introduced to me. We spoke of books we had read and places he had traveled. And later, we danced together and dined side-by-side on the supper that Agatha Preston served to us. Dressed in servant's clothes, she had even put tallow on her face as the slaves do to make it shine, but it had the unhappy effect of showing up her sallow complexion. Despite the unpleasantness with Mr. Poole, I enjoyed myself immensely.

Both Thomas and Carolina said little on the drive home. Thomas went straight upstairs, and when I asked Carolina if she would sit up with me, she refused. She said pettishly that it was clear I had more interest in talking to Mr. Emory than to her. I was annoyed, for she knows what I suffer over Henry still. I retorted that if she envied me my pleasure in an intelligent man's conversation, she might enjoy it for herself in her own husband's companionship. She laughed scornfully and said I should cease trying to bring about "an impossible romance" between herself and Thomas. I moved to go then, but she begged me to stay and abused herself for upsetting me so heartily that I relented.

Like any two people living together, Temple reflected, everything wasn't always smooth between the cousins. Carolina and Jane were like college roommates, and exactly the age for it had they lived in another time.

She had just started on the next entry when Al banged through the screen door without knocking and came into the living room, a six-pack in one hand and a paper bag in the other. He handed Temple a can of beer and a sandwich and threw himself beside her on the couch. Picking up the television remote, he flipped channels until he found a golf special.

Temple reluctantly set the diary aside. "What's up?"

"My house is full of campaign volunteers, all talking at once, and Frank Poe won't tell them to shut up because he doesn't want to suppress anyone's truth." Al rolled his eyes.

"Frank is at your house? Maybe I'll go down and meet him." *It might be a good idea to reach out to Frank before he solidifies his ideas about reparations for slavery,* Temple thought.

"Don't. He doesn't want to hear *your* truth, believe me. Besides, the news is on."

Chip Davenport made the most of a possible relationship between King and Carolina, inviting a panel to comment that included Dr. Montgomery Tate, Temple's old mentor at Folly Park, and two historians from the university. She knew them both and was not surprised by their remarks. One said he would be interested to see if the "keepers of the general's flame" would continue to reveal evidence painting "their hero and his wife" in such an unfavorable light. The second, echoing Beau, expressed his belief that Folly Park's management was pandering to political correctness. Relishing the opportunity to attack the academics, Dr. Tate vigorously defended Temple's actions in language that was less than diplomatic, and the conversation devolved into a shouting match. Overall, Temple was pleased. Though three old men fighting about history wasn't exactly great entertainment, it might help keep Folly Park in the news.

But Al was scowling. "Why do you keep stirring the pot? When Folly Park goes under, I don't have a rich father who can bail me and Betty Jean out."

"You won't have to worry about your jobs if we can stay

in the news. You've seen all the extra visitors we're getting."

Al shook his head sharply. "Race gets everyone riled up, and you can't control what happens. Hell, you've already got a Confederate army camped on your doorstep."

"I'm working on a plan for the long term," Temple said to reassure Al.

"What are you talking about? What plan?"

"Convert the old tobacco barn into a group home for girls like Wanda in exchange for funds to restore Folly Park."

Al stared. "You've got to be kidding. Girls like Wanda? You mean those juvenile delinquents you tutor? You're going to bring criminals here to live?"

"Wanda's not a criminal. She was in the wrong place at the wrong time."

"You believe that?" Al snorted. "She's been playing you from the start."

"That's not true! It was my idea to give her a job and get her released early."

"Are you sure?"

Al was always suspicious of everyone. "Well, I'm sorry you don't support my plan," Temple said stiffly. "Betty Jean will think it's great."

"Don't bring her into this," Al snapped. "You really think the White folks will tolerate those girls polluting the sacred ground at Folly Park?"

"Not all White people are reactionary bigots."

"The ones that aren't just feel guilty. Until it's not convenient."

"Are you describing me?"

"You mean well, but you're being stupid, Temple," Al said, shaking his head. "You've got to stop all this before someone gets hurt."

"I can't. The girls—"

"I won't listen to this nonsense." Standing abruptly, Al stepped on the six-pack, and a can burst and spewed a frothy stream across the wood floor. Skirting the spill, he shook his head and stalked out of the room, letting the screen door bang shut behind him.

Temple turned off the TV. The only sound in the quiet house was the hiss of beer seeping through the cracks in the floorboards.

AFTER AL HAD LEFT, TEMPLE received eight calls from people who had seen Dr. Tate's television appearance. Like Al, some objected to her stirring up old secrets. Others accused her of betraying her heritage. Temple listened politely and said she hoped they would be open-minded about what she might discover, but the calls ended in mutual dissatisfaction, and in one case what sounded like a veiled threat.

Jack called too. Temple was so relieved he didn't mention how she'd behaved the last time she saw him that it took her a moment to realize he was warning her that Senator Alden was nervous about the recent publicity. After the call, she stared at the ceiling through a sleepless night wondering whether her plan had failed and if Jack was distancing himself from her.

The telephone in her office was already ringing when Temple arrived at work the next morning. The call was from her adviser, Dr. Belcher. He was irritated that he'd been tracked down on his vacation by colleagues who, he claimed, were upset she was "emasculating" the general.

"General Smith would never have allowed his wife to misbehave in the manner you are suggesting," Dr. Belcher said.

Temple knew it would be futile to point out how sexist that was or to remind Dr. Belcher the general could hardly have kept watch over his wife when he was off fighting a war.

Dr. Belcher continued. "I'm seriously disappointed. If you persist in digging up old slave quarter rumors and treating them as legitimate sources, I will feel compelled to share my concerns with your publisher. There are times when it's best to let sleeping dogs lie. You of all people should have had the sense to leave things alone."

Temple's stomach lurched. The man was sexist and arrogant, but never before had she heard him say something so overtly racist.

"I'm shocked that you seem to have let your bias get the better of your scholarship," Temple said and hung up, surprised at herself as much as she had no doubt surprised him. The man had the power to end her academic career before it had even begun.

Just then, Stuart barged into her office. "Guess what? *Our Country* magazine is going to do a cover story on us! They want a new scoop. What've you got?"

Given Senator Alden's misgivings, Temple wasn't so sure that a story in a popular magazine was such a great idea. She was about to try to put Stuart off when Hunter Glass stepped into the room behind him.

Temple hadn't seen the chairman of the board of Folly Park in weeks, and that had been fine with her. Hunter was a fit, patrician-looking man her father's age with keen blue eyes and short, silver hair. His small, pointy teeth reminded Temple of a shark, but since he rarely smiled, they rarely made an appearance. Despite knowing her since she was born, he always treated her with stilted formality. Today, he acknowledged her only with a slight nod.

Temple turned back to Stuart, who was fidgeting with impatience. "I do have a lead on something."

"Is it juicy?"

Temple appreciated that, like her, Hunter Glass winced at the crude expression. "A Union dispatch carrier named Benjamin Elliot fought in the battle near Folly Park. I think he was Jane Elliot's brother."

"The abolitionist cousin?" Stuart frowned. "What does she have to do with the baby?"

Temple supposed it was finally time to tell her boss about the box. She took it out of her bag and showed Stuart and Hunter the diary and the photograph, pointing out the Folly Park ring that had been carried to Boston by Carolina's purported child.

After Temple had finished, Hunter stared over her head without expression. Stuart, however, was so excited his face turned red, and he squinched convulsively.

"Excellent, excellent!" he exclaimed. "Hunt, did you hear that? We've got something!"

Hunter nodded but said nothing. Stuart didn't notice. The good news had overpowered his jealous paranoia about including Temple in conversations with board members. Showing off his insider knowledge, he said expansively, "Oh! Temple, I just found out Hunt and your father won the club golf tournament five years in a row! When was it again, Hunt?"

Hunter Glass shrugged dismissively, and Temple bit her lip, but Stuart was oblivious. "Well, you can ask your dad and let us know."

"No, I can't. We're not speaking."

Stuart's eyebrows shot up, and his glasses slid to the end of his nose.

Hunt turned and looked Temple full in the face for the

first time in her life. She stared back defiantly. After a moment, to her surprise, he revealed the shark teeth in a surprisingly warm smile. He nodded, as if with approval, and strode out the door, Stuart trotting at his heels like a faithful dog.

Temple was relieved to see them go. She wasn't ready to tell Stuart or Hunter or anyone else that Benjamin Elliot might be the key to understanding the general's strange actions on the night he was killed.

"WHAT ARE YOU LOOKING AT?" Temple read the label on the box beside Vee. "The Tulane collection?"

Vee pulled back from the microfilm reader and nodded. "I wanted to find out more about Linda after she was sent to Louisiana, but there aren't any records for the plantation past 1845."

"I know. Later stuff is at the Marais County Historical Society outside New Orleans. Why are you focusing on Linda?"

"I found a letter from Lavinia to her sister Harriet. She describes Linda as 'uncommonly lovely with straight hair flowing down her back.' Lavinia wrote that their sister-in-law, Annette, 'so marked from the smallpox as she was,' must be angry Thomas had taken Linda into the house as a nursemaid."

"How did Lavinia find out about it?"

"Apparently James was trying to get her to write to Thomas and tell him to leave Linda alone, but Lavinia told Harriet she'd refused to get involved in the feud between their brothers."

"I don't blame her."

"Me either. Lavinia thought it was a good thing James had been made to send Linda away. She reminded Harriet how he used to read his favorite books to her, like 'Richardson's horrid novel that no doubt had the dual purpose of tormenting poor Anna and readying the girl for her fate.'"

"What did she mean?"

"Samuel Richardson's book *Pamela* is about a maid whose employer tries to seduce her."

Temple wrinkled her nose with disgust. "No wonder Anna insisted that James sell Linda."

"I've been thinking about the Janus ring," Vee continued. "We know it disappeared at the same time Linda left Folly Park. Maybe she stole it, or maybe James gave it to her as a parting gift. If she took it to Louisiana, then maybe it came back to Folly Park sixteen years later with Thomas Temple Smith Jr.—the general. Maybe everything starts with Linda." She looked earnestly at Temple. "I want to find out what happened to her. I want to go to Louisiana."

Temple didn't think Vee was aware that she'd clasped her hands together in an imploring gesture. But this was a perfect opportunity to get Vee away from the unpleasantness and potential danger swirling around Folly Park. Temple's stomach knotted at the thought of being left alone without her ally, roommate, and friend. Before she could change her mind, she said, "Go. I'll foot the bill."

Vee jumped up and hugged Temple. "Thank you! This means a lot to me."

"Sure." Temple smiled weakly.

"You should come," Vee said impulsively. "Get away from those nasty phone calls for a few days."

"You've heard about those?"

"Yes. I know you've been trying to protect me."

"I'm really sorry."

"I'd rather know what's going on," Vee said. "If there's

one thing my dad taught me, it's the importance of being prepared so you can plan how to respond before you're caught up in the heat of the moment."

"It's good advice. I wish I felt like I had the time to follow it."

"Come with me."

"I need to hold down the fort here. I'll take you to the airport in the morning."

"Thanks, but I'm going to drive." Vee looked self-conscious. "I told a friend I was hoping you'd let me go, and he offered to take me."

"That's a very long drive." Temple raised her eyebrows.

"It's not what you think. Matthew's gay. He's one of the other campaign volunteers. He lives in San Francisco, but he grew up here. He built Frank's whole digital platform."

"He sounds smart."

"He's great. We met at my first meeting. He told me he left the tech company he worked at because he got tired of his coworkers assuming he was just a diversity hire. And I told him the other grad students assume I was an affirmative action admit. We bonded over our mutual frustration at not being recognized for how truly brilliant we are."

"It sounds like a strong basis for a friendship," Temple said, smiling.

Vee laughed. "It is."

"I'd like to meet him. Let me take you both to Clyde's for dinner."

"Thanks! And you should invite Jack too."

A POPULAR PRESTON'S MILL institution, Clyde's Barbecue was located across from the town square, sandwiched between two churches. A century ago, when it was operated by Clyde's grandmother, the building had been an inn that euphemis-tically offered "horizontal refreshments." Before that, it was the site of the local slave market. The remains of the auction block had been removed long ago, but a plaque affixed to the brick wall in the corner of the property noted where it had been. Temple always felt it was a bit eerie to be eating where so many people had once suffered.

Jack texted to say they should start without him, so Temple and Vee ordered enough food for four and sat down at one of the picnic tables. Soon, Matthew arrived in a battered Corolla. Short and compact, he had light-brown skin and hair cut with a high fade. He was wearing a graphic T-shirt, khaki shorts, and a well-seasoned pair of flip-flops. He shook Temple's hand with a ready smile and sat down just as a server brought out the plastic baskets of food.

Matthew's roots in the area were as deep as Temple's own. When he told her his last name was Spencer, Temple assumed his father's people had come from a plantation called South Cut, and when he said his mother was a Blair, she knew those roots were at Manor Hill. The White Blairs were attached by marriage to a branch of the Preston family. She realized that Matthew must know all about her and her connections, too, and so must his entire family, going back generations. Their survival depended on knowing all they could about their powerful White neighbors.

Pushing aside those uncomfortable thoughts, Temple said, "Your family must be happy you're home."

"Yes. My dad offered my services to Frank Poe—without checking with me." Matthew laughed ruefully. "He thinks being a contractor is just a nice way to say I'm unemployed. But it was good to come back and spend time with my folks, and I respect what Frank is trying to do, even though I think challenging racism in Preston's Mill is a losing proposition."

"You sound like my dad," Vee said, adding a dollop of coleslaw to her sandwich. "He thinks the entire South is irredeemable. Although he might change his mind if he tried this pulled pork."

"I hope things are changing here," Temple said. "How is living in San Francisco?"

Matthew dipped a french fry in ketchup. "I like it. It's a great city," he paused. "But everyone wants a Black friend to show off how progressive they are. It's exhausting."

"Being popular is a lot of work," Vee teased.

They were laughing together when a middle-aged, White couple in matching denim shorts approached the table. They looked vaguely familiar to Temple, but she saw so many tourists, she often had that feeling.

The man said, "You're Temple Preston, right? From Folly Park?"

"Yes. Can I help you?"

"You sure can. You can start by not letting yourself get jerked around by these people." The man stabbed a beefy forefinger at Vee, then Matthew. Clutching a quilted purse to her chest, his wife stuck out her jaw and nodded emphatically.

Shocked, Temple grasped for something to say. Matthew stood up.

Suddenly Jack was there, inserting himself between the couple and the table. He and Matthew exchanged a look, and Matthew nodded.

Jack turned to face the couple while Matthew stepped behind him, backing him up. Without thinking, Temple had picked up her plastic fork. She looked across the table and saw that Vee had instinctively done the same. At any other time, it might have been funny.

"Are you sure you want to do this here?" Jack asked the couple evenly.

"We just want to tell her what we think, that's all," the man said belligerently.

"Do you really want to do this here?" Jack repeated.

"Come on, I'm not—" the man began in a milder tone, but Jack interrupted him.

"Make up your mind. Do you really want to do this?"

The man glanced at the other patrons, some of whom had turned to stare. He held up his palms and backed away, but his wife leaned forward. "It's terrible, what's going on!" she hissed. "What right do they have to come here and make trouble?"

Jack shifted as she tried to peer around him, and Matthew shifted with him. "You need to stop."

"They want to ruin America! They hate our country."

"Stop. Right now. I'm not going to ask again."

The woman opened her mouth, but her husband muttered, "Come on!" and pulled her arm. They left the eating area and climbed into a large SUV parked in front of the restaurant. Temple saw them arguing in the front seat as they drove away.

Jack watched them go before he sat down. "Everybody okay?"

Matthew shrugged, frowning. Temple nodded. Vee slowly shook her head.

"Can you stick it out a few minutes longer?" Matthew asked gently. "So it doesn't look like they scared us away?"

Vee didn't answer, but she sat up straighter as she stared down at her food. Jack began to eat, deliberately casual. Matthew took a sip of lemonade, but Temple saw his eyes scan every one of the tables, assessing. She picked up a french fry and put it down again. She couldn't eat.

Across the square, a group of people appeared in front of the courthouse, waving signs decorated with peace symbols and slogans: SAY NO TO HATE and LOVE IS NOT A COLOR. They seemed to be chanting, but the breeze carried their voices away. As Temple watched, a pickup truck careered around the corner. When it passed the group, someone in the passenger seat threw a spewing bottle. It shattered on the pavement, and many of the demonstrators fled, leaving their signs behind.

HUNCHED LOW IN HER SEAT, Vee was silent on the drive home. When they arrived back at Folly Park, she went immediately to her room. Temple followed a few minutes later, and she could see Vee fighting back tears as she packed. Chick whined anxiously.

"Snacks for the drive." Temple handed Vee a bag of nuts and dried fruit.

"Thanks." Vee stuffed the bag in her backpack. "I'm sorry about leaving you." She took a shaky breath. "But I just want to get away."

"I know. I'll be fine. This is my town, and these are my people."

"I don't think they see you as one of them anymore."

"It'll all work out," Temple said with more conviction than she felt. "Matthew's coming early, and you need to get some sleep. I'll say goodbye now."

They hugged each other. "Be safe," Vee said.

Calling to Chick, Temple went outside and wandered over to the mansion, where she sat down on the veranda. Chick leaned against her leg. Petting his shaggy head helped ease the hollow feeling in her chest. She wished she could take a trip, and she wondered what it would be like to go away with Jack. Just then she heard a car coming up the drive. Stones pinging on its undercarriage sounded like the striking of little bells, and for one happy moment, she thought it might be him. Maybe he was coming to check on her and Vee after what had happened.

Headlights caught Temple full in the face, and she flinched like a startled possum as the car veered toward her and stopped with a jerk. Julia erupted out of the driver's seat. With a whimper, Chick disappeared.

Julia faced Temple, legs wide, hands on hips like a diminutive gunslinger. Temple was pretty sure she didn't want to know why Julia had come. She waited.

After a while, Julia flung herself down on the steps. Temple felt, rather than heard, that she was crying. "What's wrong?" she asked.

"Pixie told me you broke up with Rich when he asked you to marry him." Julia's voice was ragged. "He lied to me. He told me *he* broke it off with *you*, and it was never serious."

Temple said nothing.

"Why did you tell my sister and not me?"

"I wasn't planning to tell anyone. Pixie saw him at the club the day after we broke up, and she thought he seemed upset, so she called me. I assumed Rich would tell you when you started dating."

"Oh, he told me. *His* version." Julia shifted restlessly. "Why didn't you tell me the truth when I said he dumped you?"

"You were engaged. I didn't think it mattered."

"You both betrayed me. He lied to me on purpose, and you lied by omission."

"We didn't want to hurt you."

"I can't trust him. But I'm still going to marry him. I deserve a house and kids."

Turning to look at her, all Temple could make out in the pale moonlight were the bumps of Julia's lips. "Do you love him?"

Julia twitched her shoulders. "I did before I found out he loved you first."

"It's not a competition. He wanted to save face with you. He's a man, not some prince in a fairy tale."

"Why can't I have the fairy tale? You do."

"Me? What do you mean?"

"Jack Early."

Julia's voice had taken on its familiar combative tone. Nothing could make Temple speak to her when she was like that.

"I could tell right away," Julia said. "When you were hiding away together behind the palms at the gallery opening. Then he kept asking about you. It was, 'What does she like to do?' and 'Where does she like to eat?' and 'What was she like when you were kids?' every time I saw him. It was *so* annoying."

Julia stood up. "What's wrong with wanting Rich to be that way about me?" She didn't wait for an answer before she stalked to her car, got in, and drove away.

Temple walked slowly back to the house, wondering if Jack was really interested in her, or if Julia was overstating things to make her point. She opened the front door, and immediately all thoughts of Jack evaporated. For some reason, the multiple drafts of her manuscript that had been stacked on the top of the dresser for over a year had chosen this night to collapse in an avalanche of paper extending from the bedroom into the hallway.

It would take hours to sort out, Temple thought with dismay. But she didn't want to sort it out. She didn't even want to touch it. Suddenly, with absolute certainty, she understood she didn't want to write the book she was supposed to be writing. And the thought of becoming an academic—competing for office space and feuding over class times with the Dr. Belchers of the world—made her feel as if she couldn't breathe. She didn't stop to think as she dumped the dirty clothes out of her laundry basket and began filling it with the pages of the manuscript.

Outside, Temple discovered the recycle bin was missing again—sometimes Martha borrowed it for the office. The rotten stench of sunbaked garbage made her gag when she opened the trashcan. It was full. She slammed the lid back down, casting about for an alternative plan. Then it came to her: she would burn it.

Temple searched the house for matches, but there were none to be found. She did discover *Help Yourself* in the back of a drawer and tossed it on top of the manuscript. When she hoisted the laundry basket, the white plastic buckled, so she cradled it awkwardly in her arms as she staggered down the drive.

The reenactors were playing cards on a tree stump beside their campfire. Their commitment to authenticity extended to their insults.

One of them said, "You're a louse on my arse. You've won every hand."

"Hello?" Temple called.

"Hush up, there's a lady present." Someone raised a kerosene lamp and called, "Who goes there?"

"It's Temple Preston. Can I borrow your fire?"

The lamp swiveled. Colonel Townsend's eyebrows rose a notch when he saw Temple, but he nodded.

Temple set the laundry basket on the ground and knelt beside it. She tossed a handful of paper into the flames. Behind her, the game resumed.

"What've you got there?" the colonel asked.

"My dissertation. I was turning it into a book."

The colonel slowly stretched out his hand, as if Temple were a dog that might bite. When she didn't react, he picked up a page and squinted at it in the firelight. Out of the corner of her eye, Temple watched him read the dense prose, his forehead puckered. "It's about the Civil War?"

"Yes."

"That's a lot of paper. A lot of work."

"Yes."

"Took you a long time, did it?"

"Four years."

"As long as the war itself."

Temple nodded.

"Four years with all that ugliness." The colonel shook his head slowly. "Why, your heart must be worn out."

Temple's throat closed. That was exactly how she felt.

"Let me help you," the colonel said, levering himself down beside her.

Neither of them spoke as they fed the rest of the manuscript, a dozen pages at a time, into the flames. But Colonel Townsend grunted and held out his hand when Temple moved to toss *Help Yourself* into the fire.

"Now, then, I don't hold with book burning. Not published ones anyway." He squinted at the cover. "I've heard of this one. I think I'll give it a read."

CHAPTER THIRTEEN

The house was very quiet without Vee's morning noises—the old pipes creaking as she ran the shower, the clatter of breakfast preparations, the sounds of a daily chore from the list they kept on the fridge. Temple hadn't heard Matthew's car or even the reenactors' bugle call. Destroying what amounted to her life's work had made her sleep better than she had in weeks. But she didn't want to get out of bed. The prospect of eating breakfast alone depressed her.

Staring up at the cracked ceiling, Temple replayed what had happened at Clyde's. She was disgusted she'd done nothing to defend Vee and Matthew. Now, of course, she could imagine all kinds of things she could have said to parry the couple's attack. But last night she'd been paralyzed, and if Jack hadn't arrived, things might have escalated. Temple thrashed off the sheets and got up. She almost stepped on Chick, wedged halfway under the bed. *He probably misses Vee too*, she thought, and gave his rump a sympathetic pat. His tail thumped once against the floor.

From long habit, Temple gingerly eased open her underwear drawer before she realized it wasn't necessary. There was no longer a manuscript stacked on top of the dresser, and the wall behind where it had been was a darker shade of yellow than the rest of the room. She probed her feelings for regret and found none.

Outside, drizzle wept from the sky, and the line of tourists waiting to purchase tickets was shorter than it had been lately. On her rounds, Temple saw that the mill folly was almost completely covered by a verdant bloom of moss. Inside the mansion, the eighteenth-century German automaton clock had stopped, which it tended to do on wet days. Temple texted Al, but she wasn't surprised he didn't answer.

Stuart bustled into the office, while Temple exchanged a one-sided greeting with Martha. "You need to find more dirt pronto. The *Our Country* magazine people are calling this week. Get Vee on it full time."

"Vee isn't here."

"Is she sick?"

"No, she's on her way to Louisiana."

"What?" Stuart bleated. "Who told her she could take a trip?"

"I did. She's been looking into the relationship between Carolina and the enslaved driver, King. The trail leads to the plantation outside New Orleans where General Smith was born. King's twin sister Linda was a nursemaid there."

"What does that have to do with anything?"

"Linda was likely the mistress of James Smith. And probably also his brother's."

"A slave mistress?" Stuart squinched, grinning wolfishly. "So, fooling around in the quarters was a habit for both the men and the women. If Vee finds something really good, we can get more than just *Our Country* interested. Maybe a talk show." He churned his hands together, and Temple's skin crawled. She escaped into her office.

TEMPLE MISSED JACK'S CALL because she was on the phone with yet another of the general's disgruntled fans. This one wanted ten years of donations refunded. Though she'd learned that the less she said, the quicker people calmed down, the incident at Clyde's had left her nerves raw, and she had to bite her tongue. When she finally had a chance to check her voicemail, she found a message from Jack letting her know he had a family emergency in New York and would be gone for a few days.

Temple texted, "I'm so sorry. Safe travels." It already felt as if he were a million miles away.

Without Vee's industrious presence, the empty basement seemed particularly uninviting, but Temple resolved to finish sorting the box Vee had been working on. An hour later, her diligence was rewarded. She found a small packet that had slipped beneath the other papers, and the rotting twine came apart to reveal three letters. The first was addressed to "Miss Jane Elliot, care of Mr. Thomas T. Smith, Folly Park, Preston's Mill, Virginia." Unfolding it, Temple noted the date: "Boston 4 Dec 1859." She began to read. "My dear Jane. . . ." At that moment, the lights flickered and went out.

This kind of thing happened often. Folly Park's perpetually deferred maintenance meant the electrical system was a mishmash of quick fixes, a portfolio of Al's ingenuity over the years. After he'd ignored her text earlier, Temple knew Al probably wouldn't answer, but she called him anyway as she made her way to the stairs. When her foot hit the first step, her legs shot out from under her, and she went down, breath kicked from her lungs. She was lying in a puddle of water that had not been there an hour ago. She got up gingerly, relieved she was unhurt. The leak would have to wait. She was impatient to get back to the letter.

Fighting her way through a prickly hedge behind the mansion to the fuse box, Temple ignored the thorns raking along her arms, flipped the basement switch, and was back at her task in minutes. She picked up the letter again.

Boston, 4 Dec. 1859

My Dear Jane,

You <u>must</u> return home! Benjamin has told us of the letter you received from your Cousin Carolina, how he drove you to the station, and that you wept the whole way. I know your sore heart led you to answer your cousin's call. But, Daughter, please come home. I have enclosed a cheque so that you may do so without trouble or delay.

Your loving,
Mother

Temple opened the second letter, also addressed to Jane at Folly Park. It was dated a few months after the first.

Boston, 8 Mar. 1860

My Dear Jane,

I was gratified to receive your letter, but I must correct your errors in understanding. I <u>do</u> comprehend that your life is rewarding, engaged as you are in educating the slaves. I wonder, though, that you can say the Folly Park people are humanely treated, when you know that the deprivation of freedom is the greatest inhumanity of all. I *cannot comprehend your vehement defense of your cousin Thomas, a Master of Slaves! Your judgment appears sorely wanting. And if your Cousins do indeed concern themselves for your welfare as attentively as you report, they must see the necessity of returning you to those who would care for you in the difficult days ahead. Take sober counsel with your conscience, Daughter, and pray for guidance. Your Father joins me in urging you to take the only proper course, and I close in confidence that we will soon see you at home. I remain—*

Your loving Mother

Temple retrieved Jane's diary from her bag and opened it to March 1860, searching for any reference to the letter. She found one.

March 18, 1860

Our days are a happy routine of household duties—just this week Carolina and I have directed the servants in scalding the bedding to prevent bedbugs, and tomorrow we are going to make beer. We ride nearly every afternoon. In the evenings, Thomas retires to the library, for he does not employ a plantation manager and performs all those tedious tasks himself. Carolina and I amuse ourselves in the sitting room until he comes. I do not feel I am intruding on their intimacy, for though they are easier together than when I first came, even quite good friends, they never appear to desire to be alone.

Mother has written again, inadvertently endangering me by mentioning my teaching the slaves—I could have been thrown in prison if a censor had seen it! Distressed by her reprimands, I went to the park, but Jewel came to tell me the quarter was in an uproar. Declaring she was only feigning illness, the overseer, Mr. Lamb, whipped a woman who had fainted in the field, though she was with child. I went immediately to Thomas and pleaded indignantly on the woman's behalf. He said I did not know all, that this Dinah had previously enjoyed a pregnancy of 11 months, and yet despite such an extended gestation period, had been delivered only of a straw-filled pillowcase.

I retorted that regardless, to whip another person for any reason was the height of brutality. Thomas replied that indeed slavery is a barbarous system, but he believes he brings a measure of civilization to his small part of it, and to do so he must have order. He cannot be either too lenient with the people or too hard, else the "barbarian hordes," as he termed his fellow slaveholders, would take notice. "And then," he said, "God help us all." I insisted that his character alone should govern his actions, not the tyrannies of a corrupt institution. He said sarcastically, "How fortunate are those who live in times and places that permit them to be entirely true to themselves. I have always believed such Utopias to be fictions."

Last night I could not sleep. When I went down to breakfast this morning, Thomas was alarmed at my state. He told me not to fret myself ill, for no matter if she feigned or not, Dr. Burroughs would see Dinah, and she would have an extra day of rest. I am still quite troubled, though touched by his pains to please me.

Temple was intrigued by this account of Jane's disagreement with Thomas and their negotiations regarding the clever Dinah. She opened the final letter.

Boston, 12 Oct. 1860

Daughter,

It is too absurd to claim that your Cousin Carolina relies on you to manage the household. Though I can well imagine her ignorance—Southern ladies are raised to no purpose but ornamentation—what do you imagine <u>you</u> know of household management? How Fanny and Dorcas, toiling for wages in our kitchen, would laugh! And it is not at all amusing to insist you also can not come home because your Cousin Thomas requires you to play chess with him of an evening! Truly, what can your company mean to such a man? His attentions must be wearying to him after so many months, and you must trespass no longer upon his hospitality. Father is certain now that war is inevitable. Your brothers are coming to fetch you home.

Mother

Temple skimmed through the diary, hoping Jane had written about the outcome of this missive.

November 20, 1860

William and Benjamin arrived yesterday. Benjamin is a serious young man now, no longer the boy I left a year hence. William has always been used to bossing me, and his manner is unaltered. Thomas was out, and Carolina, seeing I was resolved to be silent, greeted them with her usual charm, making much of our family connection. She settled them in the drawing room and had the servants bring refreshments.

My brothers stared openly at Jewel. She is quite a beauty, with a joyful air I attribute to the fact that— at great detriment to her lessons—she has lately taken up with one of the Prestons' boys, who answers to the name of Bub-Bub. I've learned he is much valued for his carpentry skills, but he does not impress me as Jewel's equal. When I asked Carolina if she would put a stop to their budding romance, she said, "Whyever for? Jewel likes him, and so does King. You should not judge him by his stammer." What could I say to that? Many of the slaves have speech irregularities, the product not of ignorance, but rather the consequence of lives lived in fear. Perhaps I judged unfairly.

My brothers sat like great lumps on the elegant Chippendale chairs. Benjamin blushed whenever Carolina looked at him. William was equally smitten, though he tried to hide it behind a stern manner. He said I looked poorly, that this climate must not agree with me, but Carolina teased him into humor.

Returned in time for supper, Thomas expressed pleasure at the "happy reunion." Carolina played and sang after my brothers partook of the best brandy. This morning, William went to the library and spoke to Thomas, and I was afraid he would prevail. But Carolina, spying on my behalf, told me she had seen William leave the room scowling. He sent word shortly after that they wished to bid me goodbye. I felt unwell and begged Carolina to make my excuses. And now, I thank God, they have gone and left me where I wish to be more than any other place on earth!

The tense exchange between Jane and her mother made clear why Jane had not gone back to Boston despite the threat of impending war. Temple thought of her own overbearing father, with his daily reminders that she was a disappointment, his demeaning comments, his quick temper and harsh punishments. She understood Jane's desire to escape. But it was interesting, and a bit disturbing, that instead of converting Carolina into an abolitionist, Jane seemed to have adapted to her cousins' lifestyle. Her minor protests and haphazard lessons probably assuaged her conscience without effecting any real change in the lives of the enslaved people at Folly Park.

Emerging from the basement just past closing time, Temple discovered the clouds had cleared, leaving behind a hot and humid afternoon. The sun glared off every surface, including a pool of water extending along the side of the house, no doubt the source of the puddle in the basement. She suspected the gutters were clogged again, the culprit a huge Catawba tree, and went to get the ladder. Al often threatened to cut the tree down because it constantly shed clusters of large, trumpet-shaped white flowers, leaves, and bark, but Temple had a soft spot for it. When he was a boy, her grandfather told her, he'd teased his mother by pretending to smoke the tree's cigar-shaped seed pods.

Temple had just finished clearing the gutters when her cell phone rang.

"Come quick!" Betty Jean's voice was pitched high with excitement. "Wanda's gone into labor, and Al's got my car. We need you to take her to the hospital!"

Minutes later, they were all wedged into the cab of Temple's truck, driving fast. Betty Jean patted Wanda's arm and said over and over, "It's okay, honey, it's okay."

Wanda hadn't made a sound, but when she dared take her eyes off the road, Temple saw the girl clutching the door handle so tight the tendons in her wrist were as taut as guy wires. "That's right, Wanda!" she called. "Just hang on."

The hospital was on the far side of Preston's Mill, and Temple was forced to slow down as she passed through town. She took a shortcut down one of the narrow side streets. Betty Jean was focused on Wanda, so she didn't see her own car parked in front of the Massachusetts Bay Development office, but Temple did. She wondered grimly what Al was doing there.

Temple squealed to a stop outside the emergency room, and two orderlies helped Wanda into a wheelchair. Betty Jean trotted beside her as they disappeared into the hospital. Relieved they'd made it in time, Temple pulled slowly into the parking lot.

Inside the hospital, Temple discovered that Wanda had been taken directly to the delivery room. Once she'd texted the news in a group message, she had nothing to do. She fidgeted with her keys in the empty waiting room.

Two older couples arrived, pink balloons floating above them. Watching them chatting together, Temple felt lonely. She listened to Jack's last voicemail message again just to hear his voice. A nurse appeared, and the gaggle of grandparents followed her away down the hall.

Picking up the television remote, Temple flipped channels until a C-SPAN program caught her attention. She recognized Barbara Trent-Holmes, a prominent Black historian.

"Of course, infidelity is an old story. But those who still idealize the antebellum South, and thus many Southern military historians, feel a personal anger and offense at the idea the general's wife could have betrayed him with an enslaved man."

The camera panned to the moderator, an earnest young woman, who asked, "Your response, Professor Belcher?"

Temple's professor smirked and made a little temple under his chin with his fingertips, a gesture she remembered well from graduate school seminars. "*I* don't feel a personal anger. It's well known that Carolina Smith was hooked on opium and had at least one affair."

"And you don't support the theory that she could have had a close and perhaps long-term relationship with an enslaved man?"

Dr. Belcher shook his head. "The nature of her past behavior speaks for itself."

"Oh, really?" The camera zoomed over to Dr. Trent-Holmes. "Were all Southern *men* who had sexual relations with slave women drug addicts?"

"That's hardly the question here," Dr. Belcher retorted. "Gender determinism isn't very helpful."

Dr. Trent-Holmes pressed her lips into a tight line. The moderator glanced down at her notes. "I see that the Association of Southern Military Historians condemns the story. Dr. Belcher, you're a member of that organization. What exactly do you object to?"

"The so-called evidence that Carolina Smith had an out-of-wedlock child has been improperly handled by the management of Folly Park. This is not objective scholarship but sensationalism at the expense of serious historical work."

Temple's face flushed. She was glad she was alone in the room.

"There's quite a stir about Folly Park," said the moderator. "Many people are giving them credit for being so open. Isn't that courageous?"

Dr. Belcher snorted disdainfully. "Hardly. I know the person responsible—an individual who allows her emotions to cloud her judgment. The supposed evidence for a relationship presented so far is purely speculative and should never have been released without painstaking verification."

Not sure whether to laugh or cry, Temple called Vee, who was still on the road with Matthew. They talked about Wanda, and Temple told her what Dr. Belcher had said. Vee called him some choice names that made Temple laugh. Feeling better after the brief call, she picked up an old *National Geographic* magazine.

A few minutes later someone said her name. "Temple Preston?"

Looking up, Temple found a middle-aged man regarding her with a friendly smile. He was of average height with dark-brown skin and hair graying at the temples. A VOTE POE button pinned to his polo shirt helped her realize she knew who he was—Frank Poe himself.

Temple shook Frank's hand. "It's nice to meet you. Have you come to see how Wanda's doing?"

"Yes. She's a popular volunteer, and word spread fast. Is there any news?"

"Not yet."

"Mind if I wait with you?" Frank Poe settled on a couch across from Temple and opened a book—a copy of *Help Yourself*, she saw. Dozens of colored Post-it notes sprouted from its pages.

"Have you read it?" Frank asked, showing her the cover.

"No, but it seems like everyone else has." Temple hesitated and then added, "Even Beau. Apparently, he's using it to plan his campaign strategy."

"You're thinking if it has something for both me and your brother, it probably has no real value, right?" Frank cocked an eyebrow, and Temple had to laugh. "I was skeptical too. Self-help is so American. The idea you can solve your problems just by reading a book. Probably the truth is we get out of it whatever we put into it."

"What have you gotten out of it? If you don't mind my asking."

"Well, the book leads you through what it calls the doors in your walls. In each so-called room, you identify the thoughts and behaviors that limit you." Frank smiled. "It was empowering. It made me decide to run for mayor."

"I'm glad it helped you."

Frank nodded and Temple returned to her magazine. They sat in companionable silence until Al appeared. He chatted with Frank and ignored Temple, clearly still annoyed with her. An hour later, a nurse came to announce that Wanda had given birth—to twins, a boy and a girl. The three of them cheered and bumped fists.

"I knew she had to have been that huge for a reason!" Al declared.

Betty Jean appeared and reported that Wanda had named the babies Barack and Michelle.

"That's great!" Temple said.

Al shook his head. "Seriously?"

"Names to live up to," said Frank.

Betty Jean planned to stay at the hospital overnight, and Al took her to the vending machines to get a snack. Frank walked out to the parking lot with Temple, climbed into a pickup even older than hers, and drove off with a wave. Arms crossed, she leaned against the door of her truck.

She didn't have long to wait. Al cast a long shadow as he approached, and she saw him scowling under the harsh lights. He was itching for a fight, but Temple didn't care. So was she.

"I'm curious about what you were doing at the developer's office," Temple challenged. "I saw Betty Jean's car there on the way to the hospital."

"I was meeting with Mr. Starkweather," Al said defiantly.

"Why?"

"You know why. I told you how I felt about you stirring up trouble."

"Don't you want to save Folly Park? You and Betty Jean need your jobs, right? Because you don't have a rich father like me."

Al shook his head. And just like that, as Temple saw the exasperated, angry expression on his familiar face, she realized Al didn't care about Folly Park. She had assumed he did because he'd made a living there for thirty-five years. And she had believed him when he said he wasn't bothered that his ancestors had been enslaved there because he didn't care about history. Maybe that was true. But now she understood that Al's relationship with the place was like that of a man stuck in a bad marriage just waiting for an out. Now he had one.

"You're not worried about losing your job anymore, are you?"

"Nope."

"Starkweather offered you one?"

"At the new golf course. I'll get an employee membership."

"You betrayed me for a golf membership?"

"And health care and a retirement plan."

"But you're always saying gated communities are elitist."

Al shrugged.

Temple knew she should walk away then, but she needed to hear him say it. "You don't care that they're going to tear it down, do you?"

Holding her gaze, Al shuffled his feet in a mocking little tap dance. "Well now, Missus, I don' rightly think I do."

Temple climbed into her truck and drove blindly out of the parking lot. A painful lump burned in her throat as anger gave way to sorrow. Her earliest memories were of tagging after Al when he worked for her grandfather, before Folly Park became a tourist attraction. He'd let her prune bushes and hammer nails and dig up pennies he'd buried for her to find. They shared private jokes and spent hours watching baseball games and golf tournaments on television. He was the first person she called when her grandfather died, and he and Betty Jean stayed with her through the long night that followed. Al was her oldest friend. And she had just lost him.

Temple pulled the truck off the road. Wrapping her arms around the steering wheel, she laid her forehead down and cried.

CHAPTER FOURTEEN

Temple averted her eyes from the rocking chair Al had made for her and turned on the news. Outside the barn that served as his campaign headquarters, Frank Poe told a crowd of cheering supporters that if elected, he would "work tirelessly to dismantle shrines to white supremacy in Preston's Mill." He called out the memorial to the Confederate war dead near the courthouse, a stained-glass window depicting a Confederate battle victory in the Presbyterian church, and the plaque at Clyde's commemorating the slave auction block, all installed during Reconstruction—stark warnings to Blacks to remember their place. Frank also named the statue of General Thomas Temple Smith dominating the town square, eloquently describing how it discouraged Black citizens from participating in local events held there.

He was right, Temple knew. Black citizens frequented Magnolia Meadows instead, a park White citizens considered "dangerous." The races didn't mix much in Preston's Mill, except at the smoker Ray Johnson set up at the gas station every Saturday morning. There were Black churches and White churches. White hairdressers and barbers and Black hairdressers and barbers. And there were names and places signaling white supremacy that Frank hadn't mentioned. Temple thought of Black Bottom, the poor section of town beside the river that flooded every spring. There was Coon Creek and Pickaninny Hill and the Little League ballpark named after "Hanging" Judge McIntosh, leader of the 1920s KKK. There was the cemetery marked by a stone archway etched with OUR CONFEDERATE HEROES. And, of course, there was Folly Park—as some might see it, a plantation-sized shrine to the Confederacy.

A reporter asked, "Do you support payments or land grants to the descendants of slaves?"

"I haven't ruled anything out. A reckoning of some kind is long overdue."

Temple felt as if Frank were looking straight into her living room. She had to explain to him how Folly Park could be used to build a better future. She had to tell him about the girls' home. But first, she needed to find out where things stood with her plan.

WHEN TEMPLE IDENTIFIED HERSELF to the staffer who answered the phone, he snapped that Senator Alden would return Judge Preston's call when he had a chance. Temple explained she wasn't calling on behalf of her brother's campaign but rather about a matter she'd been working on with Jack Early. Clearly distracted, the young man said he'd pass along her message and hung up. Temple wondered uneasily why her father had called Senator Alden.

Betty Jean was waiting by Martha's desk when Temple arrived at work. Dressed simply in white Capri pants and a black T-shirt, she hadn't put any effort into devising a signature outfit. She sounded tired when she said, "Can we talk?"

"Of course." Temple ushered Betty Jean into her office. "How was your night? How's Wanda?"

"Wanda and the twins are doing great," Betty Jean said as she sat down. "But that's not why I'm here."

"What's up?" Temple wondered if Al had told her about their confrontation.

Betty Jean looked directly at Temple. "Al asked me to tell you he wasn't coming in today because he's sick. Well, he isn't sick, and I think you know he isn't, and I won't be part of that nonsense."

"Thanks," Temple said, annoyed with Al.

Betty Jean shook her head. "I don't know what happened between you—Al won't tell me. But I know he doesn't like that you're making public what you and Vee are discovering, so I suppose that's the root of it."

Betty Jean held up her hand as Temple opened her mouth. "I don't agree with him. You should find out whatever you can about what happened here and tell the world."

"I wish Al felt that way. But he doesn't care about history."

"Oh, honey." Betty Jean shook her head with a somber smile. "Of course he does. That's why he says he doesn't. You know Al."

It did indeed sound like Al.

"History has hurt him," Betty Jean said. "And I don't mean he's had disadvantages because he's a Black man. I mean his own history, here at Folly Park, hurt him deep down when he was very young."

"What do you mean?"

Betty Jean sighed. "Al's mother used to do your great-grandmother's laundry. And his grandmother, Mary, worked in the kitchen here for years. You knew that, right?"

"Sure. My grandfather told me about Aunt Mary. He loved her fried chicken. But he never mentioned Al's mother."

"Her name was Olivia," said Betty Jean. "Al's first memory is of coming to Folly Park with her when he was four years old. He was going to help pick up the laundry, and he was so proud. They went to the back door, where the kitchen was then. Your grandfather was there with Mary. He was home for Thanksgiving, and he was telling her all about college. Your granddaddy gave Al a cookie—gingersnap, he remembers—and said, 'Aunt Mary, introduce me to this handsome young fellow.' And she said, 'This is my eldest grandbaby, Mr. Chauncey. You tell him your name, child.' Al stood up straight like he'd been taught and said, 'My name is Abraham Lincoln Smith, sir.'"

Betty Jean shook her head slowly, and in her kind brown eyes was an ancient and heartsick weariness. Temple could tell something bad was coming. She picked nervously at the edge of a file folder.

"Your granddaddy looked at that little boy, and he said, 'Abraham Lincoln is the name of a dirty baboon, and I don't ever want to hear it in my house again.'"

The folder slit Temple's finger with a sharp sting. She stared at Betty Jean.

"That night Mary and Olivia stayed up late talking over what to do. They only had the two rooms, and all the kids could hear them. They were afraid they'd lose their places. You know what that would have meant back then. Mary's husband was dead, and Olivia's had gone up North to find work and was killed in a factory accident. If either of them lost a job without a reference, they would never get another one. So, the next day they told Al his name wasn't Abraham Lincoln. From then on, he would be called A.L.—Al."

Temple imagined the little boy coming to the big house to help his mother, skinny and too tall for his age and so proud. And she imagined her grandfather, who had loved her without limit or reserve, saying those hateful words to that little boy. She felt like her heart might shatter.

"Why didn't Al tell me?" Temple's voice was a whisper.

"Don't play the child with me," Betty Jean said sharply. "You know he would never turn you against your granddaddy. He wouldn't want me telling you now. But you needed to hear it before you lose each other for the wrong reasons."

Mutely, Temple watched a drop of blood beading on her finger. Betty Jean fished around in her big woven bag. She pulled out a Band-Aid and set it on the desk. Then she left.

Temple bandaged her finger, trying not to think. If she did, she would start to cry, and she wasn't sure she could stop. She took out Jane's diary. It fell open at November 7, 1860.

Mr. Lincoln is elected. I fear there must now be war.

A few months later, on May 25, 1861, two days after Virginia seceded from the Union, Thomas declared his intention to join the war.

Thomas says he must fight to protect all of us at Folly Park. I argued that protecting slavery is not a just cause, and he said, "I have not the luxury of causes. I am a pragmatist like your Mr. Lincoln. What would become of my people if I did not answer Virginia's call? Do you imagine I could manumit them all and that my neighbors would allow them to pass out of this country unmolested? No, Jane, as they ever have, the pawns will be made to serve the kings." And he swept our pieces from the chessboard and stalked from the room.

Temple put the diary down. The mention of Lincoln had reminded her of Al.

"You look sick," Stuart said from the doorway. He didn't wait for Temple to respond. "There's a flea market or something by our entrance. It looks tacky. Find out what's going on."

Four or five cars had pulled over by a cluster of tables, and other vehicles had to maneuver around them, creating a traffic jam on the narrow road. The situation wasn't helped by people slowing down to take pictures of Colonel Townsend's entire company, lined up in formation across the street.

As soon as they saw Temple, both Colonel Townsend and Jerry Hoyle hurried to intercept her. The colonel was in better shape, and his military quickstep got him to her moments before Jerry's labored jog.

"What's going on?" Temple asked.

"We tried to look past it, we really did." The colonel pursed his lips. "We didn't mind Jerry's nails, because at least he tried to make them look authentic, but the rest of the stuff they're selling is just plain junk. Junk and crafts they're pretending are historical."

Jerry leaned over with his hands on his knees, sweating profusely. "Private property. We can do what we want," he gasped.

"That may be true, Jerry," Temple said, "but the road isn't your property. And the traffic backed up around our entrance is dangerous. Can you please get those cars to pull farther onto the shoulder while I take a look at your stuff?"

"Sure, no problem." Jerry smirked at the colonel and stepped into the road waving his arms.

"Show me what's bothering you," Temple said to Colonel Townsend. He nodded and led her along the row of tables, his distress evident by how hard his jaw was working at a plug of chewing tobacco.

In addition to the fake nails, a quick perusal of Jerry's offerings showed various unidentifiable objects whittled inexpertly from wood. Two tables nearby displayed a variety of cheap "antiques" dating from roughly the mid-twentieth century. Temple recognized Ted, one of Folly Park's volunteers.

"Hi, Temple. I'll give you a discount if you see something you like. How about this?" Ted pointed at a chrome toaster, its cord wrapped with electrical tape.

"No thanks, Ted."

Under his breath, the colonel muttered, "Mountebank."

The next table had an umbrella shading jars full of pickles and preserves made from, according to a sign, FOLLY PARK RECIPES. A table piled high with patchwork quilts advertised they'd been handmade by Folly Park slaves. The last table offered knitted baby booties, caps, and bibs. The proprietress, a fit older woman with short, iron gray hair, vigorously plied a pair of knitting needles. Her sign read: BABY CLOTHES BY CAROLINA.

"See what I mean?" the colonel said in a strangled tone.

"Hi!" Temple said. "You must be Carolina."

Beside her the colonel choked on his tobacco. The woman stood up and stabbed the knitting needles into a ball of yarn. Ignoring Temple, she narrowed her eyes at the colonel and demanded, "Are you here to buy something?"

"Certainly not!"

"Good, because I won't sell anything to you anyway," the woman said loudly. "I don't do business with racists."

Colonel Townsend recoiled as if he'd been shot. "Racists?"

"That's right! Out here in your Confederate uniforms trying to intimidate folks."

Clearly the woman's agenda went beyond selling baby clothes. She was drawing the attention of the tourists.

"I don't—"

"Oh, I'm on to you!" the woman interrupted, shaking her finger. "I grew up here! People like you shut down the schools so they wouldn't have to let the Black kids in. Folks marching for civil rights got beat up. But you don't scare me. I'm an American, and I know my rights!"

At this, Colonel Townsend recovered himself. "Madam, I, too, am an American. I fought for your rights in Vietnam and so did many of those men over there."

"What rights? Whose rights? You're a walking, talking symbol of what's wrong with this country!"

"Hey, lay off!" one of the reenactors called.

"Dot's right!" Jerry shouted back. "You're the reason everyone thinks the South is backward." He gestured toward the camp. "It's embarrassing."

"Oh, let it go," said Ted.

"We always let it go," Dot shot back. "Someone has to stop it." Suddenly she reached across her table, grabbed a handful of Colonel Townsend's beard, and yanked hard. He yelped in pain. Seconds later, someone across the street yelled, "Incoming!" and Temple felt a distinct breeze as a large object whistled past her ear headed straight toward Dot.

The colonel flung himself in front of the missile before it reached its target. Hit on the side of the head with a sickening *thunk*, he fell heavily to the ground. A large potato landed next to him.

Temple dropped to her knees beside the colonel, and

Dot hurried out from behind her table. She grabbed a handful of baby caps and blotted at the blood darkening the hair on one side of his head. Someone shouted, "Call 9-1-1!"

A moment later, a tourist touched Temple's shoulder. "I'm a doctor," she said.

Temple moved aside and looked up to see a teenaged boy hanging out of the window of an SUV filming the scene on his phone. He was laughing.

Five minutes later, a fire truck screamed up, followed soon after by the police. The EMTs conferred with the doctor and the now-conscious colonel, did a quick examination over his protests, and then roared away. Two reenactors helped Colonel Townsend to his tent. One of the policemen went off to direct traffic while the other addressed Jerry, his neighbors, and the reenactors.

"Look, folks. You're going to have to get a business license to keep this yard sale going after three days, but only if the zoning ordinance says you can. In the meantime, you have to get along, or I'm going to shut it all down—the sale and the camp. And you're going to turn over that potato launcher right now," he added sternly.

The reenactors and neighbors grumbled and eyed each other morosely. Temple stepped forward. "Maybe I can help them come to an agreement."

"Is that okay with you all?" the cop asked. A few heads nodded. The cop shrugged. "Good luck."

THE REENACTORS HAD LIT THEIR cooking fire and the neighbors packed up their tables for the night by the time Temple had worked out the final terms of the cease-fire. She'd shuttled back and forth across the road a dozen times and missed lunch to talk to Jerry, who had nominated himself the leader of his group, and Major Hollowell, who was standing in for Colonel Townsend. She listened patiently to every petty grievance.

In the end, Jerry induced his friends to remove false claims of age, attribution, or authenticity from their signs. The reenactors promised to ignore whatever was going on across the street. In return for these concessions, Temple had agreed to sell some of Jerry's nails in the Folly Park gift shop—properly labeled as reproductions—and the reenactors would be permitted to station a representative up at the house to speak with the tourists about the Civil War. The policemen, Tim and Bruce, skeptical the truce would hold, assured Temple they would check back soon.

Exhausted by the negotiations, Temple walked slowly back up the drive. Passing the overseer's house, she kept a wary eye on the door, half dreading, half hoping that Al would come out. But the door remained closed.

Temple thought about her grandfather. How could he have treated Mary and Olivia and little Al so badly? She was ashamed of him and of herself. For only now, only because of what Betty Jean had told her, did she finally admit that the way her grandfather had talked about the past, ever since she was a child, betrayed his fidelity to the cult of the Lost Cause. Its proponents painted the Civil War as an epic clash between two civilizations—the materialistic, industrialized North tragically defeating the honorable, pastoral South. They were nostalgic for a past that never existed, where benevolent masters, devoted to their "people," cared for them throughout their lives. The war had been fought, they claimed, to preserve their culture or to protect states' rights. But Temple was a historian. She knew better. The lost cause they never talked about was the right to buy and sell other human beings.

TEMPLE WAS PICKING AT HER dinner, wishing Vee were there to talk things over with, when her father yanked open the screen door. She hadn't even heard his car. As usual the judge got right to the point.

"What do you think you're doing? I just saw Stuart Sprigg on the news yacking about slave mistresses passed between brothers! What is that nonsense? You're going to foul up this election if you don't shut up."

Her father wore a golf shirt, so Temple figured he must have seen Stuart's interview at the club.

"You mean keep quiet so your developer friends aren't scared off? I can't. I'm trying to save Folly Park."

The judge crunched savagely down on a breath mint. "You're so lost in the past you don't see that Beau could save this whole region's economy, not just one stupid house no one gives a crap about. When are you going to learn that people don't care about history?"

He's wrong, Temple thought. *Al cares about history. The tourists care. And all the people texting and calling and leaving comments on social media. The reenactors and Dot care enough to fight about it.* Temple picked up her plate and set it in the sink before she turned to face her father. "What exactly do you think people care about?"

"To be entertained," the judge snapped. "To forget about their crappy lives and everything that's going wrong in this country. You can't entertain people with this place. All the stuff you've been making up to keep Frank Poe at bay is pathetic. It reeks of desperation."

"I'm not making it up."

The judge's eyes were like chips of flint. "What you don't get is that nobody cares whether you are or not."

"Lots of people care."

The judge snorted derisively. "They only act like they care because they think it makes them look progressive and enlightened to be interested in some biracial baby who was born so long ago nothing about it matters. Pretty soon everyone will get tired of the whole thing and move on to the next scandal or injustice the media is screaming about. And after they've posted their stupid opinions all over social media, they'll just go back to binging on garbage streamed to their phones."

Temple didn't know where to start to combat this barrage of cynicism, but her father wasn't finished.

"Beau's base isn't happy about this. I'm telling you to stop now or there's going to be trouble."

Is that a threat? Temple wondered as she heard another car pull up. She went outside, her father at her heels.

Hunter and Mrs. Glass got out of their white sedan. So did Beau. Like the judge, Hunter and Beau were wearing golf clothes. The Glasses had apparently given Beau a ride from the country club. It was immediately obvious he was quite drunk. Lurching out of the car, he stumbled a few steps before he fell hard on his behind. His dental plate popped out and landed in his lap.

The sight of Beau in the state he was in seemed to snap whatever was left of the judge's self-control. He turned on Temple and let loose a volley of invective. He accused her of purposely sabotaging Beau's chances of winning the election. He declared he was sick and tired of her sentimental liberalism and gullible ignorance. He criticized her profession, her lack of ambition, her embarrassing causes, her personal appearance, and her colossal stupidity in letting Rich get away.

The others appeared to be stunned. Hunter Glass looked back and forth between Temple and her father. Mrs. Glass stared, her face white, while Beau sat slumped on the gravel. Temple did not move and tried to stop hearing. But when her father mentioned her grandfather, his words were like a hot needle stabbing at an open wound.

"You're just like your grandfather. Hiding out here feeling sorry for yourself, mooning over the past, and pretending to write a book no one wants to read. You make me sick!"

Mrs. Glass rushed forward and grabbed the judge's arm. "Stop! Do you hear me? Stop it!"

The judge wrenched out of her grasp. "Stay out of this, Ava."

"I will not! For God's sake, it's downright cruel!"

The judge glared at Mrs. Glass. "It's only your own guilt that makes you stand up for Margaret's daughter."

"Margaret's daughter? Temple is your daughter, too, Harrison, and if you weren't such an ass, you'd know it!"

Hunter put out his hand, as if to restrain her, but Mrs. Glass ignored him. "All the time you thought others were betraying you, you were the one who was cheating. Look what you've done—destroyed your marriage, pushed Harry so hard you may as well have killed him. You're doing the same to Beau, and you're treating Temple just like you did poor Margaret. You've betrayed everyone you love!"

"You talk to *me* about betrayal in front of your husband? That's rich." The judge laughed harshly.

Temple saw Hunter Glass staring at her father with unconcealed loathing.

"Hunt knows about our affair, Harrison," Mrs. Glass said. "I told him the truth—that you were the worst mistake of my life. I told him the same day I told Margaret and drove her to the airport and put her on a plane to New York."

"*You* told her?"

Mrs. Glass didn't seem to care that the judge's fists had clenched, his face twisted with fury. "Yes, I did," she said defiantly.

"You bitch."

Mrs. Glass's hand flew to her mouth.

"That's enough!" Hunter snapped. He put his arm around his wife and led her to the car. After he had settled her in the passenger seat and shut the door, he turned to face the judge. "You're banned from this property, Harrison," he said with cold authority. "I'll have you arrested if you set foot on it again. You and Beau leave right now. I'll be following you."

Stalking to his car, the judge threw himself into the driver's seat.

Hunter handed Beau his dental plate and helped him to his feet. Beau stared blearily at Temple as he fumbled the plate into his mouth. The judge blasted the horn, and Beau shuffled past her.

After both cars had driven away, Temple tottered into the house on legs that felt like rubber. She sank to the floor just inside the door. Her father's viciousness, Mrs. Glass's revelation—she couldn't seem to process what had happened. The whole thing felt unreal. She curled up in a ball on the cracked linoleum.

After a while, Chick yelped at the screen door. Temple got up slowly and let him in. Sensing something wrong, he whined and pushed at her with his wet nose. He was such

226

a nuisance, Temple took a shower to get away from him. It didn't help clear her mind. Her father had a special talent for finding fresh ways to express his cruelty, and one of his barbs had hit the mark and festered. He'd mentioned her grandfather's book.

For as long as Temple could remember, her grandfather had been writing a comprehensive history of the family. They'd had a pact to trade manuscripts when she finished her dissertation, but he didn't live to see that. She hadn't had the heart to look at his book, but now she wanted to. Reading what he'd written about their shared origins might help her somehow regain something of what she'd lost that day. She went to her closet and dug out the sturdy hat box that held his manuscript.

The typed coversheet of the thick stack of yellowing paper read: FOLLY PARK PLANTATION: A HISTORY OF THE LAND AND PEOPLE, BY CHAUNCEY TEMPLE SMITH. Temple turned to Chapter 1. On the first page were two long, single-spaced paragraphs describing, in great detail, the genealogical roots of her ancestors going back to fourteenth-century Great Britain. For the general reader it was probably dull stuff, but the litany of familiar names passed down through generations soothed Temple's raw nerves like a child's favorite bedtime story. Reaching the end of the page, she turned it. The next page was blank. Assuming the paper was stuck together she turned another page. It too was blank.

It took five more randomly selected pages to convince Temple of the truth. Those two paragraphs were the sum total of her grandfather's life work.

CHAPTER FIFTEEN

Eyebrows lifted high, Martha silently handed Temple the *Preston's Mill Progress*. Temple's own copy of the Monday morning paper had been so soaked by dew she hadn't even tried to unroll it. The front-page headline was printed in letters five times their normal size and read: THE WAR IS ON! The accompanying story reported that Beau was calling upon all like-minded people, near and far, to come to a rally in the town square on Saturday. He was fighting back against Frank Poe's "scheme to destroy Southern heritage by removing treasured historic monuments to honor and sacrifice—like his own ancestral home, Folly Park."

Temple felt sick. Beau had chosen to hold his rally on Juneteenth, the holiday commemorating the end of slavery in the United States.

Martha shoved her cell phone under Temple's nose. She'd taken over Folly Park's social media channels for Wanda, and as she scrolled through them, Temple's worst fears were confirmed. Like a contagious disease, news of Beau's rally was spreading fast. Already, the event had been branded the "Rebel Rally" by a white nationalist group recruiting a busload of supporters. The Ku Klux Klan was fielding a contingent, and a biker group called The Cause was traveling from their home base in Georgia.

In response, racial justice advocates posted dire warnings about violence, and Frank Poe's supporters exhorted people to confront "the racist heirs of Nazism." The civil libertarians posted fervid homilies about the difference between free speech and hate speech. These voices were countered by the Heirs of Confederate Veterans, who lauded Beau's efforts to "prevent the erasure of the history and legacy of the Southern cause." There were also profanity-laced cries to "shut down lying liberals once and for all." A number of reenactors planned to come out to support Colonel Townsend and his men in response to a viral video titled REDNECK CONFEDERATE SHOT IN HEAD that neglected to note the incident was a case of friendly fire. Various pundits and talk-show personalities had also lobbed their soundbites into the online melee.

Appalled, Temple hunted desperately for an official announcement or any other sign that Beau's campaign denounced the venom of the public discussion or discouraged the participation of hate groups at the rally. She found none. Beau didn't answer when she called his cell, and Pixie and Julia's phones went directly to voicemail.

WHEN TEMPLE PULLED INTO Frank Poe's yard twenty minutes later, the barnyard was buzzing with young men and women talking urgently into phones or frenetically tapping on laptops. A group of older campaign volunteers had been sidelined to stuff envelopes at a picnic table.

The young people swarmed around Temple. "What are you doing here?" one of them challenged.

"I just want to talk to Frank. I'm not involved with my brother's campaign."

"You expect us to believe that? You live in a shrine to white supremacy!" a young woman scoffed, and others added jeers and insults. Temple stood silently under the barrage.

Emerging from the farmhouse, Frank Poe waded through his supporters. "What's going on here?"

"Can we talk?" Temple asked.

His manner quite a few degrees chillier than it had been at the hospital, Frank brusquely agreed to give her five minutes.

"How are Wanda and the twins doing?" Frank asked when Temple sat down across from his desk in a cozy room lined with bookcases.

Temple assured him they were fine. Then she got to the point. She told Frank that Beau had no real interest in saving monuments. He and her father had been talking to developers about Folly Park, proof they were just using the issue to drum up votes. She said she hoped Frank could see his way to leaving the house off his targeted list. Not only would it escalate tensions to go after such a popular local site, it could derail an initiative she believed he would support. Temple told Frank about her plan for the girls' home, and Senator Alden's interest. She offered to share credit with him when the deal was done.

Behind his desk, Frank listened impassively. "I appreciate you telling the truth about Folly Park's history," he said. "And the girls' home is a nice idea. But it's too late now."

"It's just a few weeks."

"I mean it's years late. Decades. A century. Do you have any idea what my folks went through to hang onto this farm since Reconstruction? They had to train dogs to keep the

230

Klan away. My great-uncle was lynched. My grandfather was beaten and left for dead. My mother had to prove title in court twice. And we're the lucky ones."

Stricken with shame, Temple said in a small voice, "I want to help."

"We're past that. Your brother started a war."

Frank stood, signaling her time was up. At the front door, he said, "We're organizing a counterprotest for the rally, and things could get ugly. Maybe you should sit it out."

DRIVING BACK THROUGH PRESTON'S MILL, Temple passed a dozen people in front of the general's statue waving signs calling for its removal. Her stomach lurched. But she couldn't think about that now. Being out of joint with Al and Betty Jean was bad enough. She couldn't lose another old friend.

Mrs. Glass was in the sun porch, lying on a chaise in a dressing gown, her silver-gray hair gathered into an untidy chignon. Without makeup, Temple could see networks of tiny lines in her face. When the green marble eyes opened, they quickly filled with tears.

"Oh, darling, can you ever forgive me?"

"There's nothing to forgive."

Mrs. Glass drew a tissue from her pocket and blotted the corners of her eyes.

Temple sat down on a rattan chair. "I need to know about my parents."

"Don't confuse needs with wants," said Mrs. Glass. "You don't need to know. But I believe Margaret would want me to tell you." She gazed past Temple, where a man was clipping the boxwood hedges in the garden.

"Your mother told me she was not happily married for a single hour. Being with your father was soul-crushing. That was the exact phrase she used. I've always remembered it." Mrs. Glass shook her head. "They married without really knowing each other. Because of her beauty and reserve, people always assumed your mother was more sophisticated than she was. Your father was handsome and charming, and he was older and used to getting his way."

Mrs. Glass told Temple that her mother had quickly discovered her husband wanted her only to be a social ornament, a prop for his career ambitions. The only time she didn't feel invisible was when he was annoyed or disappointed in her, and that was often.

"After years of failing to please him, Margaret realized she would never succeed. She withdrew, went back to painting, and spent more time in her studio at Folly Park. She loved you and your brothers, but she said it became harder and harder for her to go back home."

Mrs. Glass shook her head. "I know this is difficult to hear. But your mother told me some part of her was relieved when she was diagnosed. It gave her an excuse to leave your father, to move back to Folly Park, where she could feel wholly herself even while she was dying."

Temple was too young when her mother got sick to understand exactly why her father's presence was so oppressive, but she knew what it was like to live with him—senses on high alert trying to anticipate what he might want her to do or say or be at any given moment. Steeling herself for criticism that always came and wishing for approval that never did. Learning to hide her feelings. But Temple felt differently at Folly Park, lighter and freer. She'd begged to go live there with her mother. But her father said it was a selfish whim, and she was not to mention it again.

"She worried about you, Temple," Mrs. Glass said. "Harry was so adept at pleasing he would always find a way to get along, and Beau had already made himself a carbon copy of your father. But she was afraid your dad would bully you because you were your grandfather's favorite."

Temple didn't want to talk about her grandfather. "Did he hurt you too?"

Mrs. Glass smoothed the skirt of her dressing gown. "I've always known that nothing about Harrison is sincere, and he's incapable of feeling deeply. But Hunter and I hit a rough patch, and I wanted to punish him. He'd never liked your dad." Mrs. Glass shook her head sharply. "I want you to know, Temple, that Hunter got involved on the board of Folly Park to try to help you in a career you seemed to want."

"He did?"

"He intended to promote you when Dr. Tate retired, but your father found out and was so unpleasant—he didn't want you tied to Folly Park—that Hunter didn't go through with it. He worried your dad would take it out on you."

Temple understood now why Hunter Glass had always been so distant. He'd tried to shield her from her father without angering him. It was an impossible balancing act. "I owe you both so much."

"Enough of that," Mrs. Glass said briskly. "Here I am lying around in my dressing gown past noon like a Hollywood starlet. Let's have lunch and catch up. I've been watching the news."

TIM, THE POLICEMAN DIRECTING traffic by Folly Park's front gate, flagged Temple down when she slowed to turn in the driveway. Colonel Townsend wanted to see her.

When she'd found her way to his tent, the colonel thanked Temple for coming and seated her on an uncomfortable camp stool. He offered her a cup of muddy-looking coffee and hardtack, a dense cracker eaten by Civil War soldiers. She politely declined.

"How are you feeling?" Temple asked.

"I'm fine." The colonel waved his hand dismissively at the bandage wrapped around his head. "This little cut is the least of it. I never meant to stir up bad feelings. The camping is supposed to be fun, to feel what it was like to be in our ancestors' shoes." He sighed heavily. "That's what I wanted to tell you. We just wanted to be sure you were doing the research to get things right."

"I understand. I've always appreciated your passion for history."

"You know, I discovered two of my great-greats fought for the North," the colonel said, cutting a fresh plug of tobacco. "The others were Confederates. One was shot as a deserter two weeks before Appomattox." The colonel chewed reflectively. "They couldn't see it at the time because they were living their lives the only way they knew how, but their cause was wrong. I've never wished the South won the war. But that woman—Dot—made me realize how what we're doing looks to people. And it can be hurtful to some folks. I told my men that."

"How did they take it?"

"Well, unfortunately, some of them decided to leave. They feel I'm betraying our heritage." The colonel shook his head. "Looking at history differently when new information comes to light isn't betrayal, it's reality. But it can be hard. The reality for a lot of them is good jobs gone, development hiking up prices. They don't have any part of the American dream, and they don't know who to blame. They're spoiling for a fight."

"My brother is using Folly Park to get votes by race baiting. Some people will fall for it."

"It's the times. Folks feel like it's okay to be ugly with each other." The colonel spat toward the open flap of his tent. He missed, and the thick brown juice hit the canvas and oozed toward the ground. "But it'll swing back the other way. We've got to believe in the better angels of our natures—as Mr. Lincoln put it."

DESPITE WANDA'S ABSENCE, Betty Jean had everything under control. She was even keeping up a cheerful running patter with the visitors while she issued tickets and gave directions. Today, her commentary included an invitation to sign a petition.

Alarmed, Temple hurried over to look at the petition posted near the door. It called for "the expeditious removal of Confederate memorials, monuments, signs, names, and any other remnants of institutionalized racism, white supremacy, and Jim Crow laws from the town of Preston's Mill and environs." Temple took it down during a brief lull when she and Betty Jean were alone.

"Come on, Temple." Betty Jean shook her head and her earrings—silver thunderbolts—danced with indignation.

"It's just not a good idea. A lot of these tourists are diehard fans of the general."

"You don't think I've had to deal with bigots before?" Betty Jean snorted. "All the little things they do? Making me put their change down so they don't have to touch my hand. Pretending they can't hear me talking to them. Flora coming to work every day dressed up like a plantation mistress, asking me why I won't wear period clothing, too, so I'll look like a slave. No, don't you worry, Temple. I can handle it."

Betty Jean had never said a word about the mistreatment she faced working at Folly Park. But Temple had never asked. She felt her cheeks flush. Her failure to ensure a safe work environment was reprehensible. But letting Betty Jean continue to promote the petition with Beau's rally coming up was downright dangerous.

"I'm sorry about what you've been dealing with. It's terrible, and I should have addressed it," Temple said. "But for your own safety, I can't let you keep the petition up, even though I sympathize with your cause."

"You sympathize? Really?" Betty Jean crossed her arms under the VOTE POE button, eyebrows raised skeptically.

Temple blinked hard to keep back tears. Snatching up a pen, she scrawled *Temple Tayloe Smith Preston* across three lines on the petition. Slapping it down in front of Betty Jean, she pushed through a clump of tourists to get out the door.

Temple blew her nose and took a moment to pull herself together before going into the administration building. It was impossible to feel right again until she could have an honest talk with both Al and Betty Jean. But that would have to wait.

Stuart's office door was open, and his voice boomed pompously. Martha rolled her eyes. "He's got some poor child from the *Progress* trapped in there with him."

Glancing into the room, Temple saw Stuart leaning against the edge of his desk stroking his tie. A young woman seated in front of him held her cell phone out to record his pontificating about how Folly Park could participate in the complex national conversation about race.

His speech didn't interest Temple, but Stuart himself caught her attention. He seemed different. She looked for a reason why and found many. He had removed his glasses and apparently replaced them with tinted contact lenses, giving his brown eyes a smoky hue. He wore an expertly cut suit in a beautiful shade of blue that somehow made him look taller and slimmer. His new tie was elegant, and he had a fresh haircut. Stuart noticed Temple gaping just beyond the door and shot her a smug grin.

"He credits his transformation to that book *Help Yourself*," Martha said sourly. "It's amazing what a tailored suit can do. He looks almost human."

Temple went into her office and shut the door so she wouldn't have to listen to Stuart. She took Jane's diary from her work bag. There were only a few entries left to read. As the two women struggled to operate the plantation during the war, Jane probably had less time and energy to write. There were months in which she hadn't written anything at all.

December 21, 1862

Some of the field hands have run off. Others are sullen and slack, and I do not know what would become of us if King did not make them work. The house servants take advantage, and Jewel goes defiantly every evening to the Prestons' to see Bub-Bub, instead of only on Saturday night. Carolina refuses to punish the girl for being in love, she says. I spoke to King about his daughter, but he listened impatiently, so I know that he, too, will do nothing.

All the servants have Carolina's leave to attend the Christmas Eve festivities at Wild Oaks. Lad Preston will be home for the holiday, and the people hope he will find a way to offer a semblance of former revelries, though of course he cannot. Like tea and coffee and salt, there are no delicacies to be had for love or money, and no one has the heart for a dance, even if musicians could be found. Those days, I fear, will return no more. Oh, those happy times that seem half an age ago! But we are thankful that Thomas, too, is to come home, and Carolina and I will stay to meet him. Declining the invitation was no doubt a relief to Agatha Preston, for Carolina's beauty still outshines all, even in gowns three years old!

December 23, 1862

Carolina and I have quarreled. She came to scold that I must rest and insists I am ill. But I cannot rest! The horses are gone to the army, we have eaten all the hogs, and our stores of grain are dangerously low. How will we feed our people if I do not labor? Carolina—worn to a shade herself, she is so thin—declared with tears and temper that I will kill myself. She is overtaxed with cares, I know, but her anxiety does scrape upon my nerves!

December 24, 1862

I am greatly discomposed. Carolina departed this morning before I woke. Never before has she held a disagreement so long. And this of all days, for Thomas comes tonight—his first visit home in nearly a year. What can she be thinking?

As if written in haste, the very last entry was sloppy, the paper marred by inkblots and water stains, perhaps tears.

2 am, Christmas morn. 1862

C—

I know you will seek answers here, and so I give them to you.

How could you have treated me so? Stealing away to Aunt Harriet's while I slept was beneath you. Whose need, or weakness rather, did you serve by leaving me to meet Thomas alone? What a bitter night that took you both from me! For he is not the man I thought he was. You and he both—whom I have loved more than my own soul—have betrayed me.

I see now that I have been foolish as well as craven, but I am resolved. I leave Folly Park forever. Do not try to find me.

J.

Leaning back in her chair, Temple stared up at the cracks in the corner of the ceiling. Then she read the entries over again, carefully measuring the words. And she came to a conclusion. She had uncovered a love triangle.

Thomas had come home for Christmas and was met by Jane. Carolina had arranged for them to be alone together, maybe because she believed they were in love. Whether generosity or spite prompted her actions, either motive explained why she herself may have ended up in the arms of another man—perhaps King. But Jane had been upset by Carolina's maneuver and by her encounter with Thomas.

Temple wondered how he had behaved when he came home war-weary and found only Jane. What did he do to make her leave, and where did she go?

Temple intended to share her discovery with Vee, of course, but she was reluctant to make it public yet. It seemed too dangerous now to suggest that the general may not only have harbored, but also been in love with, his abolitionist cousin.

ARRIVING HOME AT THE END of the day, Temple found Julia's car parked in front of her house. She was not in the mood for another confrontation about Rich, but when her cousin got out of the car, she saw that this was going to be worse. When they were six years old, Julia had accidentally broken a crystal trophy in the judge's office and told him Temple had done it. He'd ignored his daughter's indignant denial, and Julia watched Temple receive a harsh spanking with the identical gloating expression mixed with a dash of pity that was on her face now. Julia was going to hurt her.

Behind the screen door, Chick whined to be let out. Temple hushed him.

"I'm sorry to have to tell you this," Julia said.

"Tell me what?"

"Jack went back to New York to be with his wife. I was dropping off campaign stuff, and I started chatting with Senator Alden's assistant. She said it was some kind of medical issue."

Temple said nothing.

Julia gripped Temple's arm. "I only told you so you wouldn't have to hear it from someone else. I didn't want to hurt you."

Temple looked directly into her cousin's slate-gray eyes. "Yes, you did." Twisting out of Julia's grasp, she went into the house and shut the door. A minute later the car drove away, leaving her alone.

CHAPTER SIXTEEN

"I can tell by your voice that something's wrong. What is it?" Temple closed her office door and told Vee what Julia had said about Jack the night before. "I feel so stupid," she said. "Not that I believed he's separated, and he may not be. Who knows what's really going on? I feel stupid because I did this to myself. Pretended there was more to it than there was because it felt nice to escape from everything that's been going on. It isn't any different from having a crush on a dead general."

"Don't be so hard on yourself. Jack is really nice, and he obviously likes you. You didn't just create a fantasy out of nothing."

"I'm not sure that's true, but thanks." Temple sighed.

Vee kindly changed the subject. "I can't seem to get away from basements," she said dryly. "The Marais Parish Historical Society happens to be located in the basement of a church. It's only open a few days a week, so I'll have time to do some research on my family in New Orleans."

Temple wished Vee luck with her research and hung up. She scrolled listlessly through her email messages, three of which suggested she resign from her job. It was hard to

242

get motivated to work after that, and she was relieved when Martha interrupted with a FedEx delivery.

The box was from the Alliance Historical Society in Ohio and contained scanned copies of Adeline Cavanaugh's correspondence, including nearly one hundred letters from her devoted fiancé, Gilbert Wheeler. Over the next few hours, Temple read them all.

Benjamin Elliot appeared frequently in the letters. According to Gil, Ben was often sickly, sometimes so much that he was unable to rise in the morning, but on other days he possessed a hectic energy. The entire camp was impressed by the young man's superior riding abilities, and so everyone was surprised when Ben was thrown from his horse one day. Brought back to camp unconscious, he was turned over to Gil rather than the camp doctor, in whom nobody had much confidence. When he attempted to ascertain the extent of the boy's injuries, Gil was shocked to discover that, he wrote, "Ben is a <u>WOMAN</u>!"

"Jane!" Temple exclaimed.

As she tried to absorb the implications of this amazing discovery, Temple recalled that she'd come across other women in her Civil War research who took on aliases and disguised themselves as men to enlist in the army. Some joined because they believed in the cause or to collect the bounty money, others craved adventure or wanted to escape an abusive home, and some wanted to be with their husbands or lovers. If they made it past lax recruiters, who rarely ordered anyone to strip for their medical evaluation, a woman could cut her hair short and bind her breasts under her uniform. She could remain undiscovered indefinitely because soldiers slept in their clothes, bathed in their underwear, and went for weeks without changing either.

One female enlistee Temple had read about even wore a false mustache, although with so many underage boys in the ranks, a lack of facial hair didn't attract undue attention.

Temple wondered again what had happened between Thomas and Jane that Christmas night to make Jane run away from Folly Park and become a soldier. *Jane was the Union dispatch carrier captured by General Smith's men,* Temple realized. *Thomas must have recognized her when she was brought to his tent, and he smuggled her through the lines, back to Folly Park.*

Reading about Jane's transformation and courage had given Temple a new sense of resolve. She didn't have time to think about Jack or worry about people who wanted her fired. She had things to do.

PIXIE WAS ON THE PHONE WHEN Temple arrived at Beau's campaign headquarters, and she waggled her fingers in greeting. Across the room, Beau lounged with his feet up on a desk while he talked at a clutch of staffers.

"Here's my lovely sister," Beau said. "Give us a minute, guys."

When his acolytes had returned to their own desks, Beau said coldly, "What're you doing here?"

"Just hear me out," Temple said. "You must know that hate groups are planning to come to your rally—white nationalists, neo-Nazis, the KKK."

Beau popped his dental plate and shrugged.

"Please, Beau." Temple put her hand on his arm. Beau stiffened, but he didn't shake her off, no doubt aware of how it would look to his staff. "I'm sure you want the rally to be peaceful, but things are getting out of control. These people are dangerous."

"I'm surprised. I'm trying to save Folly Park, but you don't seem to appreciate it."

"This has nothing to do with Folly Park."

"Oh, I disagree. You might want to pretend you're above it all, but Folly Park is a target. I'll call off the rally if Frank Poe stops trying to tear down our monuments." Beau narrowed his eyes. "But I'm guessing you already begged him to leave the place alone, and it was a no-go. That's why you're here talking to me. Right?"

Temple said nothing.

"I thought so. And pandering to him with that biracial baby story didn't work either. Well, we've got a right to free speech too. You might finally want to get on board with my campaign, Temp. We're your last chance to save that dump."

Has it come to this? Temple wondered. *Folly Park can only be saved by aligning with neo-Nazis?* "At least take precautions," she pleaded. "The local police can't handle it. Reach out to the governor."

"You've got to be kidding. I'm running for mayor, and I call in the National Guard for my own rally? I'd look like an idiot."

"Can't you forget about how it looks for one minute?" Temple's voice rose. "People could get hurt!"

The campaign workers were openly staring. Beau hissed, "Keep your voice down. You're overreacting. You libs are afraid of regular folks just because they disagree with you."

"This is different, and you know it. The Ku Klux Klan is coming."

"Those guys are all hot air. They're not out to hurt anyone." With an icy stare, Beau added, "As long as you don't drag the general down in the dirt with his wife."

DRIVING BACK TO WORK, Temple tried to convince herself that Beau knew his constituents better than she did, but she was sure he was wrong. Anxious and distracted, she barely registered the strange car parked in front of the administration building.

Martha put her finger to her lips when she saw Temple and tilted her head toward Stuart's office. The door was open, and inside Temple saw the back of a large, muscular man in some sort of military uniform. His deep voice had an intensely irritated tone, and Stuart stood with his head hanging before this commanding presence. Martha nodded decisively at the end of every sentence the stranger delivered with a smile of grim satisfaction.

". . . slipshod operation you're running here. Out of the blue, I get a notice from my insurance company that someone named Ward Hand has filed a claim for an accident involving one of my cars at this address—Vee's car. But she doesn't answer my calls or my texts. In the meantime, I'm hearing all kinds of crazy talk about a white supremacist rally. I fly down here to find out what the hell is going on, and the first thing I see after I pass a goddamn Confederate army camp is my daughter's banged-up car. I'm asking myself, 'Is she hurt or, God forbid, worse?' I come in here—reasonably expecting answers from the director of this place—and all you can tell me is that Vee works here and lives here too, but you have no idea where she is?"

When Vee's father paused for breath, Stuart risked a wary glance up at him and caught sight of Temple. He bounded to the doorway and pulled her into the room. "Ask her!"

"Vee is absolutely fine, Colonel Williams," Temple said. "I promise."

"Who are you?" The colonel looked her up and down.

Behind the sharp tone, Temple could see, was a very worried father.

"Let me explain." Quickly and concisely, Temple told the colonel about Vee's fender bender and inviting Vee to live with her. She described their research and said that Vee was smart and conscientious and that they had become good friends.

The tension ebbed from the colonel's face as Temple spoke. When she finished, he said, "You say she's in Louisiana?"

"Yes. I thought it was better that she go. Better for our research, I mean," Temple amended hastily for Stuart's benefit.

The colonel's lip twitched as he glanced at Stuart. "I understand. She can get so buried in the past, I worry sometimes she doesn't see what's going on around her."

Temple smiled ruefully. "I do the same."

Colonel Williams nodded. "Well, I'm glad *you* seem to have things under control." He looked pointedly at Stuart, who squinched nervously.

Temple was acutely aware she didn't have anything under control, but it wouldn't help to say so.

"I should leave you to your work," the colonel said, hesitating.

"Would you like to talk to Vee?" Temple asked. "I can call her right now."

"She'll be upset I came here."

"I'm sure she doesn't want you to worry." Temple texted a quick message to Vee. "Let's go outside."

When Vee answered, Temple handed the phone to Colonel Williams. Stepping away to give him privacy, she watched the tourists wandering up the drive.

When the colonel returned Temple's phone, he frowned. "Vee asked me to make sure you're all right," he said. "She thinks you might be in some sort of danger."

Temple shook her head. "I'm fine."

A teenage boy wearing a rebel flag T-shirt stopped a few feet away. He stared insolently at Colonel Williams while he slowly chewed a wad of gum with his mouth wide open. The colonel stared stonily back until someone called from up the drive. The boy made a crude gesture and sauntered away.

"I'm so sorry," Temple said wearily.

"Goddamn South," the colonel muttered as he turned back to her. "I can make a few calls. Get some private security for you until after that rally."

"Thanks, but it's not necessary."

Colonel Williams pressed a business card into her hand. "You put my number in your phone right now. And you call me if you need help. Day or night."

Temple smiled weakly. "Yes, sir."

By the time Colonel Williams's car had disappeared around the bend in the drive, Temple had added his number to her contacts. Then she hurried after the boy who'd challenged him, hoping to forestall any unpleasantness at the ticket office.

Temple arrived to hear Betty Jean say, ". . . special tour with our head guide Flora. If you'll just wait outside, she'll be with you shortly."

It didn't appear as if the boy had given Betty Jean any trouble, but she called Temple over as soon as the family left.

"Flora's having some sort of a meltdown, and I've got a line of guests backed up. You know I send folks like them to her." Betty Jean jerked her head toward the door. "And there are more around lately because of your brother."

"I'm so sorry," Temple said for the second time in five minutes. "I'll talk to Flora."

Temple found Flora with Fred in the docents' lounge.

Her satin gown was rumpled, and her mascara had run, as if she'd been crying.

"What's going on?" Temple asked.

Immediately Flora started to sniffle. Fred threw up his hands. "Guests are complaining she won't answer any questions about the baby. I had to give six refunds this morning."

"I don't want to spread that nasty gossip," Flora moaned. "The house and grounds are so beautiful. The general was a hero. Why do people only want to tear things down?" She blew her nose into a lace handkerchief.

"Betty Jean assigns guests who want a more traditional tour to you," Temple said impatiently. "But we also need you to do the updated one. We don't have enough guides."

"Why can't we just go back to the way it was? Everything was fine before that girl came."

"This is not about Vee. We owe it to the public to tell the truth. And that means making changes when we find new evidence."

"But it's not the most important thing about the house. The servants are only a small part of the story."

"'Enslaved people,' not 'servants,'" Fred said, exasperated. "We've talked about this a thousand times."

"Ignoring the baby is not an option," Temple said. "And we'll be updating all the tours because the enslaved people were always a very big part of the story. Should I assume you don't want to continue working here?"

Flora gasped and stared. Thinking of Colonel Williams, Temple crossed her arms and stared stonily back. After a moment, Flora shook her head.

Craving solitude for her frayed nerves, Temple found refuge in the basement. It was looking much better since Vee had taken charge. Nearly every file cabinet, shelf, and box had a color-coded label in her neat handwriting. Temple chose a plastic bin of plantation records. Dull accounts and business letters were about all she could handle. But, after an hour spent scanning dozens of documents relating to a variety of nonevents in the commercial life of the plantation, Temple found a shocking letter that changed everything.

Carolina's father had written to his new son-in-law a few months after Thomas and Carolina had married.

Sept. 27th, 1859

Dear Nephew,

I am indeed sorry that you are displeased by the measures I have taken to safeguard my daughter's health and honor, but you have no right to accuse me of deception in the matter. I have never sought to conceal Carolina's faults, and I believed I had told you all you desired to know. However, as you insist on pursuing this indelicate subject, I will do my best to satisfy you.

You will recall that at the time we arranged the dowry, I informed you that my daughter was not virgin. You assured me it did not dissuade you from marrying her, and you evinced no curiosity about the circumstances of her despoliation. Recall that I asked you twice again if you were certain that at some future time you would not wish to know, and that each time you demurred. Now, however, you demand a "full accounting." The reason for your application, you maintain, is because Carolina avows that laudanum "forced upon her at the time" has clouded her memory of the particulars. Whether this be truthful or not, I leave to your own judgment.

Now, here is your <u>full accounting</u>. It pains me to say so, but Carolina has always been a flirt. To no avail, the usual remedies were applied: camphor compresses, cold water enemas, seaside bathing, etc. My wife endeavored to keep a close watch over Carolina, but failed in the case of the man Steele, an itinerate music instructor, who ingratiated himself with the families of this neighborhood. A libertine and a cad, he compromised my daughter. After this regrettable incident, our family physician, Dr. Theophilus Gunn, who has served us with care and discretion for many years, advised that Carolina's propensities be curbed medically. On my behalf, he wrote to Dr. J.D. Sykes, a Specialist in Female Disorders engaged for many years in experimentations on slave wenches, who are immune to pain. With the utmost delicacy and privacy, Dr. Sykes performed his operation on Carolina, though with the use of Ether, of course. He was confident that the procedure, in concert with the laudanum he prescribed, would keep her modest, mild, and of proper feminine temper. I applied to him recently on your behalf, and he again assured me that the risk of the surgery rendering her permanently barren was slight, and he saw no indications of such an outcome in my daughter's case.

I do not hesitate to assure you, therefore, that though they may be considered a credit to your sensibility, your scruples are misplaced. You must take a stronger line with Carolina if you wish to consummate your marriage. Do not be dissuaded by her protests and cries, for it is likely she dissembles. She appears to have also deceived this Richmond physician you have consulted. His assertion that "she can never bear children, nor even engage in the marital act without considerable pain," is utter nonsense.

*I believe this explanation must satisfy you. It remains
only to be said that the offensive manner in which you judge
my actions—"monstrously inhumane" are your precise
words—leaves me no choice but to break off further communication unless strictly related to matters of business.*

Yours & c.,
William Gilmore

Temple threw the letter aside, disgusted. She got up
and paced around the basement. Given the sickening details
she'd read, and disregarding the self-serving arguments of
Carolina's father that the operation had not affected her, it
seemed unlikely poor Carolina ever could have given birth.
That meant they still had no idea who was the mother—or
indeed the father—of the child, Robert. They were right
back where they'd started.

Temple's phone rang. When she answered, Stuart
barked, "Get down to the reenactors camp now!"

Hurrying down the driveway, Temple wondered what
she would find. Jerry Hoyle had managed to obtain a sales
permit, quashing the reenactors hopes for a bureaucratic
end to the standoff. He and his neighbors, Dot in particular,
had been rubbing it in for days. *Did someone finally snap?*

Later, Temple learned that the cops, Tim and Bruce,
had been called away to deal with a protest by Frank Poe's
supporters at the Southern Comfort Café. Dot had taken
the opportunity to cross the street and dismantle one of
the tents. When the reenactors attempted to stop her, she
screamed that she was being attacked, and her neighbors
came to the rescue. Soon people were yelling and shoving.
Tables overturned and tents collapsed under wrestling

bodies. Horns blared and tourists abandoned their vehicles in the middle of the street to join the fight.

When she arrived on the scene, Temple pushed into the crowd, shouting for people to stop. No one paid any attention. She looked desperately for Jerry or Colonel Townsend, but she couldn't find them. Beside her, someone yelped with surprise, and she turned to see the woman who sold quilts attach herself to Major Hollowell's back like an oversized tick. Temple wrapped her arms around the woman's waist and tried to pull her off.

A moment later, everyone froze in shock, gasping under a deluge of cold water. Al had arrived with his portable watering cart and turned the hose full on, abruptly ending the altercation.

The *woot-woot* of a siren signaled the return of Tim and Bruce. They herded the tourists back to their cars and the two groups to opposite sides of the road. Temple straddled the yellow line, soaked and bedraggled, until Tim pulled her to the shoulder. Anybody who crossed the road again, he warned, no matter what the provocation, would be charged with assault. The reenactors and Jerry's group glared at each other across the asphalt divide.

That night, someone hung bananas on nooses from the lampposts surrounding the town square. The next morning, the town council held an emergency meeting, and while Frank Poe and his supporters rallied outside the town hall, a vandal spray-painted a swastika on the side of his barn. In the evening, a fraternity at the university staged an "ironic" minstrel show, resulting in the retaliatory breaking of every windowpane in their house. Closer to home, Temple found a dead rabbit on her doormat and tried to convince herself it had expired there of natural causes.

Then the biker group The Cause arrived. They tore up the grass on the square and did wheelies down side streets. Three of them were arrested when they started a fight in the Thomas Temple Bar. Everyone was on edge. The only tourists at Folly Park had come to town for the rally. They seemed to view themselves as crusaders, and some treated the house as if it were their own. Fred found one man sprawled in the general's chair in the library smoking a cigar. They challenged the tour guides about the biracial baby, driving one to quit in tears. Thankfully, Betty Jean agreed to temporarily stop wearing her VOTE POE button, and she'd arranged to have Wanda and the twins stay with her aunt temporarily when she was discharged from the hospital. Temple took over the other cash register whenever she could to keep an eye on things. The nightly news was filled with the upcoming rally. Temple did not sleep.

CHAPTER SEVENTEEN

Setting down her orange juice, Temple stared tensely at the phone buzzing on the table until it stopped. She needed an update on her plan, but she wasn't ready to talk to Jack. Unable to finish her breakfast, she left for work.

When Temple arrived at the office, Stuart was haranguing Martha about expense reports—his default complaint if he was upset about something else.

"Nice of you to finally show up at. . . ." Stuart made a show of consulting his watch, "Nine thirteen. We need to go. Hunt wants to see us."

Temple followed Stuart outside, where his vintage Mercedes station wagon was parked in his designated spot closest to the door. As the car chugged down the drive, Stuart speculated about why Hunter had summoned them. He was worried the trustees had decided to shut down Folly Park for good. Temple feared he might be right.

At the end of the drive, the reenactors' camp was quiet, the tents closed up tight. Jerry Hoyle and his remaining neighbors were doing a lively trade, and Jerry waved cheerfully as the car inched out onto the road. The police cruiser was not there this morning.

Driving half on the accelerator and half on the brake all the way into Preston's Mill, Stuart squealed to an abrupt stop in front of the town square. The car's engine promptly died.

People milled around in the road, ignoring traffic. Up ahead, Temple spotted a cluster of men in gray. Colonel Townsend's troops had come into town. Police cars were parked at the corners of the streets entering the square.

"What the. . . ?" said Stuart, and then Temple saw it. Or rather, didn't see it.

The statue of General Smith was gone. The concrete pedestal etched with HE FOUGHT FOR FREEDOM still squatted in the middle of the grassy square, but the bronze statue had vanished.

Temple stared, and Stuart stared, and after a while they realized a policeman had cleared the intersection and was waving them on. With the cars behind honking and the cop glaring, Stuart finally managed to start the engine after four tries. Wrenching at his tie as if he were choking, he didn't say a word in the few short blocks to the Glass mansion.

The young woman who answered the doorbell led them to the library, a dark-paneled room in the rear of the house overlooking the swimming pool. Cool and inscrutable as always, Hunter Glass ushered Temple and Stuart to a set of comfortable chairs. Fruit and muffins were arrayed on a low table, and the young woman poured coffee into china cups. As soon as she had gone, Stuart burst out, "Did you hear about the statue?"

"Yes," said Hunter as he gestured for them to sit.

"It must have been Frank Poe's people." Stuart distractedly dumped heaping spoonfuls of sugar into his coffee. "But it's hard to believe those stoned-out hip-hopsters could pull it off without anyone seeing." He stirred his coffee frenetically, the metal spoon striking the fine bone china with the *rat-a-tat* of a miniature machine gun.

Wincing, Hunter said, "No doubt people did see but are choosing not to say anything. That kind of operation would require quite a few individuals and some heavy equipment. But the statue isn't why I asked you both to come here today. I have other news."

Stuart froze, spoon suspended.

"The board wants to sell," Temple said. "The developers have gotten to them."

"Actually, no," Hunter replied. "But the crux of the matter remains. The mansion's condition is bordering on dangerous. Even if the recent influx of tourism dollars continues indefinitely, which seems unlikely, it would be years before we'd have enough funds to do the necessary work." He glanced at them before he went on. "However, the trustees are committed to holding on to Folly Park. We had a special meeting last night, and the vote was unanimous."

"That's great!" Stuart blurted, spewing crumbs.

"I don't understand," Temple said blankly.

"I was surprised myself," Hunter admitted. "As it turns out, the other trustees are rather annoyed at Frank Poe's petition. They feel it's the wrong way to go about this kind of thing—a bit aggressive and fomenting discord among neighbors. Coming on top of the relentless pressure from the Massachusetts Bay Development Company, it was the last straw. They feel besieged and are inclined to double down."

"I thought they'd come around," Stuart said smugly. "You didn't think they would, Temple, but I know them better."

Temple doubted the trustees would have characterized Frank's bold strategy as aggressive and unneighborly if he were White.

"In any case, it gives us a bit of breathing room to see if we can make the place financially viable," said Hunter. "And, of course, there's also Temple's plan."

"What plan?" Stuart asked.

Temple wondered how Hunter had found out about her plan. "I've been working on a way to save Folly Park," she said and quickly explained.

"That's a terrible idea!" Stuart said.

Hunter raised his brows. "I don't agree," he said, to Temple's relief. "I think it's a good idea. I told Senator Alden so when he called last week."

Stuart choked and tried to cover it up with a cough as Hunter continued. "But I'm sure the senator is watching the mayoral race closely."

"He won't take a side until he sees who wins," Temple said.

Hunter nodded. "Yes, but I hear from a reliable source you have some influence with Jack Early, Temple. Perhaps you can persuade him to convince Senator Alden to stick with us."

"A reliable source?" Temple echoed blankly before she realized he must be talking about Mrs. Glass.

Hunter winked—an odd gesture coming from him—and Temple wondered uneasily if she should have answered Jack's call that morning.

Stuart drove very fast back to Folly Park, pushing the old car until its engine screamed. Hunched tensely over the steering wheel, he maintained a sullen silence until he pulled into his parking spot. Then he rounded on Temple. "I'm doing my best here," he said. Before she could answer, he had flung himself out of the car and stomped into the administration building. She heard his office door slam.

Temple followed slowly. *Our relationship might never recover from this*, she thought, and she realized she was sorry for that.

"Do you know what your brother's done now?" Martha asked as soon as she saw Temple. She held up her phone, where a stream of posts flashed so quickly Temple couldn't read them.

"What is it? What did he do?"

"Beau's calling for the town of Preston's Mill to secede from the Commonwealth of Virginia. He says it's the only way to ensure local heritage monuments can be protected from left-wing terrorists like the ones who stole the general's statue."

This grotesque stunt was so outrageous Temple was at a complete loss. She went into her office to call Pixie, but she didn't have a chance before her phone rang.

"Are you sitting down?" Vee's voice was breathless with excitement.

Temple's stomach lurched. "Why?"

"It's big. Really big."

"What is it?"

"General Thomas Temple Smith was not who you think he was."

"What do you mean?"

"The man who came to Virginia after his family died on their plantation in Louisiana, and lived with Uncle James, and went to West Point, and inherited Folly Park, and married Carolina, and fought for the South in the Civil War...." Vee took a deep breath. "That guy was not really Thomas Temple Smith."

Temple was thoroughly confused. "I don't understand."

Vee took another audible breath and spoke more slowly. "*That* man was the real Thomas Smith's personal slave, Cass. And Cass was Thomas's cousin—the son of Linda and Uncle James."

Temple's mind reeled. Cass, the general's enslaved boyhood playmate, had always been a minor character in the family story. But Vee was suggesting Cass had taken Thomas's identity—impersonated him—and the man known as General Smith was born a slave.

"Are you sure?"

"Yes," Vee said firmly. "One hundred percent."

"Tell me everything."

"There aren't many records related to the Marais plantation at the historical society, but they were helpful," Vee began. "Linda was recorded in the tax lists as a nursery maid. She gave birth to twins, a boy and a girl, in November 1836, a few months before Thomas Jr. was born. She was pregnant when she left Folly Park, just as Thomas Sr. wrote in his letter to James. Linda named her twins Cass and Pamela. The girl's name probably came from the title character in the novel James used to read to her. The next year's tax list includes Cass but not Pamela. She may have died."

"This is the same Cass who was the general's companion?"

"Yes. There's no record of Cass working in the fields, even when he got older. Given how well he succeeded in passing as an educated White man later on, I think he was probably present during Thomas's lessons with his tutor."

"What evidence do you have that Cass survived the epidemic but not Thomas Jr.?"

Vee explained that she'd found the records of the doctor who had treated the family for the "black vomit," as yellow fever was called. Dr. Palmetier went to the plantation nearly every day to administer doses of vinegar and quinine, but the treatment didn't do any good. The two daughters died first, then Thomas Sr., then his wife, Antoinette. Thomas Jr. was also on the point of death. The doctor didn't think he would live through the night.

"According to Dr. Palmetier, all the other house servants

had died, and Thomas was being nursed by Cass," Vee reported. "Some of the slaves took advantage of the epidemic to run away, and the doctor thought Cass might abandon Thomas Jr. But when he went out to the plantation the next day, he was surprised."

"Why? What happened?"

"The house seemed deserted. Dr. Palmetier goes to Thomas's bedroom and finds the door locked." Wrapped up in her story, Vee didn't seem to notice she'd switched to the present tense, as if she were witnessing the events. "He knocks, and a voice identifies himself as Thomas and says his fever broke during the night. He's recovering, but his servant Cass succumbed, and he's already buried him. The doctor asks to be admitted, wondering why Thomas would lock his door."

Temple nodded, forgetting Vee couldn't see her.

"According to the casebook, Thomas—really Cass—tells the doctor he's afraid of catching the sickness again and intends to stay barricaded in the room until the epidemic is over. The doctor tells him if he doesn't open the door, he'll break it down. So, Thomas lets him in. Right away, the doctor says, 'You're not Thomas, you're Cass.' But the young man insists he's Thomas Jr. and that Cass died during the night. The doctor wrote that he 'spoke feelingly of the slave's devotion, faithfully nursing his master even as he himself must have been harboring the disease that killed him.' And, by the time Cass is through with his story, the doctor doesn't know what to believe."

"Wait a minute," Temple broke in. "How could the doctor confuse Cass with Thomas once he saw him in person?"

"The doctor addressed that point in his casebook—he was trying to figure it out for himself. He wrote that Cass and Thomas looked enough alike as brothers, which was no surprise since their fathers were brothers themselves, and everyone knew it. If you didn't know them well, they could be mistaken for each other because, the doctor said, 'Cass was very nearly White.'"

"Go on," Temple urged.

"Dr. Palmetier noted that Thomas was a little bigger than Cass. But Thomas had also wasted so much from illness that without seeing them side-by-side, it was impossible to determine who it really was. And he wrote, 'the young man spoke impeccably, in his usual forthright manner, not with Cass's servile ignorance.'"

"The doctor wasn't quite sure."

"No. But then he realized he hadn't seen a particular scar on Thomas's chin from a childhood fall. He'd been distracted earlier, he wrote, by the sight of a gold ring with emeralds the young man was wearing on a chain around his neck. He asked about it, and Thomas—or Cass, rather—told him it was a family heirloom."

"The Janus ring?"

"I think so. Maybe Linda gave it to him, or he found it in her things after she died. James must have given it to her, or else she stole it, before she left Folly Park."

Temple thought about the diamond necklace her mother had given her, a portable emergency fund.

Vee continued. "When he remembered the scar, the doctor was convinced the slave was impersonating his master. But he couldn't do anything about it. He caught yellow fever himself and died two days later. I found his headstone in the cemetery."

"So, the slave Cass, posing as his cousin Thomas Temple Smith Jr., came to Folly Park," Temple said slowly. "He took over the plantation when his uncle James—really his father—died. He married a White woman and fought for the South in the Civil War."

"Or maybe not. He'd been enslaved. He may have lost the battle near Folly Park on purpose."

"I suppose." Temple still hadn't taken it all in. "When do you think you'll finish up there?"

"Soon. I just want to check out a few documents related to the liquidation of the plantation at the New Orleans public library. And Temple?" Vee cleared her throat. "There's one more thing. Since the general was biracial, the baby Robert could have been his and Carolina's." She added quietly, "I caused a lot of trouble for nothing."

"I wouldn't say that." Temple told Vee what she'd just discovered about Carolina's inability to have children and how Jane ran away after spending a night alone with Thomas, posing as a man to join the Union army. She offered her theory that Jane and the general had been lovers.

"Wow," Vee said. "So, the baby was Jane's with the general?"

"Maybe. Gil Wheeler didn't mention she was pregnant when he discovered she was a woman, but it was early for her to be showing anyway."

"But if it's true—it's incredible."

Putting down her phone, Temple stared sightlessly out the window, feeling both amazed and duped by Vee's discovery. She'd been raised hearing stories of the general's exploits, spent countless hours in his home, researched his life as thoroughly as anyone could, and yet she had not even suspected his secret.

Taking out the tin box, she looked at the photo. It was impossible to detect that the general was at most one-quarter Black. As she returned the artifacts to the box, she noticed that the photo of Folly Park opposite her desk was hanging crooked.

Temple straightened the photo and went outside. She passed tourists strolling along the gravel paths in the park and beside the pond. Others came and went through the outbuildings, exploring the exhibits on brewing beer, smoking meat, and boiling laundry. An elderly couple sought relief from the heat under a shady tree beside her house.

Temple wondered about Cass, the enslaved man who had freed himself. How did he feel coming to Folly Park to claim his property, including slaves like him? He'd been known as a liberal master, but he never freed a single slave. He advertised for those that ran away. He whipped them for punishment. He sold them when they were unruly or unproductive or when he needed cash.

Walking along the side of the mansion, Temple passed the windows of the library full of books, now priceless, and precious even in their time. She passed the dining room, where fine French Burgundy wines, the general's favorite, were served every evening. Wine and books were commodities out of reach of the vast majority of Americans in the nineteenth century. They may as well have been on another planet for a slave. The comforts and pleasures Cass enjoyed were purchased through the forced labor of others. Temple tried to imagine what he felt when he sipped his wine and turned the pages of his books. Entitled? Avenged? Grateful? Guilty?

In the front of the house, Temple gazed down at the battlefield, shimmering with heat. Was the general fighting against slavery during the war, biding his time to deal a fatal blow? Or did he fight to protect his house and a lifestyle he didn't want to lose? Did he know his uncle James was really his father? Did he know King was his mother's twin, his uncle? Did King have special privileges because of his relationship to the general rather than Carolina? And was Cass sympathetic to abolition, or not? Did he share his secret with Jane? Was that why she ran away—saying he was not the man she thought he was—because he was a slave who fought to keep others enslaved? There were so many unanswered questions.

Temple faced the house, imposing in its mass but decaying from foundation to eaves. She thought of the enslaved people who had lived under its shadow, their voices lost to history, and she thought of their descendants—Al and his mother Olivia, his grandmother Mary, and countless others. Temple thought of her mother and grandfather. She considered her duty to the place that had belonged to her ancestors since they'd first taken possession of their vast land grant. She thought about the news that the trustees were not going to sell Folly Park after all.

TEMPLE WAITED FOR MARTHA to leave for the day before she knocked on Stuart's door. They had a long conversation, and then they called Hunter Glass. After that was done, Temple walked down to the old overseer's house and spoke with Al and Betty Jean. She called Vee on her way home.

Chick whined impatiently while Temple ate leftover pasta standing at the kitchen sink. After she was finished, she took him out for his run. While he darted through the trees chasing things she couldn't see, she climbed slowly to the top of the bridge folly and sank to the ground. She watched a black beetle slipping and sliding through the grass.

After a while, Temple's phone buzzed. It was Jack. This time she answered.

"Temple?"

"Hi," she said, trying to ignore the rush of pleasure she felt at the sound of his voice. "How are you? How's your family? Is everything okay now?"

"Yes, thanks. My mother-in-law has dementia, and she doesn't understand that Liz and I split up. They were trying to move her into a long-term care home, and she was upset and kept asking for me. But she's all settled now."

"That's good. It was nice of you to help."

"Thanks. Listen, Temple, I'm sorry I can't tell you this in person."

As Temple watched the sun sink behind the trees at the edge of the park, Jack broke the news that her plan for the girls' home was dead. Senator Alden would not be moved from his decision.

"I don't blame him," Temple said. "The timing of Frank Poe's petition was really bad for us."

"It's not about the monument petition."

"Oh. What is it about?"

Jack hesitated. "I wish I didn't have to say it, but you deserve to know."

"Know what?" Temple got to her feet, as if to be ready for whatever was coming.

"Your dad told the senator something that disturbed him. Something about you."

"What?"

"Your father reminded Senator Alden about an incident a number of years ago when a teenager picketed the Horse and Hounds Country Club. He told the senator it was you."

"What does that have to do with anything?"

"The senator's father founded the club."

Temple felt a sudden chill as the sun disappeared behind the trees. She remembered the frightened, grief-stricken girl she'd been when she planned her campaign to picket the club. She had withdrawn from her friends as her mother grew sicker, and everyone else avoided her, as if she were contagious. Temple felt bereft, misunderstood, and angry. But the long, lonely summer days of her protest had given her the time and space to heal just a little bit.

"Temple? Are you all right?"

"I'm okay. It's not like I don't know what my father is capable of."

"Speaking of that," Jack said, "I've been hearing about Beau's rally and the counterprotest. You aren't going, are you?"

"I haven't decided," Temple lied.

"Yes, you have. I can tell you're planning to go."

"I have to be there. I can't really explain."

"It could be dangerous."

"I'll be careful."

"I hope so," Jack said. "Because I'd really like to have a chance to get to know you better. If that's okay with you."

Temple smiled. "It's okay with me."

"Good." Jack paused. "There's one more thing I wanted to tell you. I've resigned from the senator's campaign. Your plan deserved a chance."

TEMPLE HAD GROWN UP IN A sprawling, midcentury modern house painted stark white with a flat roof and sharp angles. She parked on the street, even though in this neighborhood, her beat-up truck was likely to be ticketed if she left it there long. But she couldn't pull into the driveway as if she belonged. She rang the doorbell.

The judge answered the door in a shabby burgundy bathrobe, silk pajama pants, and slippers. He was holding a bloody handkerchief, and his cheek was swollen. He'd obviously had another bad day at the dentist. When he saw Temple, he shoved the handkerchief into the pocket of his robe and without a word stalked down the gloomy hall to his office like a wolf returning to its lair.

"Sit." The judge waved at the chair in front of his massive desk and sat down behind it, a position of strength from which he dispensed commands and meted out punishments.

Temple remained standing. "You sabotaged my plan for Folly Park."

"It was for your own good."

"I don't see it that way."

The judge launched into a detailed summation of how his actions were designed to mitigate the fallout from Temple's own bad judgment. She didn't listen. She could have written that speech herself. She was much more interested in a new and unfamiliar feeling radiating through her body—a deep sense of self-assurance, of confidence and faith in herself. She could feel it now because she was no longer afraid of her father.

"That may all be true," Temple said when he finished. Her voice was steady and calm, and she saw him register it with surprise. "But it doesn't matter. I'm done. I don't want to see you anymore."

The judge's eyes strayed to the formal portrait of Temple's mother hanging above the cold fireplace. He set his jaw with a contemptuous expression and a drop of blood appeared in the corner of his mouth. He'd decided to give her the silent treatment, a technique that usually made Temple say anything to appease him. Tonight, though, she didn't speak. He had destroyed her last chance to save Folly Park—her home and her livelihood. But she would no longer fight with him about it or anything else. And without an ever-present conflict, there was nothing to bind them.

Temple noticed a worn leather slipper poking out from under the desk. It had a hole in it, and one bare toe was exposed. She looked up to see her father holding the stained handkerchief against his mouth. When he saw Temple looking at him, he lifted the other hand to shield his eyes from her. It was trembling, and with sudden shock Temple realized he was old. He was old and in pain and alone.

Walking around the desk, Temple rested her hand gently on her father's shoulder. She wondered what it would have been like to have been able to lean on him, to have his arm around her, to feel protected and loved by him. She would never know. She quietly left the room, went down the hall, and closed the front door behind her.

Driving slowly back to Preston's Mill, Temple felt bone-tired and at peace, as if she had just finished a long race for which she'd been training a long time. It was a beautiful, warm evening, and she rolled down the window and took a deep breath. She smelled smoke. A half mile farther, she discovered what was causing it.

Scores of people marched along the road toward Preston's Mill. Temple slowed the truck to a crawl as the crowd thickened around her. She saw ordinary people in polo shirts and khaki shorts, cutoff jeans and tank tops, sundresses and camouflage pants. They had long hair and short hair, ponytails and braids, and some of them were bald. Some had beards or mustaches. They were tall and thin and short and fat and old and young and middle-aged. The crowd looked like central casting for a cross section of White America. But many also wore hats and T-shirts with the Confederate flag printed on them and cheap buttons with the seals of seceding states.

There were also bikers in leather vests and studded boots with rebel flag do-rags on their heads. A grim phalanx carried guns openly—on their hips, slung across their backs, in their hands, some with bayonets. And a group of men marching together in lockstep raised their arms in the Nazi salute. Up ahead the peaked white hoods of the KKK stabbed the dark sky.

Tiki torches used for backyard pool parties sent thick gray smoke snaking into the night air. In the flickering flames, eyes glittered beneath signs with hateful words. Temple caught the last strains of "Dixie," the unofficial Confederate anthem, before the singing stopped and the crowd began to chant with one raw vicious voice. "Free the South! Free the South! Free the South!"

CHAPTER EIGHTEEN

The day of the rally, Stuart called an emergency staff meeting at seven thirty. Even Al showed up. Like other local businesses, Stuart announced, Folly Park would be closed for the day because of concerns the rally in Preston's Mill could turn violent. After Fred and Betty Jean asked about posting signs to notify the tourists, everyone expected to be dismissed. Instead, Stuart waved at Temple. She told them what Vee had discovered about the general's true identity. They stared at her, stunned.

Fred was the first to speak. "You mean to say General Smith was actually a slave?"

"Yes."

"So, he fought a war to keep himself enslaved, too, though nobody knew it?"

"Yes."

"That's kind of funny."

"I think you mean ironic," Martha corrected.

"I don't think it's funny," Flora declared. "It's sickening. I have spent years telling folks what an honorable gentleman General Smith was, and it was all a lie."

"Hold on," Betty Jean said. "He was still the same man even if we weren't right about who his parents were."

271

Flora shook her head. "He was a liar. And a cheat."

"Well, I think he deserved what he got," Fred said. "He was James Smith's son, so he should have inherited Folly Park."

"But he wasn't *legitimate*." Flora's lip curled.

"That wasn't his fault," said Martha brusquely. "He was making the best he could out of his situation."

"Or making the situation," Al said. "Maybe he helped the real Thomas along to his death so he could steal his identity."

"Come on," Temple cut in. "There's no point speculating about something we can't know."

"He was a bastard, we know *that*," Flora said, sniffing.

"That's a mean word," said Betty Jean.

"I'm just calling it like it is."

"But, Flora," Fred said. "His mother was a slave—"

"Stop!" Flora cut him off. "I'm sick and tired of hearing about the goddamn slaves." She stood up. "I quit. Don't try to stop me." She moved slowly toward the door, sneaking a look to see if they would call her back.

Temple said nothing. Martha raised her eyebrows, Fred shook his head, Al rolled his eyes, and Betty Jean shrugged.

"That's that then," Stuart said.

Flora burst into tears and pushed past Vee in the doorway.

"You're home!" Temple jumped up, arms wide.

WHEN EVERYONE ELSE HAD LEFT, Temple told Vee about Jack's call and the end of her plan, her break with her father, and the people she'd seen coming for Beau's terrible rally.

"Well, I've got better news for you," Vee said when Temple had finished. "I found out what happened to Linda's other child—Cass's twin sister, Pamela."

"She didn't die at birth?"

"No. Remember, I told you the public library in New Orleans has records related to the liquidation of the plantation, when Thomas sold everything and came to Folly Park?"

Temple nodded.

"The sale records show that the Smith's neighbor in Marais Parish, Pierre Delacroix, bought some of the land and tools. So, I looked into the Delacroix plantation records too. In November 1836, Thomas Smith Sr. paid Pierre Delacroix to board an infant and for the services of an enslaved wet nurse. The infant's name was Pamela."

"Linda's daughter?"

Vee nodded. "The payments lasted for two years, probably until Pamela was weaned. But she never left the Delacroix plantation. She was trained to be a house servant, and when she was nine years old, Pierre began paying rent to Thomas Smith for her. The receipts are all in the Delacroix papers—Pamela is written in parenthesis after the name 'Jolie.'"

"They gave her a nickname?"

"Yes. Jolie means pretty in French."

"She must have inherited Linda's beauty. I think you're about to tell me that wasn't necessarily a good thing."

"It depends on how you look at it. Thomas—or Cass rather—put Jolie up for auction when he was selling everything off."

Temple grimaced. "He sold his own twin sister?"

"To be fair, he may not have known he even had a sister."

"Who bought her?"

"The owner of a brothel in New Orleans."

Disgusted, Temple shook her head, but Vee had more to tell. "Jolie left the brothel a year later, when she was seventeen, to become the mistress of a White man. They lived together in New Orleans as husband and wife. And they had a daughter, who had a daughter, who had a daughter. . . ."

Vee was grinning, her face bright and expectant.

Temple understood. She smiled broadly. "You told me you traced your genealogy to a New Orleans brothel. To a woman who became the mistress of a White man and lived with him like they were married. Was she. . . ?"

Vee nodded. "I'm descended from Jolie. Folly Park is my heritage too."

HALF OF THE CROWD GATHERED on the town square cheered and the other half booed when Beau bounded on to the temporary stage set up for the rally. The opposing sides were separated by a line of police officers and a token force of state troopers wearing mirrored sunglasses. They snapped gum and tapped batons against their tall boots.

Grouped to the left of the stage, many of Beau's supporters wore camouflage and blended into the shadows under the trees. But their glinting white placards stood out starkly, printed with racial slurs and swastikas and messages like, DON'T MONKEY WITH MY HERITAGE. Many openly carried firearms.

Counter-protestors were massed on the unshaded side of the square, sweating in the heat. Many waved signs denouncing racism, and some carried sticks and had suspiciously lumpy pockets. Jerry Hoyle's sign, painted with blue and gray read, DIDN'T WE ALREADY FIGHT THIS WAR?

A dozen news vans ringed the square, heavy cameras pointed at the stage. Beau waited for the cheering and the booing to die down before he raised the microphone to speak.

"You know, I don't like political jokes . . . because I've seen too many of them get elected." Beau grinned. Despite the heat, he looked cool and relaxed in jeans and a red polo shirt.

"But seriously, folks, I invited you here because I'm concerned about the future of our town."

The tension in the crowd was palpable. People strained forward like leashed dogs catching a scent. The policemen took a wide-legged stance and hooked their thumbs in their gun belts.

"It seems like some people won't be satisfied until they've beaten down every last vestige of the Confederacy."

Temple turned to Colonel Townsend standing beside her and touched his sleeve. He nodded and signaled his men. As one body, they surrounded Temple and swiftly escorted her to the stage. Before anyone could react, she had climbed the steps. She was wearing a simple white dress Mrs. Glass had bought her for a garden party, and except for a few wolf whistles, the crowd was silent, unsure what to make of this interruption.

"Let her speak!" Colonel Townsend called.

"Let her speak!" the reenactors echoed as they fanned out in front of the stage, antique Enfield rifles at arms, Bowie knives bristling from their belts.

Beau's crowd took up the chant. "Let her speak! Let her speak!"

Beau seemed put off-balance by Temple's appearance and confused about her relationship with the reenactors. Covering the microphone with his hand while he flashed a phony smile, he hissed, "What the hell are you doing?"

"I just want to say a few words about Folly Park," Temple said. Behind her the chanting grew louder. Frank Poe's supporters had joined in, happy to derail Beau's speech.

"Keep it short, goddammit." Beau turned back to the crowd and said into the microphone, "I want to introduce you to my sister. Temple is the curator at Folly Park, the historic house of our ancestor, General Thomas Temple Smith, that some people want to tear down." Beau waited until the cheers, catcalls, and boos stopped. "She's had a crush on the general since we were kids, and she knows more about him than anyone else alive." Beau gestured toward her. "Temple wants to say something."

The lonely sound of a few people clapping echoed in the square. Temple spotted the small contingent from Folly Park huddled together in the very back. Betty Jean and Al, Fred, Martha, and Stuart were all there. They stopped clapping abruptly when no one joined in. Just below the stage, Julia, Pixie, and the judge stared up at her.

As Temple reached to take the microphone, the crowd shifted restlessly. She had only a moment to capture people's attention before they went back to the business of hating each other. Stomach roiling, she swallowed and spoke quietly into the microphone. "I've just discovered that General Smith was born a slave."

In the shocked silence, people looked at each other, unsure of what they'd heard. At the same time, there was a rustle of movement from Frank Poe's supporters near the corner of the stage. Matthew was pushing his way through the crowd . . . with Vee. Temple froze in horror as she realized that Vee intended to join her on the stage. Afraid of what Beau's crowd might do, she tried to raise her hand or call out to stop Vee, but she was unable to move. She watched Hunter Glass lead Vee up the steps.

Wearing her Folly Park uniform, Vee crossed the stage slowly, as if she expected to be stopped at any moment. Temple finally came to life and reached out to take Vee's hand. Their eyes met, their fear and courage mirrored for each other.

The crowd stirred. Beau started toward them but stopped when Colonel Townsend held up his hand. Beau shook his head and gestured with a broad sweep of his arm, as if politely yielding the stage.

Temple found her voice. "Vee and I just discovered that General Smith was born a slave." Terrified of what would happen if she failed to hold their attention, she continued, without order or eloquence.

She told them the man known as the general was really his enslaved boyhood companion Cass. That his enslaved mother, Linda, and her many sisters had been bred at Folly Park to be sold to New Orleans brothels when they were twelve, thirteen, fourteen years old. Like Linda, they were the daughters of the master of Folly Park. She looked at Vee, and Vee nodded and took the microphone.

"I'm descended from one of those girls," Vee said. She stood stoically before the crowd's assessing gaze, but Temple could see her trembling as she began to speak.

Vee told the crowd that Cass had traveled to Folly Park after the White family on his Louisiana plantation died of yellow fever and had taken on the identity of his cousin. She said that while Cass, now known as Thomas, was in school at West Point, his father, James Smith, passed away. The old man was so reviled that when he fell paralyzed with stroke, his enslaved servants left him lying alone until he died days later.

"He deserved it!" someone shouted. "White supremacist!"

Beau's crowd muttered, and a few people touched their weapons, eyeing the policemen and the troopers. The reenactors stood unmoving and impregnable in front of the stage.

Temple took the microphone from Vee. It squealed as she spoke, momentarily stilling the crowd. Into wincing faces she threw the fact that Thomas Smith, himself born a slave, returned to Folly Park and became a master of slaves. There were stories of his overseer nearly drowning people in the pond to make them confess crimes, accounts of salting raw wounds from whip cuts, and a case of a pregnant woman fainting in the fields and forced back to work under the broiling sun. There was a story, still told, of an enslaved girl throwing herself down a well, desperate to end her misery. Here, Temple looked straight at Al, where he stood beyond the blur of White faces. She handed the microphone back to Vee.

"Thomas Smith married his first cousin, sight unseen," Vee said and continued the story. He wanted her money, land, and slaves. Before marrying her off, Carolina's father forced her to have an operation that prevented her from ever having children—an excruciating operation tested on enslaved women without anesthesia. Vee described an unhappy marriage and Carolina's plea to her cousin Jane— an abolitionist—who arrived at Folly Park in November 1859. She was still there when the war came.

The stage was stifling, the air thick and heavy, and it felt as if the whole square were holding its breath. Below, someone moved sharply, and the cameras swiveled. Judge Preston, glaring up at Temple, took a step toward the edge of the stage, but two reenactors blocked his way. Julia clutched the judge's arm and whispered. He twitched his shoulder but did not move as Vee passed the microphone to Temple.

Temple told the crowd that Thomas Smith collected rare books and drank fine wine and rode only thoroughbred horses. These luxuries came to him through the unremitting labor of enslaved people, and when the Confederacy called, he answered. Temple glanced down at Colonel Townsend as she described the war's desolation and the carnage of men and boys.

The faces of the crowd wavered in the heat, and Temple squinted in the harsh sunlight. "Folly Park is my heritage," she said. "Some people use that word to make the past sacred, something you can't criticize. They're proud to own their heritage—the good parts anyway. They don't take responsibility for the bad. But you can't pick and choose. You have to own all of it or none of it. And if you make your heritage a part of your identity and let it shape who you are, then you bring the past into the present. And the past can hurt if it ignores injustice or excuses wrongs."

Temple saw Al nodding his head, slow and steady, a drumbeat in time with her words. "Beau is right," she continued. "I used to have a crush on the general. I imagined dashing men and charming women at Folly Park, and I felt special because of my family's history. I felt like I belonged."

The crowd stood motionless in the dappled shadows of the trees.

"When I think of my heritage, I see the blue hills and the red dirt. I smell lavender and wood smoke. I remember the way the sun gleams through the wavy glass in the windows at Folly Park and warms the old wood floors. But I can't imagine dashing men and charming women there anymore."

Temple turned to face Vee as she gripped the microphone. She looked into her friend's eyes and held her gaze like a lifeline. "Now I see the other side of my heritage—the thousands of people my people owned. I see them sweating in the fields and freezing in the cabins. I see them chopping wood, slaughtering hogs, mucking out stables. I see them hauling laundry, cooking, cleaning, sewing, and serving. I see people crippled, beaten, and branded, men castrated, and women raped over and over again. I see people given away as wedding presents, sold to pay debts, separated from husbands and wives, mothers and fathers and children."

"Vee is my heritage, and I am hers." Temple's voice wavered, and she stopped, panic rising as she felt the full force of the crowd's attention aimed directly at her. Then she found Al again. He slowly raised his arm, pointed straight at her, and nodded once—a final cue.

Temple took a deep breath and steadied her voice. "Every single day for two centuries, in my family's home, on my family's land, in this great country, people were tortured and abused, denied their humanity, denied freedom." She shook her head. "And it's never stopped. Look what we're doing right here, right now. We've turned each other into enemies."

Temple's voice broke on her final words. "We have made this beautiful land rotten from the inside out." The microphone dropped from her nerveless fingers.

Vee held out her hand, and Temple took it and walked unsteadily to the edge of the stage. When they reached the steps, Hunter Glass helped them down, and Colonel Townsend and his men fell in on either side. The colonel called out an order to march, and the crowd parted silently before them.

Temple's legs felt as heavy as lead as they passed along the aisle of blurred faces. She held tightly to Vee, and Vee held tightly to her, like weary soldiers helping each other off the battlefield.

When they finally reached the group from Folly Park, Colonel Townsend called a halt. Al's long arm wrapped around Temple's shoulders. He led her to her truck, boosted her into the driver's seat, and waited while Captain Hollowell opened the passenger door for Vee.

"I'm sorry," Temple said to Al.

"I know." Al grinned wickedly and said in his exaggerated drawl, "Ah reckon we're about even now, Missus." He tipped his head toward the pedestal where the statue had stood and winked.

Temple's eyes widened. "You mean. . . ?"

Al nodded. "We put him in the river at Black Bottom. Bill Edderly brought his tractor. Lots of people helped. She knows," Al said approvingly.

Astonished, Temple turned to Vee. "You knew?"

Vee crinkled her nose and nodded, and Temple started to giggle. It had a hysterical edge, and she covered her mouth with her hand.

"Go home, both of you, and rest," Al said. "You deserve it." As the truck pulled away from the curb, he slapped the hood twice.

Behind her, Temple knew, Hunter Glass would announce that the next mayor of Preston's Mill would have sole power to determine the fate of Folly Park Plantation. But there was one stipulation. It could no longer be a tourist attraction, and the house would be demolished. Hunter had called just before midnight to tell Temple the trustees had agreed to honor her request.

CHAPTER NINETEEN

B ack at what would soon no longer be her home, Temple stepped inside the front door and stopped short in front of Lad Preston's smirking visage.

"What's the matter?" Vee asked behind her.

Temple didn't answer. She lifted the photograph off its hook and set it on the floor, facing the wall.

Vee raised her eyebrows. "I'll call Matthew. Tell him we're back safe and find out what happened."

Temple sank on to the couch in the living room, the magnitude of what she'd done sinking in. It was she, Temple Tayloe Smith Preston, who would witness the loss of the land that had been in her family for nearly four hundred years. She had destroyed Folly Park.

Chick thumped his tail against the floor and cocked his head at her. Temple smiled, a crack that opened her wide. She began to cry. Chick whined and pawed at her, and when she didn't respond, he jumped on to the couch. Temple put her arms around him and let the tears come.

When she had recovered, Temple wiped her eyes and caught sight of the curio cabinet where she kept her family mementos and the Civil War artifacts that had belonged to her grandfather. She looked away. Her grandfather had lost her respect. And she was finished with her father and brother. She had no close family left, she realized. To top it off, she was about to lose her livelihood and her home. It was all so Southern Gothic. Temple suppressed a strange urge to laugh as Vee came into the room.

"Did you say something?" Vee asked.

"No." Temple shook her head. "What did Matthew tell you?"

Vee shrugged. "Apparently, the rally just fizzled out. After Hunter Glass's announcement, Matthew said no one knew what to do. Beau said a few words about economic development, thanked his supporters, and told everyone to go home. It sounds a bit anticlimactic."

Temple was relieved. "Anticlimactic is good."

"Yes. In real life, drama is usually overrated," Vee said dryly. "Why don't you change out of your dress and come for a walk?"

Without visitors in the middle of the day, Folly Park seemed eerie to Temple, as if something apocalyptic had happened. After a stroll around the pond, Temple unlocked the back door of the mansion, and she and Vee stepped into the hall, where the hole in the ceiling still gaped. Their steps echoed through the entrance hall, the dining room, the music room. Stopping briefly in the parlor, they looked at the paintings. Dust motes floated in the still air.

In the library—the beating heart of the plantation, as Jane had described it—Vee touched the worn leather chair at the massive old desk. Temple ran her finger along the cracked spines of three centuries of bound ledgers. On a shelf near the desk were half a dozen books she had never noticed before. Small enough to fit inside a pocket, they looked humble and homey beside the oversized ledgers.

Opening the first book in the row, Temple noted the date written on the flyleaf: May 1859. Below it, two columns divided the page. One listed bushels of beans, apples, okra, peas, heads of lettuce and cabbage, baskets of potatoes and squash, eggs and trout, turkeys, ducks, and rabbits. The opposite column recorded the sums paid out to the enslaved women who grew the produce and the enslaved men who hunted in the woods and fished in the streams: Sallie, Trixie, Betsy, Jewel, Mab, Queenie, Cujo, Caesar, Rufus, Damon, and Samuel. She handed the open book to Vee. The leather cover had left rust-colored residue on her fingers. "Carolina's household account book," Temple said. "From the year she was married."

Vee turned the yellowed pages. "Look at the handwriting," she said a moment later, handing the book back.

Temple frowned down at the open oval *d*'s and *b*'s and the *t*'s so carelessly written the cross could sometimes be found spearing a word in the line above like an alphabetical shish kebab. She wasn't sure what Vee had noticed, but then she saw that the messy, childish scrawl with its uneven columns and numerous smudges and cross-outs had evolved over time. Beginning in November 1859, errors in addition were carefully corrected, and by the end of the book, the script was quite legible.

"I see," Temple said. "The entries started to improve when Jane arrived and began helping her." Vee nodded.

Temple took the last account book in the row off the shelf. It ended in September 1863, when General Smith was killed. She wondered if Carolina had lost hope or was too consumed by her responsibilities to keep up with the household accounts.

Then, as if she were seeing the room anew, Temple's attention sharpened on the heavy ledgers ranked on the shelves—1863, 1864, 1865, 1866 . . . one book for each year, extending all the way to 1934, when Carolina died at the age of ninety-three.

Holding her breath, Temple opened the 1863 ledger. It began in September, where the last household account book had left off, the month the general had died, and the mistress become the master. And there it was, the familiar handwriting, recording the painstaking details of the plantation's management. She closed the book and slowly opened the last ledger, from 1934. And there it was again, shaky with age but unmistakably the same. Day in and day out, season after season, year after year—Carolina had run Folly Park for seventy-one years.

Two letters lay folded on top of the first page in the ledger—as if they had been placed there awaiting this day in the future. Temple looked at Vee, whose eyes were wide behind her glasses, and read the first letter aloud.

Boston, 18 Jan. 1863

Mrs. Smith:

Imagine my acute distress upon receipt of yours of the 7th informing us that Jane has gone from you, and that your efforts to discover her whereabouts have proved fruitless.

What an evil day it was that led her to you! My poor child was heartbroken when she received your invitation. Her father had just released her fiancé from their engagement due to her hopeless condition, and your selfish appeal was her excuse to run away. Likely, it was a passing whim to have her with you, but you quickly learned how she could be of use. I most assuredly did not wish her to remain at Folly

Park these past three years. And I strenuously objected to my husband's connivance with you and Mr. Smith to willfully ignore Jane's illness—to play along with her fantasy. Had she been forced to face the truth, she could have sought whatever earthly relief she might from the ravages of Consumption and more strenuously prepared to meet her Maker. But playacting served your ends.

How dare you "confess" that seeing her working herself to death, you finally "could stand it no longer, and told Jane she could not live through another year?" What mattered your feelings? It was your clear duty to carry the farce through to the end if it would keep her safe. Instead, you urged your husband to impress upon Jane how her disease must prove fatal. And you tell me that he succeeded in that bitter task so well, that upon hearing it, Jane could not bear to stay at Folly Park one more day!

Because of your wicked carelessness, my poor child will die among strangers in your cursed land. I pray you will— as you claim—be tormented by anxiety and remorse for the cousin you profess to love as a sister every minute of every day for the rest of your life! That Folly Park may be crushed under the force of our righteous Army, and that you may burn in Hell for your sins, Carolina Gilmore Smith, is the fervent wish of—

Charlotte Smith Elliot

Temple opened the second letter. She handed it to Vee, who read it aloud.

Boston, 21 Sept. 1863

Mrs. Smith:

I write to acknowledge the receipt of yours of the 8th inform-ing me of my Daughter Jane's return to Folly Park, and of her death shortly thereafter.

You term it a "miracle" that Jane's favorite—the slave girl Jewel—birthed a baby boy in the very same hour that my child passed from this earth. But, conceived in violence as it was, on the Eve of our Savior's birth, I deem it rather a curse.

You have demonstrated a criminal want of care for those under your charge. Even in my generation, it was common knowledge that the Preston men are shameless libertines. But you report that Lad Preston was murdered in his bed on Christmas Day, avenged by the girl's father. What a barbarous country it is for which you fight—a land rotting from the inside out!

Charlotte Smith Elliot

Temple stared at Vee, knowing her mind was churning with the same thoughts. Jane wasn't Robert's mother, after all. She and the general had never been lovers. Jewel had the baby after she was raped by Lad Preston the night of the Christmas party at Wild Oaks. She named him after her boyfriend. "Bub-Bub" was "Bob," spoken by a man with a stutter. *What happened to Bob?* Temple wondered. *Did he run away during the war? Did he abandon Jewel, and was that why she took her life? And Lad Preston's murder, a mystery for 150 years, is solved. King killed him.*

"So, after all our theories and research, it turns out the biracial baby wasn't much of a mystery at all." Temple shook her head. "We missed the most obvious explanation—that he was the result of a White man raping an enslaved woman. There's nothing new about *that* story."

"Well, we did discover an incredible story about an enslaved man passing as a Confederate general," Vee said. "And a woman abolitionist turning herself into a soldier."

"I'm not sure Jane was a very committed abolitionist. She was just running from the truth. She was in such denial she didn't even admit she had tuberculosis in her own diary."

"It must be terrifying to know you're dying," Vee said thoughtfully. "With that looming over her, I don't think we should judge Jane for hanging on to her fantasy world as long as she could. And, when she was forced to face her death, she chose to go out fighting to end slavery. She didn't go back to Boston to die in her comfortable home." Vee nudged Temple's shoulder. "You realize that if Thomas was taking Jane back to Folly Park the night before the battle, it means he didn't sneak away to make a deal with the Union general."

Temple shrugged. "A month ago, I would have been relieved. Now I'm disappointed he didn't betray the South after all." She placed the letters inside the ledger and slid it back onto the shelf. Outside the wavy-paned window, the tall trees swayed in the park.

CHICK LOPED AHEAD AS TEMPLE slowly made her way to the family cemetery. Vee had tactfully left her by the gazebo. But, despite the familiar melancholy peace, Temple felt no bond joining her with departed ancestors today. And, for the first time, the sight of her mother's headstone and those marking the graves of Harry and her grandfather did not grip her heart with grief.

Though certain she'd never seen any sign of it, Temple searched for Jane's grave among the mossy stones. *Perhaps Carolina had managed to send Jane's remains back to Boston,* she thought as she reached the far side of the cemetery, where generations of pets were buried under the brooding trees.

Temple had never paid much attention to the pet cemetery, recognizing only the name of her mother's childhood dog, Wilkes. But today, she noticed a stone larger than the others, nearest to the human graves.

KING

BELOVED COMPANION OF C.G.S.

D. 1906

Temple dropped to her knees. C.G.S. was Carolina Gilmore Smith, she realized. A woman abandoned by her lover, mistreated by her family, married for her fortune, unable to have children. And King, his face scarred by the fire that had taken his wife, his beloved daughter raped, dead too young by her own hand. Had those two wounded people found a true love? A love that sustained them as they built a life? Temple remembered that when Robert Smith arrived in Boston, he'd told the Stannards he could hunt and fish and was good at mathematics—King's renowned skills allied with Carolina's hard-earned aptitude. They had raised Jewel's baby, King's grandson, together.

Tears of shame burned Temple's eyes. She'd looked at the photograph from the hidden box and really seen only the White trio on the veranda, the two enslaved people more props than equal actors. But if it was Carolina who had placed the box in the crack opened by the cannon blasts of the Civil War, then the photograph inside it was a precious relic. And the photo showed four beloved companions, both White and Black—Jane, Thomas, Jewel, and King.

The shadows of the trees were just beginning to creep across the park as Temple returned to the gazebo. She told Vee she'd discovered King's grave and shared her belief that Carolina and King had raised Robert together.

"I thought your theory that Carolina might have had a relationship with a Black man was crazy." Temple said ruefully. "I thought you were delusional to think that you'd ever get an article out of it. I felt sorry for you. But it doesn't even seem all that surprising anymore."

"A lot has happened in a few weeks."

Temple laughed shortly. "The understatement of the year."

"What made you do it in the end?" Vee leaned forward and regarded Temple earnestly. "Let go of Folly Park, I mean."

Temple sighed. "I just couldn't stand knowing that no matter what I did to try to make this a place where people could learn about the full history of the South, some would come because it belonged to a Confederate general. I didn't want to be that place for those people anymore. I'm sorry it took me so long to realize it."

"That's understandable. It's your home."

Temple shook her head. "I should have questioned if saving Folly Park was the right thing to do.'"

"Well, you did. And you've been willing to lose everything for it. That's brave."

"No. I should have gotten there sooner. I've hurt people I love. Losing the house is nothing next to that."

"I still think it's brave," Vee said. "And we were brave on that stage. I'm proud of us."

THE NEXT MORNING, TEMPLE woke late. She hadn't realized she'd come to rely on the reenactors' morning bugle call. But Colonel Townsend and his men had broken down the camp yesterday, after the rally. Temple stretched and slowly got out of bed. It was Sunday. The house was closed. She had nothing to do.

Tomorrow, Stuart would hold the final staff meeting at Folly Park and distribute severance packages to the employees. He and Hunter were working through the details that day. Vee would continue to organize the archives until the end of her internship, to make it easier for Laureen and Claiborne when everything was donated to the Special Collections Library. Temple had to pack up her own family mementos. She would keep a few, give a couple to Beau, and the others would be sold. She intended to donate the proceeds to the detention center, so they could purchase a group home for the girls she'd hoped to help at Folly Park. But she wouldn't tackle that chore just yet. She would take time to say goodbye before she boxed up her past and stepped into the unknown.

In the kitchen, Vee was typing on her laptop, Chick lying across her feet. The coffee pot was nearly empty. She must have been up early.

"Working on your article?" Temple asked.

Vee shook her head. "No. Something totally different. I have an idea about what we should do with our research. I'll tell you about it later."

Temple took a granola bar from the cabinet and patted her leg for Chick to come. He raised his head but didn't move, so she went outside and walked up the drive by herself. She sat down on the veranda and ate her granola bar while she watched the sun rise above the blue hills.

Her cell phone buzzed with a call from Tim. He and Bruce were stationed at the front gate to keep anyone from removing the cones that blocked the driveway. Some of Beau's supporters were still in town.

"Your brother wants to see you," Tim said.

In the background, Beau shouted, "Come on, Temp, I just want to talk!"

Temple sighed. "You can let him in."

A few minutes later Beau's car pulled up, and Temple watched him warily as he walked over to the veranda and eased himself down on to the steps.

"Thanks for letting me past your goons," Beau said sarcastically.

"You're the reason I need them," Temple retorted.

After these opening volleys, they fell silent.

"That was some speech," Beau said after a while. "I didn't think you had it in you. And that intern of yours turned out to be a real pistol."

"I'm just glad nobody got hurt," Temple snapped.

Beau twitched his shoulders and squinted out at the edge of the lawn. "What's that sound?"

"Bullfrogs down by the river. Don't you remember catching them and letting them loose in the pond when we were kids?"

Beau didn't answer.

Temple sighed. "Why are you here, Beau? What do you want?"

Beau popped his dental plate. "I never caught frogs by the river. That was you and Harry. And you and Mom and Granddad were like a private little club." His voice was wistful. "I always felt left out. I just want it to be my turn."

Dad did this, Temple thought. The judge had bulled an innocent boy into becoming a casually careless, self-serving, unprincipled man. But perhaps she, too, was culpable. She had never let Beau belong in her world. In her own childish carelessness, she had deemed him unworthy of time and attention. She had considered his presence irritating, his problems inconvenient, his existence altogether lesser than her own. She wondered who Beau might be today if she had treated him like she treated Harry—as a beloved brother. Temple felt sick with regret. She touched Beau's arm. "I'm sorry."

EPILOGUE

In the basement green room, Temple stared down at the new book. Her name was on the cover along with Vee's. They had written it together over the course of six months, between speaking engagements, where they talked candidly about Folly Park's history and their tangled heritage, a Black woman and a White woman—cousins. They hoped people would see that the country's racial divide was fiction. That the true story was a land where, from the very beginning, all sorts and colors of people mixed in a multiplicity of ways— in love and passion, with power and violence, openly and in secret, proudly and with shame. Wanda booked their appearances and handled their social media, and Matthew had built their website.

Over a year ago, Beau had won the mayoral election with a very slim margin. It was a pyrrhic victory. Only months later, Frank Poe had run for the State Assembly and won Harry's old seat. Betty Jean had gone to work for him, and she and Al had moved to a new condo, halfway between the city and Preston's Mill. They were taking care of Chick while Temple traveled around the country. Temple had recommended Fred for a job at Cleveland Hill, and

Hunter Glass had coached Stuart into a new position at an arts organization.

Beau had not yet been able to deliver on his promise to bring development and jobs to Preston's Mill. Though Folly Park had been sold to the Massachusetts Bay Development Company, Mr. Starkweather was still trying to get permission from the state's labyrinthine bureaucracy to build on the site. In the meantime, Beau was applying his frustrated ambitions to a class action lawsuit against Dr. J. J. Dodge, representing readers of *Help Yourself* who felt duped by their failure to achieve success.

TEMPLE WAS EXCITED TO SHOW Vee their book, and they were due on stage in fifteen minutes. She was about to go look for her when Vee appeared in the mirror behind her. Temple turned and handed her the book.

"It came?" Vee ran her hand lightly over the cover. "It's real."

"I can hardly believe it," Temple said.

"You know what's next now, right?" Vee asked, grinning.

"The book tour. It won't feel much different from what we're already doing," Temple said, wondering what Vee was grinning about.

"Our first appearance is in Philadelphia."

Now Temple understood. Jack was in Philadelphia working as a civil rights lawyer.

"Well?" prompted Vee.

Temple smiled. "I think I'll send Jack an invitation."

TWO DAYS LATER, AL CALLED. Temple thought he had probably received the copy of the book she and Vee had inscribed for him and Betty Jean. She was wrong.

"I wanted to tell you before you heard it from someone else," Al said.

"What?" Temple was alarmed. "Is Betty Jean okay? Did something happen to Chick?"

"They're fine. Just let me talk, will you?"

"Sorry."

"Folly Park is gone," Al said. "They were blasting for a new swimming pool at my club, and the house collapsed."

In her mind's eye, Temple saw the wooden beams cracking and giving way, the wavy-paned windows shattering, the red bricks crumbling into dust.

"It's just a pile of rubble. You remember those World War II shows we used to watch? It looks like those buildings in Dresden after the Allies bombed it. Now you can see all the way across the river from the park. There's a big, open clearing."

An empty space where her home had once been. Temple had thought she would have more time before she received that news, expecting the end would come from a long-scheduled wrecking ball. But it was done, and Al was waiting for her response. She said, finally, "Thanks for calling to tell me. I appreciate it."

"So, are you okay?" Al's voice was gentle. It brought tears to Temple's eyes—gratitude for the care in which her oldest friend was trying not to hurt her.

"You told me the house was too much of a burden," Temple said. "You were right. I'm glad it's gone."

"Me too."

They were quiet. Then Al said, "They'll clear away the rubble and fill in the hole, and it'll be ready for something new."

"Something better," Temple said.

"It's a low bar." Al snorted. "But you're right. It feels different up there."

"What does it feel like?" Temple asked, curious. "Hope?"

Al said nothing for a moment. When he spoke, Temple could hear the smile in his voice. "Let's just go with change for now. And take it from there."

ABOUT THE AUTHOR

Heidi Hackford is a historian, writer, and editor. She has a PhD in American history and has worked at a number of historical sites and museums, including Thomas Jefferson's Monticello. She lives in Half Moon Bay, California with her husband, who is a fellow historian, and a very old cat. You can find her at heidihackford.com.

Author photo © Douglas Fairbairn

SELECTED TITLES FROM SHE WRITES PRESS

She Writes Press is an independent publishing
company founded to serve women writers everywhere.
Visit us at www.shewritespress.com.

South of Everything by Audrey Taylor Gonzalez. $16.95, 978-1-63152-949-8. A powerful parable about the changing South after World War II, told through the eyes of young white woman whose friendship with her parents' black servant, Old Thomas, initiates her into a world of magic and spiritual richness.

The Alchemy of Noise by Lorraine Devon Wilke. $16.95, 978-1-63152-559-9. In this timely and provocative drama, an interracial couple's new and evolving relationship transcends culture clashes, police encounters, and resistance from select family and friends, only to have a violent arrest leave them questioning everything—including each other.

The Trumpet Lesson by Dianne Romain. $16.95, 978-1-63152-598-8. Fascinated by a young woman's performance of "The Lost Child" in Guanajuato's central plaza, painfully shy expat Callie Quinn asks the woman for a trumpet lesson—and ends up confronting her longing to know her own lost child, the biracial daughter she gave up for adoption more than thirty years ago.

Beginning with Cannonballs by Jill McCroskey Coupe. $16.95, 978-1-63152-848-4. In segregated Knoxville, Tennessee, Hanna (black) and Gail (white) share a crib as infants and remain close friends into their teenage years—but as they grow older, careers, marriage, and a tragic death further strain their already complicated friendship.

In the Shadow of Lies: A Mystery Novel by M. A. Adler. $16.95, 978-1-93831-482-7. As World War II comes to a close, homicide detective Oliver Wright returns home—only to find himself caught up in the investigation of a complicated murder case rife with racial tensions.